FROM SEA TO STORMY SEA

Crak! by Roy Lichtenstein

FROM SEA TO STORMY SEA

17 STORIES INSPIRED BY GREAT AMERICAN PAINTINGS

EDITED BY
LAWRENCE BLOCK

PEGASUS BOOKS
NEW YORK LONDON

FROM SEA TO STORMY SEA

Pegasus Books Ltd.
148 W 37th Street, 13th Floor
New York, NY 10018

First Pegasus Books cloth edition October 2019

Interior design by Maria Fernandez

Frontispiece: *Crak!* by Roy Lichtenstein, 1963. Pop art lithograph,
48.9 cm × 70.2 cm (19.25 in × 27.625 in). From The Artchives / Alamy Stock Photo.

Library of Congress Cataloging-in-Publication Data is available.

ISBN: 978-1-64313-082-8

10 9 8 7 6 5 4 3 2 1

Printed in the United States of America
Distributed by W. W. Norton & Company

CONTENTS

FOREWORD

BEFORE WE BEGIN . . .

t's my pleasure to present *From Sea to Stormy Sea*, a collection of seventeen new stories by seventeen stellar authors who've been inspired by seventeen American paintings.

Does this ring a bell?

It very well might. A couple of years ago, I was struck by an idea, and it couldn't have had more impact upon me had I been sitting under a tree, be it of the Newtonian apple or of the Siddharthan bodhi persuasion. (It was, I'll concede, rather less consequential for the rest of the world. Never mind.)

"Stories inspired by Edward Hopper's paintings." That was the thought, and it was followed in no time at all by a title: *In Sunlight or in Shadow.*

Bingo.

Now, I don't get that many ideas, and when one comes along, I generally give it a little time to germinate. If it's a good idea, it will profit from a few days' or weeks' or months' attention from my unconscious mind. If it's a bad idea, time will allow its lack of merit to make itself known to me.

And, however good or bad the idea may be, there's a very good chance I'll forget it altogether. That's increasingly apt to happen as the date on my birth certificate edges ever further into the past, and I can't tell you how much burdensome work it spares me.

In Sunlight or in Shadow. I didn't give myself a chance to forget it or grow disenchanted with it. An hour after that comic-strip lightbulb had formed over my head, I was busy making up a list of potential contributors. By day's end I'd drafted an invitation and begun sending it out, and I was delighted to discover what a high percentage of positive RSVPs I received.

I was no less delighted when the book filled up with outstanding stories and when Pegasus published it in a handsome volume that drew unanimously enthusiastic reviews and generated strong sales. (I could add that the icing on the cupcake came when my own contribution, "Autumn at the Automat," received an Edgar Allan Poe Award from Mystery Writers of America, but I'm far too modest to mention it.)

But how to follow such a success?

I couldn't think of another artist who could carry an entire volume the way Hopper did. The capacity of his paintings not to tell a story but to suggest that there were stories waiting to be told—what individual's work could match it?

So *Alive in Shape and Color* widened the focus. Each author was invited to choose a painting by a favorite artist, and the range was considerable, from the prehistoric cave paintings at Lascaux to the abstract expressionism of Clyfford Still, from Hokusai and Hieronymus Bosch to Magritte and Norman Rockwell.

Again the stories were quite brilliant. (That's a natural consequence when you're lucky enough to persuade brilliant authors to write them.) And again each story was very different from its fellows. A real danger with any themed anthology is that all the participants will write the same story, a result of the theme's pointing everyone in the same direction. That didn't happen in *In Sunlight or in Shadow*, nor did it happen in its sequel.

Alive in Shape and Color got a heartening reception. Reviewers liked it, and readers bought it.

So *now* what would we do for an encore?

More of the same, of course. Seventeen stories, inspired by paintings from seventeen different artists.

But one thing I'd learned from *Alive in Shape and Color* was that freedom of choice can engender problems of its own. With the entire art world there for the choosing, some writers had difficulty zeroing in on a selection.

A bit more specific a theme, it seemed to me, might better serve writers and readers alike. And a bit more editorial direction might be useful as well.

For starters, I decided to confine the volume to American artists. And then I chose thirty paintings, from which writers were invited to make their selections. (That part was especially gratifying, as I got to pick some of my own personal favorites.)

I made one more change—to the guest list. Most of the writers in *In Sunlight or in Shadow* wrote stories for *Alive in Shape and Color*, and they were every bit as excellent the second time around; the urge to invite them all again was a powerful one, but I forced myself to resist it.

For two reasons. First, I didn't want to make too many trips to the well. The economics of the anthology game are such that one is asking a favor when one invites a writer into an anthology, and there's a point when an invitation can become an imposition. Besides, I was eager to see what other writers might bring to the party. Once again I drew up a wish list and took a deep breath and sent out invitations, and once again I was blown away by the proportion of positive responses—and, as the stories came in, by their quality.

The title took some tweaking. I wanted to convey the essentially American nature of the artwork, and its reflection of the country in full. I thought of the song, "America the Beautiful," and the line that suggested itself as a title was "From sea to shining sea."

And that would have been fine, but too many authors and publishers have already slapped it on too many books. And wouldn't it be useful to come up with a word to suggest the conflict and drama and intensity that found its way into both the stories and the paintings?

You know, a touch of alliteration wouldn't hurt, either.

From sea to—what? Shimmering? Scintillating? Silvery?

Ah, of course. *From Sea to Stormy Sea.*

As I may have mentioned, I wrote a story for *In Sunlight or in Shadow*. And I tried mightily to write one for *Alive in Shape and Color*, one that started with Matthew Scudder and Mick Ballou and their wives standing in front of a Raphael Soyer painting at the Whitney Museum, and something about it reminds Mick of a story, and—well, I don't know where it might have gone from there, because it never went anywhere. It fizzled out, and I resigned myself to the fact that it was not going to get written, and neither was anything else from me, and *Alive in Shape and Color* would have not seventeen stories but sixteen. I so informed Pegasus, and they reworked the cover accordingly.

And then Warren Moore, who'd contributed to both of the books, pointed out to me that my body of work already included a story that fit the book's requirements. It was called "Looking for David," and Michelangelo's statue had indeed been its inspiration. While it was certainly not a new story, neither was it one that had been widely published. So we included it, and Pegasus adjusted the cover accordingly.

For *From Sea to Stormy Sea*, I didn't even have the intention of contributing a story. I had seventeen superb writers to do all that heavy lifting for me.

And then one of them was unable to deliver.

This happens. Ordering a story from a writer is not like ordering a sandwich from the corner deli. You don't always get what you asked for. (And, now that I think of it, that's also occasionally true of the deli. Never mind.)

I tried to think who might step into the breach, and a little voice suggested that I write the requisite story myself. I've become quite adept over the years at tuning out that little voice or telling it to go to hell, but this time it was persuasive.

I sat down and started writing. I didn't have a story consciously in mind, or characters with whom to people it, but one word led to another, and one sentence led to another, and I found myself wholly caught up in what I was writing, the happy result being "The Way We See the World."

And the painting from which it took form? *Office Girls*, by Raphael Soyer. Yes, really. The very painting that didn't work out as a story for Mick and Matt, which we used instead as a frontispiece for *Alive in Shape and Color*.

The world's a strange place. But you probably already suspected as much.

And I could leave it at that, but after I'd written my story, another writer was forced to pull out late in the eleventh hour. As I said, these things happen, but time was short and finding a replacement likely to be challenging.

So I broke my own rule and turned to a writer who had in fact participated in both earlier books, and other anthologies of mine as well. He's the aforementioned Warren Moore, and I was confident of two things—that if he took the job he'd be able to handle it in a timely fashion, and that I'd be more than happy with what he delivered.

And he was, and I am. He selected a painting and wrote a story for it, and the artist (whom I won't name here, or anywhere else, ever) denied permission, deciding he didn't want his painting in our book. And Warren realized there was another painting that fit the story he'd written quite perfectly, a painting by his late father that very much resonated with the theme of his story.

Sometimes it's really nice the way things work out. . . .

—Lawrence Block

FROM SEA TO
STORMY SEA

Patti Abbott *is the Edgar-, Anthony- and Macavity-nominated author of* Concrete Angel, Shot in Detroit, I Bring Sorrow & Other Stories of Transgression, *and the soon-to-be-reprinted* Monkey Justice *and* Home Invasion, *and she won the Derringer Award for* "My Hero." *Her story's title is from a poem by Darla Biel, included in* Feminine Images, *ekphrastic poetry inspired by Harvey Dunn's images of women.*

The Prairie is My Garden by Harvey Dunn

THE PRAIRIE IS MY GARDEN
BY PATTI ABBOTT

1884. DE SMET, SOUTH DAKOTA.

D o you think this plat will do?" Knocking off his straw boater with his gesture, Martin took the opportunity to mop his forehead. Their eyes swept the expanse of land. The house was modest but solid, the outbuildings mostly sod. "I don't know, Ellie. I'm away so much, and it's a long ride into town. It's so lonesome out here. Menacing, almost."

"Is it that cow or the milkweed and hyssop you find threatening?" Smiling, she visored her eyes. "Will you look at those coneflowers."

"I would if I knew which flower they were. So many flowers, so much grass, but so few trees." He ran a hand through the waving grass. "I would want to take a scythe to this so we can see who's sneaking up on us."

"You sound like my father, finding fault with my prospective garden. That Lakota told me that though the tall grasses kill off budding plants, the summers are too dry for most trees anyway. It's the tall grass that makes it a prairie, Martin."

"What Lakota is this?"

"One of the guides in town. Akecheta. He came by with a wagon filled with jewelry and potions. His wife does beautiful work with beads." She knelt down to examine what looked like a weed to her husband. "It's a bluestem."

"Your father would not approve of you and the children out here, Eleanor. Talking to primitives. Imagine. He reads the newspapers too. Jesse James, Sitting Bull. Gold Fever. These are not calming stories."

"The Indian was in town and no more a primitive than me. And if he was out here, you could spot him coming for miles. It's in town that men lay in wait."

They both fell silent, remembering a recent night.

"Father has more respect for 'potions' than you might think. His pharmacy is filled with herbal concoctions." She stood up. "Children, stop running before you are overheated. There's no way to cool off. And leave that skipper alone. This is her land more than yours."

"Robbie Olafson has a box full of them," Harriet shouted back, her voice getting caught up in the wind. "I just need a net and—"

"There will be no nets," Martin hollered back. He looked at his wife and, failing to see the irony, said, "I will leave you a shotgun just in case. You are eight miles from town or from a neighbor."

"I hope that is distance enough," she said.

"We are at cross-purposes, Eleanor. I want to fence you in, and you want to tear the fence down. Children, it's time to go. Your legs will be aching tonight."

1875. CHICAGO.

Eleanor Carpenter took a walk on her lunch hour every fine day, amazed at the speed with which new buildings arose from the ashes of the Fire. Chicago, built from lumber, was ripe for the flames incinerating the hodgepodge of rickety firetraps in hours.

The Palmer House, which used terra-cotta to rebuild, rose regally in front of her. It was said to have a barbershop with a floor made of silver dollars. She had ducked inside once to see, but the door she had pushed through led to the haberdashery. A plush emerald carpet, mahogany trimmings, and a row of wax heads modeling fashionable hats was all she saw.

Tired of city vistas, Eleanor vowed to find her way to a woods, a meadow or a riverbank before too long. But such a landscape was miles away, even by horsecar, and her father held her to the forty-five minutes he allowed his other clerks.

The odors of the pharmacy, with its liniments, camphor, cod-liver oil, ammonia, rubbing alcohol and various cosmetics extracted from an assortment of sources was difficult to tolerate ten hours a day. How could an establishment purporting to cure illness be so poisonous to the nose? Many of their patrons claimed the smell was curative, but to her it was harsh and suffocating.

"The university in Urbana is admitting women, Eleanor," her father repeatedly reminded her. "You can study medicine downstate or pharmaceutical science right here in Chicago and be a bigger help."

As she rounded the corner of Monroe, a young man, redheaded and wild-eyed, nearly knocked her down. Eyes fixed on the ground, he was mumbling in an agitated way. He offered no apology, did not even glance at her. Since the Fire, desperate people roamed the streets. The *Tribune* had recently listed the names of every person brought before the insane court, also publishing the basis for their appearance. Many had been driven mad by losses suffered in the Fire: lost family, lost homes, lost pets, lost businesses. Or just plain lost from the look in their eyes.

Seconds later, the redheaded man ran full-tilt into an elderly man turning away from a newsstand. This time the fellow had to stop because the victim of his carelessness was lying flattened on the sidewalk. Eleanor swooped in, and together they helped him to his feet. The young man was full of apologies as they led the man to a bench.

"Quite all right, no need for concern," the old man said, brushing cinder from his forehead. "I was, no doubt, too much occupied with the headlines."

"Don't try to stand until you catch your breath," Eleanor said, using her handkerchief to clean the dirt from his hands and face. She held it under his mouth, and obligingly he spat.

"I can't apologize enough," the young man said. "Should I look for a physician?" He looked to Eleanor for an answer, somehow assuming she possessed an ability to take charge.

"Takes more than a tumble to damage an old soldier like me." The injured man rose despite their protestations. "Look, no harm done." When he gave signs of breaking into a jig to prove his fitness, Eleanor grabbed his arm.

It seemed best to end their intercession then, as the man seemed embarrassed by the fuss. Nodding goodbye, all three went their separate ways, the young man turning back to mark the spot for future reference.

As fortuity would have it, two days later Eleanor came in contact with the redheaded man again. The Carpenter family was occupying their usual pew at the First Congregational Church of Chicago when Reverend Patton stepped up to the pulpit and told his congregants a guest speaker would deliver that day's sermon.

"Mr. Martin Tyler, a graduating student at the Theological Seminary will be delivering his first sermon. His talk takes its inspiration from Henry Ward Beecher's famous 'Poverty and the Gospels' sermon," Reverend Patton said, his voice pitched high with excitement.

A growing buzz accompanied the student's approach to the pulpit. It had been the congregation's good fortune to hear Reverend Beecher speak only a year before. Reverend Beecher had been among the first abolitionists and was now a defender of the right of women to cast a ballot. Both causes were dear to the hearts of the Congregationalists.

Eleanor didn't hear a word of Mr. Tyler's sermon, although she would later learn it demonstrated neither a facility for public speaking nor a grasp of his topic. From Eleanor's vantage, Martin Tyler stood poised before the church's solitary stained-glass window—one composed of gold and blue panels—and his hair, the most vibrant red she had ever seen, seemed lit by the light flowing through the glass. Or perhaps illuminated by the beneficence of the Lord.

In either case, Eleanor was transfixed and failed to notice the hum that began to weave through the church. It was difficult to be certain amid his shaking voice, his fluttering hands, the rumble of his stomach, but it seemed probable that Martin Tyler had misunderstood Reverend Beecher's words completely and was advocating a stoic acceptance of poverty and an acknowledgment that perhaps such a condition was part of God's plan. This turned out to be a tragic miscomprehension of the tangle of words emanating from his mouth, but many would continue to believe it for days to come.

If the delivery of a modestly successful sermon was a test, Mr. Tyler had failed. But flush with a mistaken belief in a victory, albeit minor, he did not detect the disapproval. He was buoyed by relief that he had managed to complete his talk without fainting, vomiting or forgetting his place, all outcomes that had seemed likely a few hours earlier. Eleanor, in the first flush of love, noticed nothing beyond the vibrancy of his hair, the firmness of his chin, the deep timbre of his voice. Never before had Eleanor been so caught in the snare of pure physical desire. Until that very hour, she had never entertained the notion of marriage at all, preferring to imagine herself free to wander unimpeded through nature. The works of Henry David Thoreau and Caroline Kirkland were especially inspirational, and she carried scraps of paper penned with particularly stirring sentiments.

It had been planned that Mr. Tyler and Reverend Patton would join the Carpenter family for a celebratory Sunday dinner. The poor evaluation of Mr. Tyler's performance had not made its way to him, so he enjoyed his chicken fricassee with rice, fresh spring peas, Parker House rolls, and a strawberry pie. Neither did he notice the conversation at the dinner table was muted and that all eyes avoided his. Mr. Carpenter and Reverend Patton talked about city politics; the Carpenter boys, home from school, spoke about the upcoming college football schedule; the girls and their mother reviewed the guest list for an impending party. Only Eleanor and Martin were quiet: she, to her shame, still occupied with his physical attributes; he feasting silently on the best meal he had been served since leaving Boston for the seminary three years before.

"I wonder if that elderly man is all right," Eleanor said suddenly. She had been struggling for a topic of conversation, and this fairly fell from her mouth. It took Martin a second or two to realize her remark was directed at him.

"I beg your pardon," he said, quickly swallowing his bite of pie.

"That man you knocked down at the newsagent?"

He looked at her carefully. Without the hat she had worn on the street, her pretty face was more evident. And her hair, strawberry blond, although he wouldn't have known the term, was worn up for almost the first time. She looked like a woman rather than the schoolgirl of a few days earlier.

"I went back to the newsstand, you know," he said, suddenly feeling a need to win her approval. "The agent knew the fellow in question and directed me to his flat."

"Did you find him well? Recovered from your . . . collision?"

He nodded. "Albert Jenkins is his name. Mrs. Jenkins made us a cup of tea, and we had a fine visit. In fact, I tried some of today's sermon out on him." Mr. Tyler bit his lip. "He didn't seem to take in my key points though. Of course, he confessed to not being a churchgoing man. You don't think—"

"Would you care for a short walk, Mr. Tyler?" Eleanor said, interrupting him. "We usually take one after a Sunday dinner. Isn't that right, Father?" Her father avoided her eyes, pretending to be in a deep discussion of the installation of a new sacristy.

Rolling those eyes, Eleanor excused herself and, taking Martin's arm, made her way to the street. No one showed the slightest interest in joining them. In the midday sunlight, Martin's hair again caught Eleanor's attention.

"Are you all redheads?" she asked. "Your family, that is."

"Just my mother's side. They came from County Cork, and most of them have a least some red in their hair. Orange, in some cases." They walked in silence for a block or two, both of them at a loss for an appropriate subject for two strangers of the opposite sex. But despite the sporadic awkwardness, their walk concluded with a plan to meet again. Something had been decided almost from the start.

1876. CHICAGO-MINNEAPOLIS.

It was only repeated assurances from Reverend Patton that Martin was not the dolt he seemed that eventually won over Mr. Carpenter.

"The boy made a hash of his thoughts that Sunday," Mr. Carpenter said. "He must have been in a panic. Maybe Eleanor can take him in hand before he steps up to the pulpit again. Elocution was one of her strong suits."

"No minister excels at every aspect of the job," Reverend Patton said. "I am all thumbs when it comes to counseling young couples." They exchanged smiles.

The courtship was quick. A call had come from a Minneapolis church two weeks before Martin's graduation. Caught in a bind, the Plymouth Congregational Church was willing to take him sight unseen, which hurried the usual process along.

"Why not a church in Chicago?" Mr. Carpenter asked.

"There's no need for another Congregational minister here," Martin said apologetically. "It would have been my first choice too. I dislike taking Eleanor away from her family."

"Then travel east. Surely there are churches to serve there. I can write to Uncle Abner. He belongs to Kensington Church in Connecticut."

"Father, you know Martin has to go where he is needed. How would it look if he tried to call in favors? Don't you think such a tactic would put him on the wrong footing?"

This conversation had been coming on like a bad cold for several weeks. She had watched her father dogging Reverend Patton, trying to find out the seminary's plans for Martin, writing letters to everyone he knew connected with the Congregational Church. It would be pure misery for George Carpenter to send his favorite daughter west, where life was bound to be more difficult and dangerous. And, most of all, she would be far from her family.

"They need help in Minneapolis. The city is growing by leaps and bounds with all the new mills," Eleanor tried to explain.

"Nothing but flour and lumber from what I hear. How mundane." Mr. Carpenter looked at Martin coldly. "You know they don't even have trees on that prairie. It will be sweltering in the summer. Freezing in the winter."

"Minneapolis isn't really the prairie, you know." Why wasn't Martin saying anything? Eleanor wondered.

"All those little lakes instead of our grand one. Oh, I've heard tell about this great Minneapolis." He caught Eleanor's eye. "You will miss the musical evenings the Philharmonic Society brings in. Summer night concerts are going to be in the Exposition Building next year. And then there's the Athenaeum and the Museum."

In order to halt the floodgate of Chicago's cultural achievements, Eleanor laughed. "And I am sure your family said much the same thing when you left Connecticut for Chicago. But you traveled to a place where a pharmacist was needed. Father, do you know Minneapolis is allowing women to both vote for and serve on the school board? Quite progressive, I'd say. And a new streetcar is in operation. We'd be arriving just as the city is making its mark." When he didn't respond, she added, "And what would you have Martin do here? Help out in the pharmacy? Make deliveries on a bicycle?"

"And you are to have your own church, Martin?" Mr. Carpenter continued, ignoring his daughter. "I have heard of men called and then made to do nothing more than serve as a janitor or choir master. Or a Sunday School teacher."

"The Plymouth Congregational Church has a new building at Nicollet and Eighth, which is quite grand I am told," Martin finally said.

Mr. Carpenter shrugged in defeat. "I guess there is nothing more to do than plan a wedding, then. It is going to be very difficult for your mother and me to visit, you know. We are too old to spend days on a train. And I will worry about you being out west with the scoundrels and scallywags I read about daily."

"Chicago isn't held in such high esteem," Eleanor said. "Many fathers wouldn't want their daughters coming here."

"People say the Chicago Fire was divine retribution for what is a modern-day Sodom and Gomorrah," Mrs. Carpenter added, incurring a scornful look from her husband but a grateful one from her daughter. "Well, I heard that at the Ladies Auxiliary! Don't look at me like that."

But the Tylers' future did not lie in Minneapolis. Martin's gifts, as evidenced in Chicago, did not rest in preaching cerebral sermons, nor in interpreting the scripture. Nor did they revolve around raising money or providing financial leadership. His gift was in pastoring, in providing solace to the bereaved, to those ill or in care, to people needing counseling. He was ill-suited for Plymouth Congregational Church. The call had been based on that church's belief that he was a man who could elevate their status, increase the size of their congregation, raise more funds. His undergraduate degree from Harvard and his study at the seminary in Chicago misled them. They just about accused him of misrepresentation. And the sort of formal sermon expected by the Minneapolis congregation was not in Martin's makeup despite extensive tutoring from his wife.

"If I could just preach from my heart, I think I could win them over."

With her own heart breaking, Eleanor said, "This isn't the right place for us anyway, Martin. It is just a smaller Chicago. We'll fit in better in another sort of town."

This was true, she told herself. But the notion that Martin had chosen the wrong profession was beginning to haunt her. Perhaps schoolmastering would be his forte. Was it too late for a change in careers? She had recently learned of a group called the Charity Organization Society that might be a better fit for Martin. They helped people undergoing financial or personal troubles.

But being a minister in the Congregational Church was important to her husband, and he wouldn't hear of leaving his collar behind. He had grown up in the church and never wavered from his desire to serve it. She listened to him practice his sermons, holding her breath. Even when the sermon was well planned and heartfelt, it tended to blow up in his face or wander off along uncharted paths. She dreaded the moment when the fidgeting in church began, when sighs of exasperation, if not consternation, escaped from the people around her. Perhaps a church in a more roughhewn place would make fewer demands on him as a public speaker, as an interpreter of the Bible. Perhaps Martin's assets would be appreciated in a town populated not by lumber barons and flour magnates but by farmers, liverymen, mill hands, small shopkeepers.

Martin looked at her worriedly. Family indeed. She was due to deliver their first child in a few months. Surely the church in Minneapolis would give him time to find a new congregation. They would not be tossed on the street.

1880S. DE SMET AREA.

The baby had come early. It was a girl, and they named her Harriet. Within a few weeks, the Tylers took the Minneapolis and St. Louis Railway to the De Smet area. Although all communications between Martin and his prospective church had been cordial and welcoming, a letter from a deacon had mentioned in a vague way that the Congregationalists would have to share the building with the Baptists and Presbyterians: "Your congregation meets the third Sunday of the month. You can gather in the schoolhouse the other weeks should you choose."

A postscript added that he might be called upon to preach in neighboring towns. If so, his congregation could attend services with the Baptists and Presbyterians while he was absent. "I am sure it will all work out," the deacon wrote. "Luckily there is no shortage of land. Just the money to construct buildings."

"So I'm to be a circuit preacher," he told Eleanor, flinging the letter down. "I didn't know such a practice existed."

"Not since the War. At least that's what we heard in Seminary."

De Smet was laid out in the typical T of most railroad towns. The first week they stayed in the Exchange Hotel, which sat a scant twenty feet from the tracks. Most of the guests were businessmen there for only a night or two. They tramped back en masse from the saloons after midnight, stumbling and paying little heed to the noise they made. Several times, strange men turned up in their room, the door having failed to lock properly. And once, a man in a bowler hat had a dance hall girl perched on his lap, two feet from Harriet's empty cot.

"I believe you have the wrong room," Martin told them, and they left, laughing wildly.

Harriet did little to make their transition easier, screaming night after night until they feared they'd be asked to leave. The lulling train ride west had been their only period of extended peace for weeks. Martin used some of their wedding money to buy a secondhand buggy so they could push Harriet around town, a difficult feat with the mud, horse droppings, and ruts from wagons to contend with. And the ride was too bumpy to serve a therapeutic purpose. It often ended with the child convulsed by her screams.

Eleanor couldn't help but think every building in De Smet looked like a box with windows, much like the dollhouses she had constructed from pharmacy delivery cartons in her childhood. Little thought had been paid to architecture. There were no parks, no green areas. She roamed the town, disheartened at the streets and backyards full of garbage. It seemed like life was too hectic in De Smet, too transitory to deal with such mundane matters. Most people stayed there only long enough to find a guide to take them to their claim and to stock up on provisions. The people setting up homes in the town itself were mostly shopkeepers, railroad employees and liverymen, although gradually a more professional class began to appear.

The only building of note was the courthouse, and even that was ordinary compared to those in Chicago and Minneapolis. Folks seemed to gather at the railroad depot, waiting for the next train to turn up. What looked like impressive buildings were often made grand by false fronts weighted down with advertising. *Lydia Pinkham's Vegetable Compound* for feminine complaints adorned the top half of the pharmacy. Inside, the shops and businesses were tiny, dark places with muddy vestibules, grimy floors, and poorly stocked shelves. The two newspapers published mostly gossip and news that the railroad furnished them with. The young couple was disheartened by almost everything they saw around them. Since most of the incoming travelers were there to claim land, their spirits were buoyed by the new opportunity. The Tylers had no land to claim, and little they saw lifted their spirits.

Martin's church had seemed striking at first . . . until they walked through the door, realizing in an instant that most of what impressed them was on the outside. And even there, the steeple was made of plaster. The bell rang only sporadically, mostly when the wind picked up.

"The congregation is saving for a real one," he told Eleanor. "Of course, this building may not ultimately be ours. I think the Presbyterians have the numbers on their side." The Congregationalist attendance changed from week to week but never exceeded forty. During a blizzard once, it was just the three of them.

There was no rectory, of course, and a home couldn't be shared anyway. So after a few weeks of hotel life, they found a two-room flat over the hardware store. "Handy if we need a hammer, right?" Martin joked. The various odors of a hardware store, not all pleasant, scented their rooms.

Slowly, the Tylers settled into town life in De Smet. Martin preached at the church on his Sunday, traveling to Brookings, Manchester, and Silver Lake to preach the other weeks. Generally he spent a few days in each town, seeing to the folks who needed him, staying at a widow's house in one town, in a miner's bunkhouse in the other. It was a life that suited him in terms of his duties, but being separate from his family was a constant hardship. And he had a deluge of letters coming from Mr. Carpenter in Chicago, asking how he could keep Eleanor safe from miles away.

"We get the news here," Mr. Carpenter wrote, "so we know the mischief that men out there are up to. Only misfits head west." Martin didn't bother to reply that he was one of those misfits, assuming that was the point.

Although the weather had been difficult in Chicago and Minneapolis, it was temperate compared to De Smet. Blizzards seem to gain speed and power over the flatlands, and there was snow on the ground from October to May. The makeshift housing was a poor match for a Dakota winter for many of their congregants, and Eleanor was put in charge of writing to various patrons and benevolent groups for blankets, warm clothing, whatever would see them through.

"Of course, I can only tap a mine so often," she reminded Martin. "People back east only have the vaguest notion of what life is like out here. They assume since our temperatures are similar, so are our houses."

It was not until May that they made their first journey to the prairie her father so reviled. Perhaps it was because the day was a perfect one. Or maybe because they had just discovered she was pregnant again. Or probably because they had borrowed a parishioner's fetching carriage for the trip, but Eleanor was awestruck by what suddenly surrounded them. When she tried to describe it to her mother later in a letter, she could not find the right words. Every word she chose was far too prosaic and diminished what she had seen.

Never before had the sky seemed so vast nor half as blue; no vista had stretched so far, seemingly meeting the heavens in an undulating horizon. The land appeared both barren and abundant with life, depending on how closely you examined it. She fell to her knees. The plants were equally tender and sturdy. What looked colorless at first took on infinite hues as she inspected it. The insects buzzing overhead were unfamiliar but immediately dear to her. The absence of trees allowed her to take it all in with huge, thrilling gulps. Unlike the wind coming off Lake Michigan in Chicago, the blow rustling the grass was almost deafening. The prairie was where she wanted to be, where she belonged. It immediately became the landscape of her heart. Its emptiness, which was what one saw first, was its greatest strength. All the things that man had added to this world were superfluous, soulless. She was unprepared for this. Why had no one told her that such a place existed? Why had people described it as lonely or inhospitable?

"Pretty stark, isn't it?" Martin said, breaking into her reverie, his tone dismissive. "I guess your father was right. Something about its size feels threatening. A storm or an Indian tribe or a blizzard could bear down on us in seconds. I guess I am a city boy. I wouldn't feel right living out here. Nor in having you and the children in such a place."

She had been about to tell him how she felt, how what lay in front of her had profoundly changed her, but then thought better of it. Martin would need to be won over. How that would happen eluded her though. It would come to her eventually. Solutions usually did, if she didn't hurry them.

Eleanor returned often to that spot and others like it, but mostly without Martin. Harriet and eventually William played more naturally on the prairie than anywhere else. They intuited the happiness it gave her and shared it. There were a million things to investigate on every square inch of land. The three of them could lie in the grass for hours, merely studying the cloud formations overhead.

Martin was away more every week. The population in Brookings proved especially challenging and in need of constant pastoral attention.

"Influenza has taken its toll," he said "And now there's another village to serve: Fountain. The deacon sent me over there today. People are claiming land by the hour. One parcel has turned over three times in a month as the owners head farther west."

Her husband's voice was excited as he packed his bag. Providing solace and both spiritual and practical advice was clearly his calling. No one in these tiny outposts demanded fancy sermons or elaborate fund-raising endeavors. It was enough to have a protector, and that was how Martin served them. She appreciated his talent for it too, never resting more easily than when he was beside her. Unfortunately, too many nights were spent alone. The sounds of De Smet were not pleasant for her: raucous saloons open too late, horses trotting down the street at all hours, arguments between various parties spilling out of boardinghouses and hotels, wagons coming and going past midnight. It was a way station on the road west.

She became more proficient in repairing things, in making decisions on her own, in being the disciplinarian—not that she wasn't always that anyway. Martin was too softhearted to deal with the misbehavior of small children. The streets stretched farther out now. The T became an H. Calumet Avenue, where they rented a small house after William came along, had a few trees shading the ground beneath them. None of this was planned. Sometimes she wondered if De Smet was not the worst of both worlds: neither a company town nor an autonomous one. The railroads simply allowed laissez-faire capitalism to shape things. They provided land, and the rest of it be damned. If her heart's desire was to be in a growing community, it might have served her. But it lay elsewhere.

Soon the children would be attending school, and the poor quality of the local one worried her. Her education and, even more, Martin's, had been superior to what her children would have here. It was little more than what farmhands were offered—a sixth-grade education at best. She was startled when the new teacher, sitting next to her in church, stumbled over several words in her hymnal. "It's my poor eyesight," she told Eleanor, embarrassed.

In December of their fourth year in De Smet, William came down with what at first seemed like croup. She constructed the usual tent and set a pot on the stove to make steam. But during the night, his fever shot up, his neck seemed to stiffen, and Eleanor feared something worse. Martin was in

Manchester, well beyond her reach. She alerted a neighbor that the children would be alone and set off for the doctor's office. It was past midnight, and the streets were as quiet as she'd seen them.

It was brutally cold. She could hear ice snapping the branches of the more delicate trees as she hurried through town. The snow was knee-deep on side streets where the makeshift plow hadn't gone. As she pushed through the drifts, her coat brushing away the outer layer, she suddenly felt an insistent tap on her shoulder. Before she could turn to look or say a word, a man, she couldn't make out his face, pushed her into a snowbank and fell down on top of her. She felt him prodding at her; it was if he was in possession of six wiry, probing hands. She knew she would have only the briefest of moments to call for help. Summoning all of the breath inside her, she let it out in a piercing scream, pushing him off at the same time. In nearly the same instant, she realized her attacker was not a man at all. It was the wire mannequin dressed like Santa Claus that had sat outside the De Smet General Store for the last two weeks. Mr. Olafson had removed the mannequin from his shop window and stationed it outside for the holiday, remarking on his clever invention to all who stopped to look. The ropes tethering it to the hitching post had obviously come loose in the blizzard, and it had wheeled or been pushed down First Street by the same wind propelling her. She thrust it aside, righting it, and the strange apparition continued its wobbly journey down the street, leaving only its top hat behind. Perhaps no one had heard her embarrassing scream. But no.

"What is going on out there? You are waking my children." Then a pause. "Was that a woman, I heard?" It was a man's voice, coming from a nearby house.

"Yes, yes, it's me. The preacher's wife," Eleanor shouted back. "I'm all right. It's just a . . ."

The mannequin was more than a block away now, the snow crunching loudly under the wheels, its red flannel coattails flapping behind it. A gust of wind propelled it around the corner and onto Joliet. And then it was gone.

"The preacher's wife?" The man's voice grew closer, and she heard feet skidding on the ice. "Mrs. Hancock?"

"Mrs. Tyler. Congregational." She was sitting up now, her back against a snowdrift.

"Have you fallen?" A lamp held high lit her face. "Or were you attacked?"

She forced herself up farther and into the light. She could still hear wheels squeaking in the distance, along with branches being weeded from trees from the weight of the ice. The night was one of those where sound carried. She hoped her savior was more deaf than her.

"Attacked?" It was a question, but he didn't hear it as that.

"Oh, my dear woman."

She could make him out now. It was Mr. Armbruster. The glasses that usually sat on his face were missing, and his eyes seemed to bobble without them. He was in his nightshirt, a coat thrown carelessly over it. His feet were clumsy in unlaced boots. "Look, here is his hat. The scoundrel." He swept the top hat off the ground. "Seems like he was celebrating . . ." He shook his head.

She couldn't force herself to clear up the misunderstanding. Her brain was too busy finding a purpose for it.

"You had better come inside before one of these flying branches hit us. My wife will see to you." He looked at her as carefully as he could, being half-blind. "Do you need to be seen to?" She shook her head. "I will head for the sheriff's office. The reprobate may be looking for his next victim." He helped her inside the house, where his wife was waiting anxiously. "Do you have any idea who it was?" Mr. Armbruster said, his hand on the door. "The sheriff is bound to ask that."

"None at all," Eleanor said. "He was swaddled in dark wool." This was true, at least. "But really I must continue on my errand. I was on my way to the doctor. My boy is very ill."

"I'll go with you," Mrs. Armbruster said, grabbing her shawl. "The horrid man may be laying in wait."

When she lay in bed later that night, Martin summoned but not yet arrived, her boy's fever dropping, Harriet having slept through it all, she considered the danger of continuing on with the lie versus the perils of admitting the truth. Was she an evil woman for seeing how her supposed attack could win her a home on the prairie? Could win her the blue sky, the rustling grass, the endless sea of flowers.

"It's not like this was the first time a woman has been accosted by the men exiting those saloons," Eleanor said to Martin later, embellishing rather than diminishing her tale. "Those men are away from their families and use the opportunity to drink to excess, gamble their paychecks away, and look for women to warm their beds."

"I am going to set up a watch for when I am away," Martin said, his chin thrust out. "We can have a patrol arranged in a matter of hours."

"Do we really want to live in a jail, Martin? I have a better idea." This could not end with her imprisoned by the fears of men.

1884. DE SMET, SOUTH DAKOTA.

The house was theirs in weeks. She could stand outside with the children and spot someone coming for miles, not that she gave such an idea much thought. Sometimes Lakotas with their wagons of goods stopped by. She was especially fond of Talutah, Akecheta's wife, who made such beautiful jewelry. Town men mostly stayed away after hearing about the De Smet confrontation. Martin was the one she usually spotted, coming home from Manchester or Fountain. His red hair was a dead giveaway. The sun lit it up like fire on a nice day. Even on a dull one it held light. It was a beacon. It was her heart.

Charles Ardai *is the author of five novels, including the Shamus Award–winning* Songs of Innocence, *which the* Washington Post *called "an instant classic." He has also received an Edgar Award for his short fiction and an Ellery Queen Award for his work as founder and editor of the pulp-revival imprint Hard Case Crime. He lives in New York City and walks through Times Square every day.*

Broadway Boogie Woogie by Piet Mondrian

MOTHER OF PEARL

BY CHARLES ARDAI

For a long time Harry Castle sold penknives, the sort with phony mother-of-pearl handles, out of a cardboard suitcase on Forty-Seventh Street, and when the police confiscated those, he tried his luck with neckties. In this, as in so much else, his luck was poor. Except for being labeled 4-F when the draft came, nothing much had ever gone right for him. But he wasn't complaining. If you're going to use up a lifetime's worth of luck in one shot, keeping out of a war was the time for it. And if no one would ever have called him a success, that was true of most men who made their living on the streets of New York. With one thing and another, he'd at least never gone hungry, not two days running.

There was, of course, one other time Harry had gotten lucky, if we're being completely honest, and it was because of this other lucky night that people kept calling him Mother-of-Pearl long after he'd lost his case of knives and switched to hand-painted menswear. That was the night of May 8, 1945, when victory had at last been declared in Europe, and for all that there was still no end to the fighting in the Pacific and men less fortunate than Harry Castle would continue losing their lives for another three months, the population of New York City was aching for a release, and the news that the Nazis had finally laid down their guns released something powerful throughout the city, like a cork from the neck of a sweating champagne bottle.

The famous photograph of the sailor kissing the nurse, that came later, when Hirohito went on the radio and handed his country over to Douglas MacArthur. But Times Square wasn't empty on May 8. We all had our corners, our places to be, the ladies and the men, the cabbies and the cops, the lucky poor who'd been picked to wear sandwich boards or hand out leaflets and the unlucky ones whose evening would be spent scraping a tin can in an empty lot. But no one wanted to stay in his place that night. We all felt the need to move, and the streets were alive with bodies. Men went from bar to bar, stopping barely long enough to down the glass the barman handed them on the house. Newsstands stood unguarded as their tenders came out from behind the counter to take in a night sky empty of air-raid sirens and blackout drills. No one set foot in the theater on time that night, not the audience and not the performers. And some ladies of the evening, not having free beer to offer but loath to ply their trade in the ordinary way on such an extraordinary night, hung a CLOSED sign in their proverbial shop window and took men of their acquaintance to their beds—men they really shouldn't have, for all the lasting pleasure it gave them, but it wasn't every night a war ended, or half-ended, and in any event that was Harry's lucky night.

The pleasure may have been fleeting for both of them, but something lasting came of it, and when nine months later the lady in question, in a moment of impishness or sheer exhaustion, told the nurse to put the name Pearl on the child's birth certificate, Harry's nom de guerre was cemented as well.

Mother-of-Pearl Castle. Harry. He kept on working his corner, selling neckties or whatever it was that came next—novelty items, I believe, probably some of them stamped MADE IN JAPAN once the shadow of the war had well and truly passed. The corner never changed, nor did the man, though a little at a time he grew gray at the temples and his suits wore shiny at the knees and seat. And then one afternoon in '63 he was struck by a yellow cab while crossing Broadway to get to the lunch counter at Howard Johnson's and died of his injuries on the way to the hospital. Bad luck—it was Harry's story to the end.

But then there was Pearl.

It was the last week in August before she found her way to me, waiting patiently while I made change for a couple in matching outfits who just had to have a memento of their visit to New York. I was set up with a folding table between Woolworth's and Regal Shoes, my usual spot. The couple headed off on the Woolworth's side, shooting me a matching pair of goodbye waves, and behind them was this well-turned-out girl in a yellow-striped sundress, her purse hanging by a braided strap from one wrist. She came forward, ignored my display of acetate playing cards and tortoiseshell combs, and braced me with a thumb-worn clipping out of the *Daily News*. It wasn't the first time I'd seen that particular clipping. Harry hadn't even been deemed worthy of an entire headline, "Local Peddler Hit by Taxi" sharing space atop the article with "Traffic Woes Cited in City Cleanup Campaign."

Did I know who she was at first glance? Maybe not. But when I saw that column of newsprint in her hand, I knew.

"I was wondering," she said, her voice lightly accented with the tones of the suburban upbringing she'd enjoyed, "if you might know anything about the man mentioned in this article. They say he was in your line of work, so I thought perhaps you might have known him or known of him?"

"Listen," I said, "if you want a canasta set, I can help you, otherwise . . ."

But she didn't move along. Something had bred stubbornness in her, despite her having been raised by an aunt in a place with soft lawns, where the only honking horns you'd hear were on bicycles driven by schoolchildren. She looked twenty-one or twenty-two, though of course she was only eighteen. And she wasn't going anywhere without an answer.

"Sure," I told her, "I knew Harry. We all knew Harry."

People talk about faces lighting up, but I don't think I'd ever seen it happen until that moment. Who knew how many people she'd asked before she got to me, how many unfriendly brush-offs she'd received? Here at last was hope. Her wide green eyes—her father's, God rest him—grew wider still, and the look of fatigue slid from her face like snow from a kicked boot. I held up one hand.

"I can tell you something about him, maybe answer a question or two. But not now. Now is when I pay the landlord, understand? Any minute I'm not selling, I'm not eating."

The sentence that had been on its way out of her mouth stopped, stillborn, and was replaced with a single word: "When?"

"You still around tonight?"

She crossed her arms over her chest. "It seems Harry Castle was my father," she said. "I'm not going anywhere until I find out more."

"Eight P.M.," I said, "when all the curtains have gone up. You can meet me over there." I nodded in the direction of Howard Johnson's. It seemed appropriate. "You can buy your own dinner, though. Matter of fact, you can buy mine."

Growing up on the sunny shores of Lake Hopatcong, New Jersey, I used to get fed off the backyard grill seven months out of every twelve, starting around Easter and running nearly through Thanksgiving, and I'll say with no hesitation that the ham steak Mr. Howard Johnson prepared in his kitchen had nothing on the one my mother used to coax out of that little device the Ford Motor Company had sold her husband. But I ate it, every bite, even the two rings of pineapple lying wistfully on the side of the plate, before I answered Pearl's first question.

"He was good at the work," I told her, and I meant it, even though "good" and "successful" are hardly the same thing. Harry had been good. He'd had the charm to stop pedestrians on their way from here to there and sometimes to persuade them that a penknife or a necktie was something they might want to own. He was less good at the necessary art of keeping one eye peeled for the beat cop who was empowered to deprive you of your entire stock of penknives and neckties without paying you a cent for it. And don't think that cop wasn't pocketing a tie for his own weekend use, and a knife for his son's, before turning in the rest at the precinct house. I wasn't in Harry's line of work then—I had other ways to turn a dollar as I tiptoed into my roaring twenties—but I dined with the peddlers many an evening and heard them vituperate the men in blue, and I learned early on to consider them parasites rather than protectors. It wasn't only knives and ties the police would sample on the arm, and I learned that too.

But we all looked up to Harry, or anyway I did. He was handsome and brash and wore his two suits well, the linen one for summer and the heavier herringbone when the chill came back each September. He was swift with a joke, but more often at his own expense than yours, and he'd buy you a coffee if he had a nickel in his pocket and you had none.

How much of this did I tell Pearl over the ten-cent mugs of coffee the waitress in the blue checks and white apron obligingly kept refilling? All of it. And she drank it down hungrily, like a second stream of java. She kept drinking, and like our good waitress, I kept pouring, until a glance at the clock on the wall told me the shows would be letting out soon. She followed my glance, and we both fell silent for the first time since those pineapple rings had fallen before my knife and fork.

"What I don't understand," she said, in that delicate little voice of hers that nevertheless had steel behind it, "is why someone mailed that article to me. How would anyone even know where to send it? Who would have? And the note with it—" She pulled from her purse a half sheet from the Hotel Astor, free in the lobby along with the use of one of their pens. *You deserve to know, Pearl, that this man was your father. I wish you could have met him.* "Who?" she said. "Who wished that? There was no name, no address."

I dabbed my napkin at the corners of my mouth. "That I can't tell you."

"Do you think," she said, and she hesitated only for a second, "it was my mother?"

"That looks like a man's writing," I said.

She shook her head. "Not to me. Look at those loops where she writes her Ys. *You* deserve to know. *Your* father."

"Your mother was—" I took a swallow; it bought me time, though no swallow would buy me enough. "Your mother was a fine woman. But she had no choice, you understand. There's no raising a child in a Times Square flophouse. Not when green pastures are an alternative."

"You knew her too?"

"I knew her too."

"What sort of person was she?"

And we were off again. Landlord be damned. Mr. Johnson served us one of his Jell-O dishes, with the fruit suspended inside, and we each ate some forkfuls while I told Pearl the story of Lilian Dressler, known as Lily on the street, and by some as Tiger Lily for the marks her nails left on certain gentlemen's backs, but I didn't mention that.

There was more I didn't tell her but plenty that I did, enough that by the time we were finished she knew what her mother had done for a living and what category of man she had done it with; she knew that her father hadn't been the best of them, but he'd been far from the worst, and what did "best" mean in this life anyway? There'd been a Broadway producer once who'd tipped her with an emerald brooch, but later it came out that the brooch had been his wife's; it was reported missed and he begged for it back, but by then it had been pawned and the ticket torn and flushed. He'd paid her the most any man ever had, that was for sure, but did that make him better than Harry Castle? Harry's nickel coffee had warmed her better than the rich man's emerald.

How did I happen to know this story? Pearl was too polite to ask, but I could imagine what she was thinking. That her mother, being equal opportunity about such things, had taken me to her bed as well and talked in the wee hours, in my arms. Let her think that. Let her think less of me, less of her mother. Let her learn about the world.

I asked her where she was staying, as we stepped out from the relative darkness of the glass-doored vestibule into the intersection where Broadway and Seventh Avenue collided and ten thousand lights, all in motion, were the thrown-off sparks. Mustard-colored Checker cabs tore down the street, followed by the flashing red-and-blue lights of police cars. I held my table under one arm, my case in the same hand, and seized her elbow with the other when she seemed as though she might step out into traffic and go the way her father had.

"Where is she?" Pearl asked. "My mother. I want to meet her. She owes me that." This, as we picked our way along Seventh toward the shabby hotel she'd checked in to, around the corner from the Astor but a universe away. Two men with guitars smoked cigarettes on the stoop, and they eyed Pearl with quiet curiosity as we climbed the steps. It wasn't a hungry look. But I was just as glad to get her away from it.

"Your mother," I said, "as I understand things, had an agreement with her sister. She'd take you in, but only if there was no further contact between you. None. You were hers to raise, as she thought best."

Something flared in those green eyes. "My mother mailed me that clipping. She wanted me to come find her. Surely you see that."

"You don't know who mailed you that," I said. "I could have mailed it to you. Any of us could."

"Did you?" she said.

I rode over her: "You don't even know if she's still alive," I said. "If she is, she could be anywhere. She could be in California, or, or—" But the look she gave me shut me down. "Listen," I said. As if she hadn't spent the whole evening listening, and me talking. "I can try to turn her up. But I can't promise I'll succeed or that she'll agree to see you if I do. No return address, no telephone number . . . you can't assume she wants to be in touch again. It looks to me like she's ambivalent at best."

"Ambivalent."

"That's right," I said. "Like she wants and she doesn't want."

"I know what the word means."

"Pearl," I said, "if you did meet her, you might not like what she's become. I don't imagine she's entertaining gentlemen anymore. She'd be in her forties now. No call for women that age in the beds of paying men. But that doesn't mean she's doing something finer."

"Why, what do you think she's doing?"

I hefted my case, my table, and made for the door. "Not necessarily anything a daughter would be proud of."

"Proud's not important," Pearl said. "I think she's looking for me. I think she wants to see me. You tell her I'm ready. Tell her I got her message and I'm ready to see her."

I told her I'd do that and shut the door behind me.

They tore down the building the other day. I saw them do it, jackhammers and bulldozers, behind a barrier of orange-and-white plastic stanchions all lined up in a row. It's a longer walk for me now, the same half block, and so I got to watch quite a lot of it, the shattering and disassembly. I don't carry a suitcase and a folding table anymore, but my hands are full all the same, and my progress is slow. Giant stone cornices and windowsills littered the ground, like the aftermath of an explosion. The beds had been removed first, I imagine, and the lighting fixtures, and the carpets and curtains, the towel rods and showerheads, until nothing remained but the building itself, the bare skeleton. And now not even that.

I never saw her again after that night, never spoke to her, but that's not to say I never went back. I did go back, once, in the small hours of the morning, after a night spent around the corner in the lobby of the Hotel Astor, pen and paper in hand, rocks glass beside them. I drank more than I wrote. And I wrote plenty.

In the morning I slipped the note under her door and quietly left.

I imagine she found it not long after I left it. I know she came looking for me. She didn't find me. I stayed in my room for the better part of a week. I had a small icebox there, a loaf of bread, some cans. I didn't starve.

When I went out again, Murray Stroganoff—who wasn't Russian, by the way, we called him that for another reason entirely, a story for another day—tipped his hat to me and said he hoped I'd been traveling rather than sick. I told him yes, I'd been out west, because why get into it? He said a girl had been asking about me, had told him I was—"Yes," I said, "I know."

"She left a telephone number," he said.

I took it. I didn't use it.

There are no more Checker cabs today, and the ten thousand lights of Times Square aren't incandescent bulbs anymore; they're huge square television screens, stacked one on top of another, blurting their candy-colored advertisements overhead. In the summer, women wearing nothing but platform shoes, panties, and feather headdresses paint their bosoms red, white, and blue and pose for tips. These are the new ways of turning a dollar half a century on—but that dollar won't buy you a coffee the way a nickel used to.

Half a century.

I still read the newspaper, though like everyone else these days I do it on a screen, where the ink never smudges and no story is too small or too local to find. I found it when Pearl Weisenbach (née Dressler, but no one told the newsman that) got married, when she had the twins, when she was awarded the Centennial Prize in Allston, Massachusetts, for devoted service. I found her husband's funeral, and her own. I didn't go.

And now the jackhammers, the bulldozers. It's all dust now, as I will be soon enough. The Hotel Astor itself barely outlasted my long night on one of its overstuffed settees. But that night it gave me what I needed, and I don't just mean the complimentary stationery or the ballpoint pen, or even the bourbon, Harry's drink, chosen in the dear man's memory.

I wrote so many drafts, some just a few words long, some pages. In the end, this is what I settled on, fifty-seven years ago, when that grand hotel still stood, and the lesser one in which Pearl lay fast asleep, when I could stand without the assistance of this aluminum contraption and all the city's lights glowed amber and crimson in the hectic unwashed night.

Dearest Pearl,

Forgive me. But this is the best way even if you won't think so. I was 18 once and headstrong and thought I could come from Lake Hopatcong to New York and make it mine. I did all right. I did the best I could. You will too. But you won't do it here, and you won't do it with me hanging around your neck, a sorry reminder of where you came from. Your father was a good man, or good enough, and I was good enough too, but no better. You be better. Just go somewhere green and fresh, where people say How do you do?, and you'll do fine.

Thank you for my dinner. It was delicious.

Your Mother

Jan Burke's *novels and short stories have garnered Edgar, Agatha, and Macavity Awards, among others. She is a proud member of LACMA, where she first saw works by Warhol.*

ANDY WARHOL, MOST WANTED MEN, MAY 1 – JUNE 30, 1988

Detail from *Thirteen Most Wanted Men* by Andy Warhol

SUPERFICIAL INJURIES

BY JAN BURKE

People ruin everything." Elena Monroe said it absently, her focus on her computer screen.

"Everything?" her great-aunt asked.

Elena glanced over at her. Valerie Monroe, who had just accused Elena of becoming a recluse, sat up against a dozen pillows on her bed, her eyebrows raised.

"Everything," Elena said, and went back to her work.

"Name three."

"Sex. Religion. Dining out. Sooner or later, some human being is going to make you regret participating in any or all of the above."

"Sounds like something your mother might have said."

She was trying to start something. Valerie loved drama. Elena did her best not to be conscripted into the cast, so she ignored that little dig about her mother.

"I'm sorry computers were invented!" Valerie said.

"You could use one if you tried. You're bright enough."

"I'm not patient enough. Besides, that's not what I meant. I wish you couldn't use them, either."

"Too much attention taken from you?" Elena said, not looking up.

Valerie gave a crack of laughter. "I suppose I deserved that. But no. I hate them because, as I said, they've turned you into a recluse."

Elena lifted her hands from the keyboard and swiveled her chair. She traced a finger down the scarred right side of her face. "This turned me into a recluse."

"Nonsense. First, that scar has never been as disfiguring as you've imagined. Second, these days, so much can be done by plastic surgeons. And third, and really more important than all the rest—you have so much to offer!"

"I'm too old for this nonsense."

"I'm old, and I haven't given up on romance. You're . . ." She scrunched up her face, doing the math.

"Fifty-two. I was born in 1963."

"Fifty-two! That's not so old. Lord, what I'd be up to if I could see fifty-two again. You just need to find the right person. I've been noticing that you've attracted the attention of—"

"Let's drop it there. Next you'll start talking of princes. Save that stuff for your next bestseller. Besides, I'm happy."

"Because you've been able to go into hiding. I blame myself for letting you do it. It's a good thing *I* wasn't afraid to appear in public. Which, until quite recently, I was faithfully doing—book tours, television, all of it—wrinkled face and sagging boobs and all, mind you."

"You're a lovely woman, and you know it. And I'll never be able to tell you how grateful I am that you allow me—"

"Now stop! We have a symbiotic relationship. You take care of me, and I torture you. If you ever want to change the arrangement—"

"Never. No matter what prince shows up to ride off with you."

"I just don't want to see you end up like your mother."

"Put your mind at ease. I'm unlikely to be an unwed mother at this stage of my career."

"Don't pretend to misunderstand me. Your grandfather was so worried that any man who courted Louisa was actually courting his money, he made her doubt that anyone would ever value her for herself."

"Hmm. My memory of her is of a very different woman. An independent, stubborn, impetuous, and—for lack of a better term—wild woman."

"People your age will never understand what the pill did to the sex lives of women of her generation."

"Hard to convince the 'accident' that she was on the pill."

"Nonsense. She wanted you. That's what you should make of that. Don't give me that skeptical look, either. Your mother and I—"

"Were almost the same age. I know. More like sisters than aunt and niece."

"It's true. Your grandfather was twenty years my senior. Now—as for the rest of it—you got to know your mother as she was after your grandfather's death. She felt set free, and who could blame her? And beneath the wild woman was an insecure one, as there so often is. If she was a bit improvident—"

"I don't think you can refuse to teach someone about money and then be surprised when they blow their inheritance."

"That's a kind way of looking at it." She paused. "Elena, about Clarence—"

"My cousin *was* taught. Uncle Titus had the good sense to get out of the garment industry and into more diversified holdings—actually increased what Grandfather left him. Brought Clarence into the company to try to train him. But Clarence, as they say, made a small fortune by starting out with a large one."

"He's the last of our name!"

Elena stared at her.

"Well, I don't mean to say you *aren't* part of the family!"

Elena went back to work.

"Elena!"

"If you want me to produce a clean copy of your manuscript, which I remind you is due at the end of the week, you had better let me work."

She stopped long enough to make dinner, and as they ate their meal, any bad feelings from their earlier conversation were set aside.

"When does your physical therapist come back?"

"Ugh. Tuesday."

"For someone who has survived two falls—minor as they may be—you are doing well."

"I know, I know."

But Elena knew that any talk of the falls troubled Valerie.

After dinner Elena gave Valerie her evening medications and returned to her keyboard, but the queen, propped up on her pillows, was in the mood for attention. "I know the name of your father."

Since one of the first things people had ruined for Elena was the hope of learning her father's name, she did not rise to Valerie's bait.

Elena's birth certificate listed her father as "unknown." Her mother, Louisa Monroe, had never married. Over the years Louisa had steadfastly ignored Elena's pleas to be told who he was.

"Neither of you would be safe if I told you his name," Louisa had said.

"Safe! Who wants to be safe if you don't even know who you are?"

"Listen to me, Elena Monroe, and listen well. No man—no man on this earth—should ever be given the power to define who you are."

It wasn't a bad piece of advice, Elena thought now, but Valerie was right. Louisa had been a rich man's much-indulged daughter, taught to mistrust the motives of those who sought her hand. She was in her thirties when she conceived Elena. That was in the early 1960s, when the stigma of having a child out of wedlock was stronger for both mother and child.

Elena had never felt fully a part of the Monroe family. Except for her height and blue eyes, Elena didn't look like any of the fair, willowy Monroes. She had thick, dark hair and was built on what Valerie kindly referred to as "more athletic lines."

At the age of seven, a car accident had scarred her face. She once overheard her uncle tell her mother that her scars were God's punishment for her mother's sin. Her mother had replied that if there was anyone less godly than Titus, Satan was going to quit in the face of the competition. They saw less of Uncle Titus after that.

When Louisa died in 1986, she left Elena an estate worth $500,000. Most would not consider it a small sum. Uncle Titus and his son Clarence thought it a pittance. She found a job as a secretary at a brokerage and lived in a tiny apartment.

Valerie invited her to live with her. She got promotions. When she decided to give in to Valerie's urging to quit her job at the brokerage, her life both expanded and stayed safe. Valerie might call her a recluse, but that was not entirely possible in the home of a social butterfly. Only Valerie's recent injuries had limited the number of callers.

Tomorrow would bring Clarence upon them for his usual Sunday visit.

After Titus's death, with no trustees to provide guidance or restraint, Clarence had run through almost all of his inheritance within five years. Now, in the sixth year, it was clear where Clarence expected to find more funds. His initial hints to Valerie about being temporarily cash-strapped had been met so coldly, he had given up future attempts. Six months ago, Elena had caught him opening an empty jewelry box.

"I'm sure you just wanted to admire the diamond necklace she used to wear," she said apologetically, "but I'm afraid Aunt Valerie doesn't keep jewelry and other portable wealth here, Clarence. A friend of hers was robbed by a granddaughter, and Valerie said she didn't want me to be tempted to commit larceny."

The next morning was a rainy one, but nothing could keep Clarence away from his weekly display of devotion to his great-aunt. Elena wasn't fooled, and she knew Valerie wasn't, either.

As Elena met him in the foyer, taking his raincoat and umbrella, Clarence said in a low voice, "Someday, you're going to have to move out of here."

"Clarence—"

"She's going to leave me everything. Everything."

Elena stayed silent.

"It's true. She doesn't discuss your wages with me, but it doesn't take a genius to figure out the deal—she lets you stay with her in this gorgeous place *now*, working for her like a servant—typing out her manuscripts, cooking, cleaning, serving her guests at her old-people parties, doing anything that needs doing. Great for you while she lives. But once she's gone, well—she wants it to be my turn to benefit. Problem is, I have no need for a typist. Have you planned for what you'll do after she dies? It won't be long now."

Something in the way he said that alarmed her. "You inherit her estate only if it's a natural death!"

"Planning to kill her?"

She frowned at him. "Try not to be so horrible."

Clarence laughed.

She thought of the two accidents that had befallen Valerie just after Clarence's visits, including one that led to her current bedridden state. Now, after his visits, Elena had taken care to make sure no rugs had been mysteriously moved or objects placed on the floor where Valerie might trip over them. And she kept an eye on his movements during visits.

Innocent until proven guilty, she reminded herself. Except that while that was fine as a legal concept, it wasn't really true outside of the legal system, was it? A guilty person was guilty whether you could prove it or not, and Valerie would be harmed all the same.

"You'll be glad to see her go, I think. Valerie is often cruel to you. I've seen that, Elena."

As if to prove his point, Valerie again taunted her as they ate lunch. "I do know who your father is, you know."

"If you do, send him a card nine months before my birthday and ask him if he remembers a one-night stand from around that time in 1962."

Valerie laughed.

"You love to stir up trouble, don't you?" Clarence said in a teasing tone.

"I do," Valerie admitted. "And I love a good lie. That's why I'm such a great writer. Isn't that so, Elena?"

"Popular, anyway."

Valerie laughed harder.

After lunch, Elena helped Valerie back into her bed in the library. It was Elena's favorite room, although Clarence was not fond of its dark paneling and heavy furniture. The scents of leather, old paper, binding, and ink that were so beloved by Elena were abhorrent to him. He stood by the tall windows, looking out at the rain-slicked street.

"Clarence, dear," Valerie said, calling him to her. "Do you see that large book—the first book on the fourth shelf there?" She pointed to a case. "Among the art books."

Moving toward it, he said, "The one about Warhol?"

"Yes. You'll find a brochure wedged in next to it and the side of the case. Remove it gently, please."

"*The Thirteen Most Wanted*," he said, reading the cover. "Police Department, New York City." He opened it. "February 1962. What is this?"

"Bring it to me, please. It's a booklet issued by the NYPD to its officers and the public. Think of it as an early form of social media. Raising the public's awareness of men the police hoped to capture."

She began looking through its pages, Clarence peering over her shoulder. "Mug shots and descriptions," he said. "Crappy design. Why is it among your art books?"

"Warhol," Elena answered from her nearby desk. "He famously—"

"Infamously, really," Valerie said.

"—silkscreened enlarged versions of their images to make a huge work of art for the New York World's Fair of 1964. *Thirteen Most Wanted Men.* It was controversial, and before the fair opened, the folks in charge painted over the images with silver paint."

"Painted over?!" Clarence spluttered. "Painted over *Warhol's* work?"

"Appalling, I agree. But some pointed out that the men were wanted, not convicted. Many were of Italian heritage, and because Rockefeller was up for reelection, he didn't want to lose the votes of the Italians. There was probably homophobia involved. It's hard to know what was really behind it. There are some other theories that may explain the outrage better."

"Fairs are meant to celebrate the pleasant," Valerie said. "Mug shots aren't."

"How do you know so much about it?" Clarence asked Elena.

"It was all part of a Queens Museum exhibition recently. We didn't make it there to see it, but there have been articles about it online and in the papers. I had no idea Valerie had the booklet—"

"Ah!" Valerie interrupted, pointing to an open page.

"What?" Clarence asked.

"Elena's father!"

There was a moment of stunned silence, then Clarence burst out laughing. "Oh, Valerie, no! That's too mean."

He brought the booklet to Elena.

It was opened to a mug shot of a young man with a full head of dark, wavy hair. He was dressed in a light-colored suit. The right side of his face was bruised and swollen, the eye nearly shut. The photo taken in profile was of that side of his face, making him look subdued. The photo taken from the front-facing view showed the beating more clearly, but . . . she placed her hand over the right side of his face.

Yes, defiance. Quiet anger. A promise of retribution.

Or was she reading that into it?

Had the police broken up a brawl when he was captured? Or had they delivered those blows? The latter seemed more likely, but she reminded herself that she knew nothing about his case.

"'Homicide,'" she read aloud. "'John Victor Guisto, age thirty-eight in 1957. Blue eyes, brown hair, five-eight, one hundred and seventy pounds.'"

"Short and a little pudgy, then," Clarence said, giggling.

She read to herself after that. The booklet gave a last known address, a list of previous occupations (laborer, chauffeur), his vices (gambling, liquor, "female entertainment"), and previous arrests (assault, robbery, grand larceny, possession of a dangerous weapon).

He was being sought as one of two men accused of murdering a union organizer in 1949. William Lurye had been stabbed while in a Manhattan phone booth and died the next day. He had been working for the International Ladies Garment Workers Union. The ILGWU was offering a $25,000 reward. Ten times that amount in today's dollars.

Another man, accused of being Guisto's partner in the attack, was acquitted of the crime.

She looked over to Valerie, saw the old woman regarding her steadily.

"The victim was ILGWU."

"Yes. Your grandfather's sweatshops were among those Lurye was trying to unionize."

"Now, Aunt Valerie!" Clarence protested.

"Sweatshops. Do not contradict me, Clarence. You know nothing about it. Your father sold them off in the 1950s, not long after you were born."

This apparently took the fun out of the game for Clarence. He went back to the window to sulk.

"The union reacted strongly to Lurye's murder. If those who hired the killers thought the ILGWU would be intimidated, they were proved wrong. They gave Lurye a hero's burial—nearly a hundred thousand people watched from the sidewalks or marched. Thousands and thousands of workers—they filled Eighth Avenue, solemnly following the hearse, marching to protest his murder, and thousands more were part of a work stoppage on the day of his funeral.

"You must understand that no one could text or email someone to ask them to show up. The union and the newspapers spread the word. They were showing the garment factory owners—even those who were suspected to be mob connected—that they would not be intimidated."

"This police case sounds shaky," Elena said. "It says the other man was found not guilty."

"Well, yes and no. Originally the police said there were three men involved, although that story changed. As did the memory of the only witness when he was on the stand. The prosecutors and judge were not amused. There were perjury convictions after the trial. I forget the name of the man who was acquitted."

"Benedict Macri."

"He confessed to Walter Winchell."

"What?" Clarence said, moving away from the window. "He confessed to a ventriloquist?"

Valerie covered her eyes with a hand and shook her head.

"You're thinking of *Paul* Winchell," Elena answered. "You mean the radio star, right, Valerie?"

"Yes. He was a newspaper reporter and gossip columnist—the latter was something new, something he started. He wrote a syndicated column for decades. And yes, he had a gossipy but extremely popular radio show. Good at attacking Nazi sympathizers in the 1930s but made the mistake of backing Joe McCarthy in the 1950s."

"So how did he get involved in this case?"

"Oh, he loved involving himself in crime stories and had a wide network of informants. He offered to donate his share of the ILGWU reward money—they were offering a huge reward—to a cancer research charity he started in memory of his friend Damon Runyon. Winchell teased out the story of making contact with Macri over a couple of his shows. He managed a clandestine meeting with Macri and ended up convincing Macri to turn himself in. Winchell went with him to the police station."

"Very dramatic."

"Winchell came out of vaudeville, not journalism school. He knew the power of drama."

The doorbell rang.

Speaking of knowing the power of drama, Elena thought, and went to answer it, checking her iPhone as she made the trip down the long hallway. She opened the door to find, as expected, three gentlemen, two of them not much younger than Valerie, the other in his forties.

They were all dressed in suits. One of the older men carried a large bouquet, the younger one a briefcase.

They greeted Elena warmly.

"Good afternoon, gentlemen," she said, smiling. "Thank you for coming out on such a horrid day."

They disclaimed any trouble as she took their coats and umbrellas.

"Please join us in the library."

The youngest of them, Aldus, glanced at her phone and asked, "Cloud or . . . ?"

"Both."

He nodded in satisfaction.

They were frequent guests of Valerie's, but since Valerie reserved Sundays for Clarence, and Clarence felt a Sunday visit was troubling himself enough, he had not met any of them. As they entered the library, Clarence was looking through Valerie's pills before hastily placing the containers back on the bedside table.

Valerie began the introductions.

"Mr. Robert Taylor, Mr. Thaddeus Fitch, and Mr. Aldus Fitch, allow me to introduce to you my grandnephew, Mr. Clarence Monroe."

The Fitches shook his hand. Taylor nodded at him and bent to kiss Valerie's cheek. She laughed and thanked him for the flowers, then asked Elena to place them in a vase. By the time she returned with it, the men were seated around Valerie's bed.

"Where shall we begin, Elena?" Valerie asked.

"You seem to have scheduled a meeting," Clarence said. "Perhaps I should be on my way."

"The meeting is for your benefit," Valerie said. "Stay."

"My benefit?"

"Mr. Thaddeus Fitch is our attorney. His son Aldus works with him. Robert Taylor is Elena's accountant and my fiancé."

"Fiancé!" He turned in anger toward Elena. "You allowed this—"

"My dear Clarence," Valerie said, "I am not addled. I am old, not incapable of making decisions. Nor of falling in love."

"Aunt Valerie, please, I just want to protect you! There are always going to be people who will be after your money!"

"She has no money," Elena said quietly.

"No money! No money!"

"Haven't had any in years," Valerie said gleefully.

"But—but—that can't be true!"

"It is."

"But the books!"

"Clarence. Take a deep breath and think for a moment. You visit me once a week. When have you ever seen me writing?"

"You go on television! You're famous."

"I haven't made a public appearance in years. The books were written by Elena."

He stared at Elena.

"The books were written by Elena, but she is not an extrovert like me. So we came to an agreement. It was not our first. She helped me out when I was about to lose this place."

"I don't understand! She only had five hundred thousand to her name! She was working as a secretary."

"May I?" Mr. Taylor asked Elena.

She nodded.

"We are discussing, with permission, matters very personal to your aunt and your cousin. You are not to repeat any of what you have heard or are about to hear today."

"I don't see how you can prevent me!"

"You will not," Aldus Fitch said quietly and firmly. "You will not."

Clarence had probably seldom met anyone—other than his own father— who had a commanding voice equal to Aldus Fitch's. For the moment, it shut him down. Mr. Taylor continued.

"When she first moved in with your aunt, as you say, Elena was working as an executive's secretary in a brokerage firm."

Elena said, "I once overhead a colleague ask him why he had hired someone with a scarred face, when his previous secretaries had been so gorgeous. He said his third and present wife was one of the gorgeous ones, and she was the one who hired me—to ensure he didn't cheat on her."

"He was an ass," Valerie said. "I'm glad you were able to quit that job."

"He's divorced, and his ex has brought him to the attention of the SEC," Aldus said.

Elena looked at him in surprise. He shrugged.

"Elena gave nearly all her salary to your aunt," Taylor went on, "but she did allow herself one indulgence—she bought an SE/30."

"A what?" Clarence asked.

"An early Macintosh computer," Elena answered.

"She liked that computer so much, she used almost all of her inheritance to buy Apple stock. It has, shall we say, done very well for her. A little later she invested in Amazon."

"I liked books, too," Elena said.

"And started writing them," Mr. Taylor said fondly. "As you mentioned, Clarence, those did well, too."

"All right, fine! Let's pretend I believe Elena is rich as a rock star. Aunt Valerie still owns this place. It's worth millions."

"Thaddeus?" Valerie said.

The lawyer opened his briefcase and pulled out a copy of the deed. He handed it to Clarence. The color drained from Clarence's face.

"Meanwhile," Valerie said, "I had been as foolish as you are, Clarence. I nearly lost this place. Elena was willing to help me. I had enough pride to refuse to simply take her handouts. I deeded this place to her."

Clarence came to his feet, his face, so pale a moment earlier, now red with anger. "So all this time—all these Sundays—"

"All the times you assured me you loved me and weren't just after my money and my real estate. Yes."

"I'm going to tell everyone!"

"Ghost writers are not uncommon," Mr. Fitch said. "The publisher and agent are fully aware of the arrangement in this case. And Miss Monroe has retired from making public appearances in recent years. This will hardly be earth-shattering."

"But he won't make any such announcement," Elena said, "because he'll know I can offer evidence that he attempted the murder of his great-aunt."

"You're lying!" Clarence shouted, but looked panicked.

Aldus rose to his feet. "Sit down and shut up."

Clarence obeyed.

Elena decided she was going to have to ask Aldus to teach her how to give commands.

"I had to come up with a way of stopping you, Clarence. I've never liked the game Valerie played with you, and I knew you'd never understand that she only wanted to see you, to stay connected. I had planned to settle some funds on you when she died. But then you started trying to kill her."

Clarence opened his mouth, glanced at Aldus, and remained silent.

"Aldus works with his father, but not as an attorney. He was a police officer for a time, then became a private investigator. He helped me to place hidden cameras after her second fall. So we have proof that just now, what you did with the substitution of her pills . . ."

They all saw him start to make a grab for the pill bottles, saw him realize that he had given himself away a second time, saw him slump in defeat.

"Are you going to have me arrested?" he asked after a long silence.

"That depends on you," Taylor said. "If it were up to me . . . but it's not. Valerie sees her role in this and also tells me that she doesn't think you'll do well in prison. She does love you, Clarence. God knows why."

"Mr. Fitch has drawn up some paperwork," Elena said. "You will agree not to contact or interfere with her or her future husband, nor to contact me. You will be given a home in Florida and enough to live there comfortably. That money will be managed by a trustee. If you return to the state of New York, if you tell anyone what you've learned about the authorship of the books, if you discuss my finances or Valerie's with anyone, you forfeit everything and a video from today goes to the district attorney and the press. Aldus?"

Aldus, who had donned gloves during this speech, bagged the bottles of pills.

He told Clarence to stand up and hand over the bottle of prescribed pills he had exchanged with whatever fatal substance was in the bottle he had placed on the table.

Clarence, to Elena's wonder, obeyed again.

Clarence signed the papers.

"You're all the family I have left," he said morosely.

"You ungrateful—You just tried to deprive Elena of all of hers!" Aldus said incredulously.

"No, she'd still have her murderer father," he sneered.

"What in the hell is he talking about?" Aldus asked, breathing hard, looking as if he was struggling not to pummel Clarence.

"Aldus, please, no!" Elena said. "Let me show what he means."

Elena handed him the brochure and briefly told him the story.

"What a load of crap. You don't look a thing like him."

Aldus paced the length of the room a few times, then turned to Valerie. "I suppose it's too late to get you to reform from this kind of mischief."

Many months later, on a bright spring day, Elena stood in the aviary of the Queens Zoo. She was not entirely surprised to see Aldus Fitch making his way down the walkway.

He had developed a habit of watching over her. She supposed it could have easily felt as if he was stalking her, but he managed not to take it that far. Or maybe she just felt comfortable in his presence. More comfortable in his presence than out of it, she had begun to realize.

He had been teaching her how to be more commanding. Her new book contract reflected that. So did her willingness to venture outside more often.

She watched the birds.

"It was easier to disappear in 1949," he said as he came up to her. "One way or another. At first I figured someone killed him not long after the Luyre murder. Now I'm not so sure. When that bulletin came out, he had been on the loose for more than a dozen years. If the police thought he was dead, they wouldn't have bothered putting him in the booklet."

"But no one has claimed to see him since, have they? His image is the one most often shown in stories about Warhol's *Thirteen Most Wanted Men.* Amazing that he could elude capture with so much publicity."

"Maybe he dyed his hair, grew a beard, went to live in a small town under another name. It has happened before. He could be a model citizen somewhere."

"Do you think so?"

He shook his head. "I don't."

"No, I don't, either."

They stood quietly together. She felt at ease. It seemed to her that she had not felt at ease for a long time.

Aldus said, "I'm not convinced he was guilty or that he was innocent. It's weird. Usually I have a better sense of things. But he's a mystery."

"Valerie's intrigues often are."

"How's the happy couple?"

"Happy indeed."

"Good," he said. "Good."

After a while he said, "I've lived in New York my whole life, but I've never been to this place before. I like it."

"This is from the World's Fair of 1964, you know. The same one that destroyed Warhol's art. This is its geodesic dome."

"They had an aviary at the fair?"

"No. It served as a gigantic futuristic pavilion; then the next year they used it to set up an exhibition to honor Churchill, who had just died. It became the dome for the aviary later. They put the mesh over it and went from there. Like just about everything from that fair, it has had a history of difficulties, but recently revived and improved, I'm glad to say."

"It's good they didn't give up on it."

"I've always wondered if the birds here would rather be free or safe," Elena said. "The only one known to escape was a magpie—I love that it was a magpie!—and the magpie came back and fed other birds through the net, until they coaxed it back in."

"Fugitives usually have a hard time staying fugitives," Aldus said, hearing her worries beneath what she said. "You can't let yourself be convinced he's really your father."

"There are a few things that ring true about it. If my grandfather—known to be quite ruthless—hired him to kill a union organizer, maybe he already knew John Victor Guisto as a chauffeur and entrusted him with that job. He was a rich man who could have hidden him from the police."

"For a dozen years, and then he gets the daughter of the house pregnant?"

"Or maybe after Grandfather died, John Victor was running low on funds and approached the wild daughter about continuing the arrangement."

"You make up stories for a living. Storytellers are always explaining the world and its questions, Elena. You can keep making up these stories about him, your mother, yourself. But they aren't necessarily true stories."

"You're right, of course."

"You could go on one of these DNA sites, spit in a tube, and see if a bunch of Guistos match to you."

She shook her head. "No, that would tie me down if I matched or leave me feeling a silly sense of loss if I didn't. Maybe I'm like these birds. I don't mind the in-between places, safe and free as I want to be."

He looked away at that. She smiled to herself.

"Some things," she said, "aren't just one thing or another, you know. Innocent, guilty. Free, safe. Truth, story."

He looked back at her.

"I want to give a command right now," she said. "But it's also a request."

"Okay," he said, starting to return her smile. "Go for it."

Some people, she thought later, make everything better.

Jerome Charyn's *latest novel,* The Perilous Adventures of the Cowboy King: A Novel of Teddy Roosevelt and His Times, *was published in 2019. A new book,* Cesare: A Novel of War-torn Berlin, *will be published in 2020.*

Twilight of Man by Rockwell Kent

THE MAN FROM HARD ROCK MOUNTAIN

BY **JEROME CHARYN**

Larson lived alone.

He had a cabin under Hard Rock Mountain, at the edge of an old mining town that had rumbled out of existence. Larson had no electricity or running water. The town had been properly wired, but he lost his dial tone one morning and couldn't get it back. He had no cable service and couldn't seem to charge his cell phone. The mailman had stopped making deliveries, and Larson wasn't even sure if there ever was a post office connected to the town. He couldn't buy groceries. The stores were shuttered. So he became a scavenger in order to survive.

He went from street to street with a crowbar, from cabin to cabin, store to store, even broke into the abandoned motel on Rock River Road. He carried a sack with him, like a demented Santa Claus. But he found a cornucopia of peanut butter, crackers, jelly, jam, beef jerky, and cans of corn giblets and tomato soup, enough to last for a year, so he didn't have to do much scouting after that. He had drinking water from an old well behind the cabin, even if the well was full of frogs and the water a little rusty. He had a supply of kitchen matches and a stove that burned balled-up paper and chunks of wood. And not all his flashlight batteries had gone to rust. There were no more radio or television stations within miles of Hard Rock Mountain, and perhaps there were none at all. Besides, what did a radio mean without a real electrical outlet?

He still had his double gauge and a drawerful of shells, but he hadn't seen the first sign of a squirrel, and there wasn't a fox to be found. All the animals had fled, even the black bear that used to scratch at Larson's trash can. He no longer left much of a trail of trash. He drank water from jars and cans and used the empty boxes of crackers as kindling to prime his potbellied stove. He still had a tiny garden; the soil had gone sour, and all his carrots shriveled in the ground. He'd once had a cat, Key Largo, but the cat had died on Larson, and he buried her behind the cabin. What would he have fed her now? Condensed milk and soda crackers? And Larson suddenly remembered that Key Largo died before the entire population fled, a little at a time.

Larson was all alone, without even the comfort of a single birdcall. He could still see the smokestacks on the far side of the mountain, but he couldn't remember the last time they'd been fired up. Yet there was a great advantage. No longer bothered by the constant plumes of smoke, he could study the night sky and its enormous quilt of stars.

He was content in his own way, humming to himself, not even searching for human company—there was none. And then the two strangers appeared, like rag dolls out of the dust. The first was a woman of twenty-seven or so, in a simple smock, and the second a little girl of five, a creature with big green eyes and rusty red hair, carrying a little jeweled purse close to her tummy.

"We're hungry, neighbor," the woman said. "Can you part with some nourishment for me and the little one?"

The idea of two companions thrilled Larson. "Where are you from?" he asked.

"From yonder," she said, "over the hill." She had a melodious voice, like the songbirds he missed.

"But are there still towns?" he asked. He remembered vague reports of a vast cyber attack, but how vast he couldn't tell. Nothing died at once. The electricity might spark for an hour, his cell phone might suddenly ring, or else Larson might receive a text from an unidentifiable caller.

HELP WILL ARRIVE

"The towns," she said, "are just like this one. Can you provide us with nourishment, neighbor?"

"Yes," he said. "Of course I can provide." And Larson was suddenly alert. He prepared a soufflé with powdered eggs. He put ketchup on the table and peanut butter.

"Scrumptious," she said, shaking Larson's hand. "I'm Emma Rothschild, and this is Kathy."

"You have a lovely daughter—with red hair."

"I hate to disappoint you. She's sort of my niece, by adoption."

"I don't understand," Larson said.

Emma was tall and had muscular arms, light blue eyes, and traces of a blond mustache. "Well, I found her in a somewhat deserted village. She was starving, and I adopted her, right on the spot. It was a snap decision."

"Didn't her mother object?"

"Oh, I answered all her objections," Emma said.

Larson persisted, and Emma grew a little surly; her eyebrows twitched.

"But a mother wouldn't give up her child to a perfect stranger, even in such weird times. That doesn't sound natural to me," Larson said.

"It's perfectly natural. I knew how to feed her, and her mother didn't."

"But you have to cadge every single meal," Larson said.

Emma didn't stall. "There's an art to that."

Larson invited this muscular woman with a blond mustache to stay on with the little girl.

"Are you sure we won't be a burden?" Emma asked, watching Larson with the clear blue eyes of a hawk.

"No," he said. "I can make toys for Kathy. I'm pretty good at carving things."

"And I'm a decent gardener."

"But the soil's sour. All I could produce was one wilted carrot."

"We'll see," Emma said.

She worked all afternoon, getting rid of the sour clay with her fingernails, while Kathy stood beside her like a toy soldier, still clutching her little jeweled purse; they found a tiny bed of dark soil in that vast coffin of clay and planted a few seeds that Emma took out of her pocket. Larson shuddered once or twice. Emma seemed like a bountiful witch. He carved a little wagon for the girl, with wooden wheels. Kathy played with the wagon, imagined it filled with the forest animals that had all disappeared from Hard Rock Mountain.

Larson worried about the nighttime and where Emma would sleep. But she climbed into his bed like a trampoline artist, took off her smock, and straddled Larson, who was astonished.

"If this is some sort of payment, Miss Emma, it isn't necessary."

"Silence," she growled, and rode him into some kind of sweet eternity. He'd never had much luck with women, couldn't seem to reveal his desires, but here she was, with that child in the same room, cuddled up on an enormous pillow, without much of an expression on her face, as if she'd been observing a pair of acrobats.

Larson couldn't help himself; he was smitten for the first time in his life, in love with a lady who'd arrived out of the dust. Their bodies never touched while they strove to stay alive, with Larson preparing the meals and Emma ripping at weeds in her garden. It was only at night, with the sweat of their toil still on them, that their bodies clapped together and made a celestial sound.

It went on for a month. And then another stranger appeared, a frog of a man who had the collapsed cheeks of the hungry and half-starved. Larson fed him beans and crackers on the cabin's tiny porch. The frog stopped chewing when he saw Emma and the child.

"Jesus, son," the little man whispered, "they're the flesh eaters."

"Flesh eaters?"

"Cannibals," the little man said. "The two of them take over a house and then move on. How the hell do ya think they've survived this long?"

"But who told you this?" Larson had to ask. His hands were trembling.

"It's common knowledge, son. Thanks for the beans. I'd best vamoose, or I might end up in a skillet."

And the frog scattered as fast as he could.

Larson was quiet for two hours. Yet he wasn't frightened. He'd had a rapturous month with Emma and the little girl. Emma's acrobatics on the bed had rekindled him somehow. He couldn't return to that warp of isolation, no matter who Emma was or what she had done.

It was Emma who broke the silence.

"What did that midget tell you, Larson? Your cheeks are pale as chalk."

"He said I'd end up in a skillet if I stayed here, in my own cabin."

She laughed, and Larson could see how yellow her teeth were, how sharp.

"I'm fond of you, Larson. Can't you tell? I've found my peace on your pissy mattress. I'm content."

"But you and the little girl chew on people?"

Her blue eyes didn't avoid his. "Yes."

"And when our food stock runs low?"

"We'll find some stranger . . . and I'll lure him into your bed—it will be over with in a minute. We'll survive."

"No," he said. "This cabin isn't a charnel house."

"Fine," she said, snapping her fingers. "But it's hypothetical, darling. We still have food. And I have *some* hope in our garden."

It was never the same after that. He built new toys for Kathy, but she couldn't seem to ignite that little playland of hers, and she soon tired of all the toys. She made toys of her own with some bent nails and shards of wood and a tiny silver hammer that she took out of her purse. Kathy's toys made no sense; no matter how hard she knocked, the bent nails wouldn't bite into the wood. She surrounded herself with scatterings and discards and refused Larson when he offered to help.

Larson still made love to Emma, savored the little tattoos she left with her bite marks. And he'd ride along as she rode on him. Yet he made love like some reptile, with one eye open. And he slept with that same sullen, one-eyed stare.

"Larson, it's that little man. He poisoned you against us."

She clutched at Larson, brought him out to her little garden, with its carrots and tomato vines.

"Well," she said, "I took your clay and revived it some. Is that God's hand, or not?"

Larson's lips moved with a pronounced whisper. "God's, I guess."

Other strangers arrived, even hungrier than that little frog, and scattered after one look at Emma. Larson had all the evidence he needed. *I'm living with a pair of cannibals.* But he was strung to them now, even if Kathy was blind to his toys and her own scatterings of wood. She was more amused by her purse, digging at the little jewels until all the ornaments were gone. She seemed different to Larson, with a greater grip on things than Larson himself had. Her hair was turning bloodred. Her teeth grew, and her jaw widened.

Larson's coffers were emptying. He no longer had powdered eggs for a soufflé. The ketchup was all gone. The portions he delivered to the table were less and less copious.

"Emma, we'll starve pretty soon. And I've been all over town. There's nothing but empty shelves."

"Don't worry, darling."

But how could he not worry? He watched while she washed the kitchen knives with little deft maneuvers. He imagined all sorts of weaponry in her hands. Would Emma and her accomplice grind him down with their teeth?

"I'm frightened," he said. "I'll have to leave."

"And where will you go?" she asked. "You're like a baby, Larson. You'd get lost climbing Hard Rock Mountain. *Stay.*"

She signaled to Kathy, and the two of them departed without a word or a kiss or a wave of their hands. Larson was miserable in his new isolation. He treasured the black soil of Emma's garden, sifted it, made a mud pie or two. He had no appetite. He lived on a few crackers and lumps of peanut butter. It was a starvation diet. He couldn't sleep. He was restless and morose without the little noises of Emma and the girl. He'd never survive.

He hiked up the mountain. There was nothing to hold him there, nothing but rock and hard clay, as if the world itself had gone sour and he was some miserable accomplice of the dead. Even that quilt of stars suggested nothing but the naked vastness of eternity. He was alone again, and he didn't like it.

Larson returned to his cabin. He moped about for two weeks, more isolated than he'd ever been. He couldn't bear to look at his own handiwork or the little girl's crazy toys. He smashed them all and shoved the splintered wood into his stove. He still couldn't get warm. Larson didn't have the temperament—or the ingenuity—to kill himself. He was a walking carcass, nonetheless.

And then they reappeared, rising out of the dust again.

Emma Rothschild was radiant, with a dark red bloom. Her flesh had filled out; she no longer looked like an acrobat; and the little girl had come back with a slight paunch, as if a five-year-old were suddenly pregnant. He wasn't fooled by their calm demeanor—the two of them had found their prey, had had their fill of human flesh. Larson was convinced of that.

"Emma," he muttered, "we'll still run out of food."

But she wouldn't let him spoil her homecoming. She fiddled with his hair, caressing his scalp with her callused hands. She and the little girl had arrived with several sacks of food—olives in a jar, dry cereal, an assortment of muffins . . .

All of a sudden, out of nowhere, Larson was as hungry as a horse. They watched him chew, listened to the gnashing of his teeth. They were content. Emma and the little girl held hands and didn't even sample the muffins.

"Will you stop brooding?" she asked.

"I'll try."

"We came back, Larson. Isn't that proof enough?"

"Proof," Larson repeated, like a deranged parrot.

"That we care for you. We could have stayed on the other side of Hard Rock Mountain. Oh, we had a million opportunities. Isn't that so, Little Kate?"

The little girl nodded her head—all that shaking might have signified nothing at all.

Larson scrutinized Emma while he tore into his fifth muffin. "And what did you find on the other side? I've never been."

Emma was evasive. "People are people, no matter where you go."

"But have they lost their electrical grid?"

"Oh, it's erratic—same as here."

And she lured him down onto his own bed. Larson didn't feel any tenderness toward her. He was savage in his need of Emma. But she didn't seem to mind, as he scratched her arms and legs with his long, wolfish fingernails and marked her with ribbons of blood.

She laughed.

"Darling," she said.

But he saw Little Kate out of the corner of his eye. The ribbons of blood had riveted her. She took the tiny silver hammer out of her child's purse. There was nothing impulsive in her moves, nothing casual. She struck Larson over the right temple with that little hammer. It wasn't the play of a child. It was a deliberate act. She struck him again, while her tongue wandered in her mouth.

He looked at Emma, appealed to her, with blood bubbling out of his left nostril. She and Little Kate hadn't come back out of any concern for Larson. He was one more chicken about to be plucked. He felt hypnotized by the hammer. Little Kate was a tympan artist, delivering blows with each lick of her tongue.

Larson reached his hand out to Emma, his fingers twisting in the dusty air of the cabin. But Emma was as neutral as Hard Rock Mountain, as puzzling as the quilt of stars. All Larson could do was wait for the hammer to fall on the tympan of his skull, watch and wait.

Brendan DuBois *is the award-winning author of twenty-two novels, including two—*The First Lady *and* The Cornwalls Are Gone—*co-authored with James Patterson. His 170-plus short stories have won him three Shamus Awards from the Private Eye Writers of America and three Edgar Allan Poe Award nominations from the Mystery Writers of America. And if the answer is "A* Jeopardy! *game show champion," then the question has to be "Who is Brendan DuBois?"*

Reefing Sails Around Diamond Shoals, Cape Hatteras by Winslow Homer

ADRIFT OFF THE DIAMOND SHOALS

BY BRENDAN DuBOIS

The interior of the Diamond Shoals Pub in Rodanthe, North Carolina, is fairly empty this late September afternoon, as the leading edge of Hurricane Grace has started to batter Hatteras Island and the pub's only visible window. The rest of the windows have been sealed up by plywood, and the pub's owner—Polly Trenton—is only keeping the place open so we'll put up the last section of wood when our business is finished for the day.

I'm sitting near the window with Till King, an old friend from grammar school and high school, and he's hunched over his Budweiser draft like he's afraid Polly is going to come and steal it. Lots of things have been taken away from Till in his life, so I guess that's a reasonable assumption on his part.

Till looks to me and says, "Don't worry, Cyrus'll be here. It'll take more than a hurricane to keep him away from this deal."

I don't say anything, just pick up my iced tea, take a sip.

Polly is behind the bar, wearing a black sweatshirt advertising her place, her thick blond hair tied back in a bun currently holding two pens. She's standing with her head tilted back, looking up at a TV screen hanging from the ceiling, playing a CNN news feed showing some brave journalist in a yellow slicker being blown back and forth a few miles away as Grace, a Category Five hurricane, hammers its way right down our collective throats.

She calls out, "TV says they're closing off Route 12 in two hours and pulling back emergency responders. Everybody who's left will be on their own, nobody coming in to rescue 'em." She looks to us, her face troubled. "You fellas gonna be done by then?

I look to Till and say, "Depends if his older brother shows up or not."

Polly says, "Fellas, don't care if the pope is showing up, I'm headin' out in an hour. You best have your business wrapped up."

Till says, "He'll be here. I promise."

"Okay," she says, seemingly not believing a word he's saying, just as another heavy gust of wind hits the pub. The air seems to throb, and the lights flicker, and even though I have planned and know what's coming up in the next hour, my skin crawls with a primeval fear of the approaching storm. I make a look of sitting here casually, sipping my iced tea, but my deep inside is telling me to *escape, escape, escape.*

Another, heavier gust of wind hits the pubs, making glassware and bottles rattle and framed photos and prints on the wall shake. There are photos of fishermen past, old trawlers, one of the destroyer USS *Roper*—which sank a U-boat not too far from here in 1942—a couple of the last remaining Texas Towers on the Eastern Seaboard (once used as light stations but now abandoned), and a framed print from Winslow Homer, called *Reefing Sails Around Diamond Shoals, Cape Hatteras* which is just up a way from here.

I know next to nothing about paintings and art, but the print of that hundred-year-old watercolor has always stirred me. I even have a similar print in my studio apartment. It shows two fishermen in an open boat, desperately hauling in sails as the water gets rough, as storm clouds gather. In the near distance is a lightboat, stationed there to warn mariners away from our Diamond Shoals, which has probably caused the sinking of more than six hundred ships over the years.

The framed print near the bar is askew. I think about going up and straightening it, but another gust of wind hits the pub, and it moves again.

Touching it would be a waste of time, so I let it be.

But I look at it again. When Till and I were younger, we'd go out in small sailboats along this whole coastline and out to Diamond Shoals, fishing and swimming and sometimes snorkeling, looking for wrecks to salvage.

Nothing much ever got salvaged during those day-trips, save for a lot of pleasant memories. But a couple of times we were just like those fishermen up there on the wall, trying to reef in our sails when the wind and waves picked up.

Outside, the parking lot of the pub has about a half foot of standing water in it, and high tide isn't due for another four hours, just about the same time the full force and fury of Hurricane Grace is due to strike.

A bad combination, meaning that about the time Polly comes back to her place, only the cement foundation will probably be left.

Till says, "I read your last book, Henry. It was pretty good."

"Thanks."

"That makes . . . what, five, now?"

I say, "Eight."

"Oh, well . . . I liked the last one pretty good."

"What was your favorite part?"

Till smiles. His teeth are worn and crooked, and on the left side a molar is gone, leaving a black gap there, as dark as dirt. His skin is worn and creased from long days of working out on the waters and long nights drinking and drugging his way to whatever sleep could come his way.

"Oh, I don't know," he says. "All of the parts were good, honest."

"How about the ending?" I ask. "Did you like that? It took some research."

He quickly nods, like a pet, yearning for approval. "Yeah, I can tell, Henry. It was pretty graphic."

The lights flicker again. I say, "It was fiction, you know, but I had a good time, writing that scene, about the U-boat surfacing and firing its deck gun at the lighthouse. Remember that?"

More quick nods. "I sure do, Henry, I sure do. Wow. Made you think you was right there."

I shake my head, smile at my old friend. "Sorry, Till. I was fooling you. There are no U-boats in my book."

He grimaces and lowers his head in a practiced move, of being caught, whether in a lie or drunk driving or fishing without a permit. He says, "Honest, I started it. I'll finish it, one of these days. Honest."

"It's all right, Till. I'm sure you will."

There's movement outside, and a black Lincoln Navigator rolls in, splashing up water, its headlights and windshield wipers working hard against the heavy rain. The Navigator pulls past the old rust-red Chevy pickup truck belonging to me and the beat-up Kia belonging to Polly. The large SUV comes close and parks in a handicapped spot.

"See?" Till says, a bit of triumph in his voice. "Cyrus is here."

I watch, feeling again that warning of *escape, escape, escape,* and I relax only when I see the door open and one man climb out.

"So he is," I say.

About a minute later Cyrus King bursts into the pub, shaking the rain off an Irish tweed cap and then taking off a dark green L.L. Bean rain slicker and then shaking that off as well.

"Sweet Jesus, I don't think I've ever driven through so much goddamn rain," he says, and then he drops his hat and coat on an empty table and strides over to see us. Polly glares as he walks in our direction, leaving his wet clothes on top of the clean table. He has on dark khaki slacks and a black turtleneck sweater, and close up, there's a clear family resemblance to his younger brother Till, although Cyrus's face is red and fleshy from lots of time indoors, wheeling, dealing, and cheating.

At our table he wipes his hands and says, "Hey, Tilly, move over. I want the window seat."

Till asks, "Why?"

His older brother snaps back, "I wanna make sure nobody steals my Lincoln, okay?"

Till doesn't say anything else, just slumps his shoulders in a practiced move, gets up, and Cyrus takes his seat. He then looks over to the bar and says, "Polly! What do you have on draft?"

She's back to watching CNN. "Nothing. I've run dry, and I'm not going to waste my time hooking anything new up. I'm gonna be closing in a few minutes anyway."

"Shit, well, give me a bottle of something."

Polly doesn't move. "Sorry. Stock's run out."

"But Tilly's got something."

"Got the last one."

The lights flicker again. The rain is falling so hard and the wind is rushing so much that it's like a hose is spraying water on the single window, clouding up our view.

Cyrus turns to face me. "Fine. Hope ol' Hurricane Grace flattens this place out."

"Doubt it," Polly says. "The pub's been here long enough, survived enough storms."

Cyrus gives me a can-you-believe-this look and says, "Okay. Henry, I'm here. So let's get to it. You're finally ready to accept my offer?"

I nod. "Yes, I am."

"Took long enough."

"As long as it had to," I say. "When my dad was alive, he'd never sell. Now, a year later, it seems to be the right time."

Cyrus says, "Well, glad to see things are working out in the right direction. Even if your dad was a dope"

Till says, "That's not fair. Henry's dad was a good sort. Just stubborn."

Cyrus doesn't turn his head, but he says, "I don't remember asking your fucking opinion, so shut up, Tilly."

There's heavy silence for a moment.

I say, "Your brother's name is Tillman. Or Till. I don't like it when you call him Tilly. I know he doesn't like it either."

Cyrus says, "Still sticking up for my loser brother?"

"Seems like it."

"Who sticks up for you, Henry? Hunh? Last I heard you barely make a living from those lousy books, your wife and kids are up in Arlington, and you waste your time trying to save the world."

"Not all of the world," I say.

He grins, his teeth white and perfect. "Sure. Recycle. Windmills. Degradable trash. All that happy hippy crap. Hey, Polly, I saw once in the paper that Henry here was backing recycled paper plates. You ever use that stuff? You think your customers would like using a plate that was recycled from used toilet paper or old paper towels?"

Polly says, "If you're against it, I'm considering it."

Cyrus is still smiling. "You always thought you were higher and mightier than the rest of us, your shit didn't stink, all the way through high school. Thought you could outlast me here. Well, who's the winner here, hunh? Who's the winner?"

There's a harsh *bleep!* and the lights blink out.

They don't come back.

"Looks like Hurricane Grace at the moment," I say.

There's not much light coming into the place, and Polly says, "That's it, fellas. We are officially closed. You remember your promise now, Henry Cutler, okay?"

"I remember," I say.

Cyrus speaks up. "Look, why waste the time anymore, okay? Over there in my coat, I got a purchase and sales agreement with a five-thousand-dollar certified check. Let's just sign the paperwork here and get the hell off the island."

I say, "You scared, Cyrus?"

Oh, that gets his back up. "There's not a goddamn thing in this world that scares me."

"Then the deal is the deal," I say. "We go out to my family place, I get one more look around, and then I sign the paperwork, and the place is yours."

"Fine," he grunts. "Let's get the hell out of here and get it done."

Outside, Polly gets into her Kia and starts up and turns on the lights and windshield wipers. Cyrus does the same for his Lincoln, leaving Till and me to do what was promised.

In front of the pub, there's a sheet of plywood on the ground, held down by four concrete blocks, and there's a nearby toolbox. I pop open the toolbox and check the electric drill; it's still holding a good charge. Till and I get the concrete blocks free, and picking up the plywood and putting it in place is one hell of a chore, with the winds whipping it around and trying to fly it over the island. Till is heavier than me, and after we get the plywood slammed into place, he leans into the plywood as I get the electric drill and six long wood screws and drill them in through pre-drilled holes.

We step back, both of us soaking wet, and I put the drill back into the toolbox, snap the lid shut, and slide it under the outside deck.

Behind us Cyrus honks the horn twice.

"Your brother is impatient," I say.

"Yeah, always."

There's another, softer horn blow, and Polly goes by in her Kia, waving at us, and we wave back and then trudge over to my truck.

Inside the Chevy truck cab the windows fog up real quick as I start the engine and slowly go out onto Route 12 and start heading north. I switch on the air conditioner to dry things out. Cyrus pulls in right behind us, and Till says, "Watch out, he's gonna stick to your ass so much, if you gotta stop, he'll ram right into you."

"That's a price I'm willing to pay."

The rain has fallen so much that most of the road is flooded, and two SUVs pass us, also going north, blinking their headlights at us—*escape, escape, escape*—and Till says, "I dunno."

We drive on a bit more.

"You don't know what?"

The wind shakes my truck, and I take my time, trying to dodge power lines that have been ripped away from the tilting wood utility poles.

"I dunno why you're doing this, right now, with this big blow coming."

"My quirky sense of humor, I guess."

"Hunh?"

Part of the road is now a turbulent stretch of a flooded area, and I take it slow as I feel for the crown of the pavement, not wanting to flood out my engine so close to our old house. Most of the houses around here are as boarded up as the Diamond Shoals Pub, with one literary person writing NOT TONIGHT GRACIE in bright orange spray-paint on sheets of plywood.

There's a slight rise, and to our right the churning Atlantic is visible, right beyond the national shoreline. I say, "Days like this, that'd be something to go out sailing, right?"

Till folds his arms. "You're not right, Henry. That's not sailing weather out there."

"I know. But still, remember all the times we'd go out after a big storm like Grace, looking to see what was tossed up on shore? Stuff from the wrecks, maybe the U-boats that were sunk out there."

"You and your U-boats."

"That valve I found had German writing on it, and you know it."

"Okay, okay, it had German writing. Doesn't mean it was off a U-boat. Could have been off a freighter. You can't prove that."

"The heart knows what it knows," I say. "And that's beyond proof."

"Oh, shut up already." Till laughs, and I laugh with him.

There's a narrow dirt road up to the right, the sign CUTLER WAY leaning over, and I turn on the directional and make the turn. I look up in my rearview mirror and, as warned, Cyrus is right behind me, like he is trying to intimidate me or overwhelm me with his big Lincoln Navigator.

Yeah, I think. Good luck with that.

The road widens some, and lots of memories decide to make themselves known, poke their heads up. Till and I bicycling along this same road, fishing gear in hand, looking for the best places up and down the narrow coast to spend a lazy day. Nights out stargazing over there by the dunes. Bicycling down as well to Callaghan's Market to get a few groceries for Mom. Bonfires at night. The people in this little stretch of Hatteras just being the best of friends, dating and marrying each other.

I see the new homes and condos.

The memories go away.

To the left and right are large, overwhelming buildings, built hard and fast into the delicate land. Two stories high with turrets and outside decks and large windows, satellite dishes attached to the roofs. There's never been written or verbal evidence, just bits of gossip and tales told around the bars and pubs up and down Hatteras, that Cyrus King had connections, had pull, and managed to knock down the old homes and put up these multimillion-dollar capitalist castles, monuments to his own greed and bitter memories of growing up poor.

I recall one night, at Newton Station, drinking hard while a fiddle player and guitar player swung out some old Celtic tunes, and one limping fisherman told me, "You know what 'Cyrus' means, don't you? From the old Persian. King. That means that son of a bitch is called King King . . . or King of Kings, like Jesus damn Christ."

But in front of us now is my home, my family's home, secure in its place like it's been for more than a century, built like lots of old homes in Hatteras, one story with heavy shingles and a wraparound deck, small windows, doing its best to blend into the scenery, heavy wooden pillars holding everything in place.

Yeah. Years ago it did blend into the scenery, but the scenery has changed, and now it sticks out like an Amish woman walking backstage at a strip club.

There are two small sheds, a kayak tucked under the rear deck, and up on the roof are old rusted struts from a project of mine that had failed a couple of years ago.

I park near the house, and Till says, "Why today? Hunh? Why today?"

"You know why."

"I don't want to know why."

I switch off the engine, and with the wipers gone, I can't see out the windshield from the torrential rain.

"Then stay in the truck, Till. Okay? You promised me, but if you're changing—"

"I said I didn't want to know why," he says, opening the door. "But I'll still go in and be there with you, just like I promised."

The Lincoln pulls right in next to us, and the wind and rain are much stronger here, without the other buildings around the pub giving some sort of windbreak. Cyrus gets out and says something, but I can't hear a damn word he says, and I just shrug my shoulders and walk up the near steps to the wraparound deck.

The door is unlocked.

For long years, until the new neighbors supplied by Cyrus came in with their ATVs, loud music, parties, and bright lights, this home's door was never locked.

It's good to be back in the past, if for only a moment.

Inside it's dim, and Till and Cyrus follow me, and by touch and by making my way through the shadows, I get into the kitchen and find an oil lamp—or hurricane lamp, how damn ironic—and, with a wooden match, light it. There are two other lamps on the round kitchen table, and I bring those into the living room, which we always called the big room.

The lamps give off some light, and I stand to one side of the sliding glass doors and look out to the Atlantic. Cyrus and Till join me, and in an awed whisper Till says, "Sweet Jesus, will you look at that."

"That" being the Atlantic Ocean out there, hardly a hundred yards away. The waves are rolling toward us, hard, wide, and deep. White foam spreads ahead of the waves, the wind carrying the foam away in long, whipping stands. Till is next to me and says, "Holy shit, the waves are already at Doyle's Dune. And the real storm surge isn't due for another four hours. Holy shit."

I admit seeing the waves hitting Doyle's Dune—where a long-ago hermit named Doyle lived in a shack made of driftwood and lumber—does make my face and hands cold. Never in my life or in my family's memories has the Atlantic ever reached in this far. Damn. And the sky . . . the clouds are low, dark, ominous, with rolls of vapor and streamers seeming ready to descend and smother us all.

The windows hum with the vibration of the wind and rain striking, and Cyrus says, "Damn it, Cutler, can we hurry this up?"

I want to say something insulting, but I can't work myself up to do so.

"Yeah, let's do it," I say.

I step back into the shadows, and Cyrus says, "Hey, Henry, too bad your solar power project didn't work, hunh? Sure could have used the lights here . . . even with the rain and clouds."

"Well . . . it would have worked, but for some reason, it kept on getting vandalized."

Cyrus says, "Funny, hunh?"

"Hilarious," I say.

"Also heard that a windmill you were making here toppled down before it was finished."

Till says, "Cyrus, it wasn't toppled. Someone drug it."

"Dragged it," his older brother corrects. "Christ, are you drinking today?"

"No," Till says, as a heavier gust even makes this old home shudder. "But I'm sure in the mood."

I light another hurricane lamp, and we go to another part of the big room, part of a porch jutting out. At the center of this place is a heavy wooden captain's chair, bolted to the floor, which my dad had sat in over so many years, keeping an eye on his beloved ocean and his lot of land.

At a near table, I put down the lamp, and Cyrus grabs the back of the chair, gives it a tug.

It doesn't move.

"What the hell?" he asks.

"Dad didn't like his chair being moved around," I say. "After a couple years of having us kids drag the chair around, he bolted it to the floor."

Till says, "Gee, that makes sense."

But I don't say what else Dad had said back then: *I'm bolting this chair to the floor because a Cutler won't move, won't budge, and a Cutler will always be here.*

I'm afraid I won't get the words out.

In this part of the porch is a worktable I've used off and on over the years, cluttered with plastic bags, tools, an old laptop, and a toolbox. Beyond that is a wall that used to have lots of family photos and now bears only two: the World War II aircraft carrier USS *Enterprise*, on which my grandfather served, and the destroyer USS *Joseph P. Kennedy*, my dad's home for a few years.

Cyrus is behind me, so close I can feel his breathing on the back of my neck. He says, "You never served, did you?"

"No."

"Why, didn't have the guts?"

"Didn't have the right heart valves," I say.

"Fine, whatever," Cyrus says. "I got the purchase and sales agreement in my pocket; let's get the damned thing signed so we can get back to the mainland."

I stand still, looking at the old black-and-white photographs.

Cyrus says, "C'mon, can we get this done?"

"Sure," I say.

I grab a hammer off the near worktable and spin around and smack it right in the middle of his forehead.

His skull must be very thick, for it only stuns him, as he backs away, so I hammer him twice again in the forehead. He stumbles back, still not falling down, and I snap, "Till! Give me a hand here!"

But Till just stands there, his mouth agape, watching me, so I grab Cyrus's right arm, tug him, and he falls back and sits down heavily in my dad's chair.

He says, "You . . . you . . ."

I go back to the workbench, get strips of a special plastic, tie off his arms and legs to the chair, and when I'm done with his ankles, he recovers some and says, "You fucker, what the hell are you doing?"

I stand up, breathing heavy.

"Getting it done," I say.

He moves his arms, his legs. They don't move much. "Get me out of here."

"Not at the moment," I say.

"Tilly!" he yells. "Get a knife, cut me free!"

His brother looks scared but defiant at the same time. "I hate it when you call me Tilly."

There's blood trickling down Cyrus's forehead, and he seems to grit his teeth and says, "Okay. Tillman. My younger brother Tillman. Please cut me free, okay?"

Till just stands there.

"I don't think your brother feels like it," I say.

His head turns to me. "You! Get me out of here right now. . . ."

I start walking away and say, "No."

Till joins me, and Cyrus yells out, "What the hell is this? You want more money? Is that it?"

"Nope," I say. "I don't want your money. I just want this," I add, sweeping my arm.

"This? Your house? You can't goddamn afford it! You know that!"

Till stands still, and I go back to Cyrus. I say, "I know. I can't afford the taxes or upkeep on the house, especially with the new neighbors breaking in and vandalizing the place. But by this time tomorrow, there won't be a house here. Just the land. And I can afford the taxes on the land."

"But . . ."

"You've wanted this place for so many years, harassed and terrified my mom, and then my dad, all in trying to force them out. Well, congrats, this place is yours. For at least a day."

He says, "You can't do this, Henry!"

"I think I will."

He pulls again at the plastic bounds. "What, you don't think you'll get caught? Half a dozen folks know I was meeting you today. And if they find my body . . . all bound like this. . . . Man, don't you think you'll be arrested?"

I walk over closer, smile at him, my tormentor from high school and from years following. I rub the plastic. "These come from a special type of plastic bag I heard about, just being developed. Very, very strong . . . but when exposed to salt water for forty-eight hours, it'll dissolve. Just like that. And your body will be discovered in the wreckage . . . and I'll tell any investigator that I changed my mind about meeting you after I left the pub. That you must have gotten here by yourself. Got scared, decided to ride out the storm here."

Cyrus tries to look to his brother, but the angle is all wrong, and his bleeding head can only twist so far. Still, he yells out, "Tilly . . . I mean, Tillman, get me out of here!"

I say, "Your brother's had enough of you over the years. Just like me. And I'm not trying to save the world."

I pat the tight plastic.

"Just this part of it."

Outside the hammering wind and rain means we can't hear Cyrus yelling, which is nice. I get into my pickup truck, and Till joins me.

We don't say a word to each other.

I start up my Chevy and make a turn in the soggy lot, and then reverse our direction down the road. We get to the intersection with Route 12, and a utility pole is down on the ground, parallel to the access road. It seems as though there's no power or utility lines attached.

It gives me an idea.

I say, "Hold on."

I put the truck in park and get out. It doesn't seem possible to get soaked through again, but sure enough, the harsh wind and gusting rain wets me even more.

In the truck bed I haul out a thick and long length of chain. I secure one end around the trailer hitch, slosh through the water, and wrap the other end around the wooden pole. I tug on the chain, and it remains in place.

Good.

Back into the truck, the windshield wipers hammering away, the air conditioning still running, the fog inside drying out, the heavy rain slamming onto the metal roof.

"Henry?"

"Just a sec."

I shift the Chevy into drive, pull out a few yards, and then stop. I go out back into the storm and see the pole is now blocking access to the road.

Nice job.

Which means any Good Samaritan who slides by in the next hour won't be tempted to go down the road to check things out.

I pull up and make a right, and we start heading north on Route 12.

After a sloppy, soggy mile, Till says, "Henry?"

"Yeah?"

"Uh . . . don't you think it's been long enough?"

I keep quiet. We come to another flooded stretch of the road, and I drive even slower than before, the water cascading up on each side of the truck. Really not the time nor place to stall out.

He adds, "Isn't it time to go back?"

"No," I say.

Till says, "I mean, I thought we were just gonna scare him. That's what I thought."

"You thought wrong."

"But, Henry . . ."

We go past Newton Junction, all closed up and buttoned tight.

"Henry."

"Yeah."

"It's not right."

I keep quiet.

Route 12 is so empty now, just water and wind and closed-up buildings.

Till says, "You hear me? It's not right."

Up ahead is the intersection of Route 12 and the Route 64 Bypass, which leads over to the famed Roanoke Island, and from there, the mainland. There are flashing red and blue lights from the state police and volunteer firefighters, manning a checkpoint.

"You know what's not right?" I ask. The traffic light poles hanging over the roadways are fluttering back and forth like windmills.

I say, "What's not right is your older brother stomping on you since you could barely walk. What's not right is Cyrus ruling this part of Hatteras. And what's not right was how Cyrus bullied my parents, tried to bully me, tried to rape this place. That's what's not right."

Up ahead a North Carolina state trooper standing by his gray-and-black cruiser is waving a lit orange baton at us, directing us to take a left and off the island. He's wearing yellow rain gear that's flapping hard in the wind.

I say, "Till? You got anything?"

He finally says, "You got me all wrong."

"What?"

"When I said it wasn't right, I meant it wasn't right for you to keep it all secret like. You should have told me. You should have told me what you were going to do with Cyrus."

We're now at the intersection. The soaked state police trooper is close enough to shout at. I look to see where Till's hands are, to see if they are near the door handle or the toggle switch to lower the window.

His hands are in his lap.

Till says, "If I knew, I would have said more back there. I would have had more fun with the asshole, told him what I really, really thought about him. That's what was wrong."

I switch on the directional, take a slow and careful left onto the Route 64 Bypass.

The trooper gives us a wave.

I wave back.

"Sorry, Till," I say. "Guess I wasn't thinking."

"It's okay," he says.

And then we're safely onto the paved road, leaving Hatteras and Diamond Shoals behind us.

Janice Eidus *is a novelist, short story writer, essayist, and writing coach. Twice the winner of the O. Henry Prize as well as a Pushcart Prize, her novels include* The War of the Rosens, Urban Bliss, *and* The Last Jewish Virgin; *her stories are collected in* Vito Loves Geraldine *and* The Celibacy Club. *Her autobiographical essays appear in* The New York Times, Purple Clover, Lilith, Tikkun, *and other leading journals. She lives in the bustling heart of New York City with her husband, their teenage daughter, and a feisty rescue cat, Cherry. Visit her at www.janiceeidus.com.*

Number 14 by Mark Rothko

YOU'RE A WALKING TIME BOMB

BY JANICE EIDUS

F ive years ago today, on my fortieth birthday, I survived a brain aneurysm. Since then, my personal mantra has been: *You're a walking time bomb*. I repeat this to myself many times a day. The phrase calms me, reminding me to live each day as though it's my last—until the day it really is.

I've got a 15 to 20 percent chance of having a second aneurysm. Most likely, I won't survive it. Surviving the first was a miracle.

"This is the worst headache of my life," I'd groaned to Jeff, my boyfriend back then. Jeff was a graphic designer for fashion and media startups. On our first date, he said, "In college, I planned to be the next Warhol, reinventing art while becoming rich and famous." He blushed at his own youthful pretentions, and he seemed absolutely content with his non-Warholian life.

It was easy for me to relate to Jeff, since my own career as a life coach wasn't what I'd imagined for myself either. I never dreamed I'd spend my days helping people to "achieve life goals and live their bliss." Or that I would genuinely come to believe in such jargon.

As it turns out, my crappy childhood made me well suited for the job. My father drank all night at bars and my depressed mother watched TV alone in her room. Feeling miserable and being ignored, I developed empathy and insight to help others.

The headache grew worse, and I rubbed my temples. Jeff and I were cuddling on his cozy, unmade bed. We'd just devoured an entire chocolate birthday cake he'd baked for me from scratch.

A flood of perspiration pooled from my forehead and beneath my arms. My neck went stiff. I rarely got headaches, so having one was surprising. Having one so painful was a shock.

Jeff was a hypochondriac, which usually drove me crazy. But he did know all the bad things that could befall anyone at any time. A stubborn zit: "It's cancer." A sprained ankle: "I'll never walk again."

Propping himself up on his pillow, his dark brown hair mussed, he squinted his hazel eyes. "I'm calling 9-1-1."

"It's just a headache," I protested weakly, "not a . . ." The pain was so severe I closed my eyes and couldn't finish the sentence.

Five years later, it's a gorgeous spring morning. I'll be celebrating my birthday tonight at Ophelia, my favorite rooftop bar because of its sweeping view of the East River. I'll be with my two closest friends, both life coaches. We like to share life techniques with one other, like, "How to Ask Problem-Solving Questions" and "Affirming Elusive Dreams."

Sunlight spills into my apartment as I await my first coachee of the day: Coachee #1. Her name is Marissa, but I often think of my coachees by number. It helps me to maintain objectivity.

As I always do before meeting with a coachee, I whisper aloud my mantra: *"You're a walking time bomb."*

My apartment is on the twentieth floor of a white brick high-rise near the UN. Prints by the late abstract expressionist Mark Rothko make my home feel both personal and professional. They hang everywhere: in the entryway;

in my living room above the black leather sofa where coachees sit; above the recliner in which I lean back almost imperceptibly during sessions; next to the wooden bookcase that displays the latest books on life coaching; in my kitchen; in both bedrooms (even the one that's so small, there's room only for a narrow bed and a bureau); and on my bathroom walls.

All the Rothkos contain blazing, luminous colors that glow from within: oranges, reds, yellows, violets, blues, greens, plums, ochres, blacks, magentas. Coachees sometimes remark on how "pretty" they are. But to me, they're ferocious. They snap, crackle, and pop like a bursting brain.

After college, I worked temp jobs and wrote two novels I couldn't sell. One was about a young woman like myself with an alcoholic father and a depressed mother, blah blah blah. The other was an apocalyptic fantasy about the last survivors on Earth, a group of psychotherapists who spend their time recounting their childhoods while scrounging for food and weapons. That was what gave me the idea that I could be a psychotherapist. Didn't I possess all that empathy and insight from my crappy childhood, after all?

But I was too impatient to return to school for an MSW or PhD. Instead, I discovered life coaching, the "fast track" way to help people achieve their goals. I studied with a life coach superstar who hosts a podcast and cable TV show. In three months, I was certified.

Some deride life coaches as second-rate therapists. But for me, life coaching is about moving forward and not dwelling on the bad childhoods we all had, blah blah blah. When one skeptical former friend said, "Now you've drunk the Kool-Aid," I replied, "No, I've found my calling."

Each day, I assign numbers to my coachees in the order in which we meet. Coachee #1, a thirty-year-old size zero whose beige pantsuit hangs on her tiny frame, greets me shyly. At our first meeting three months ago, she and I established her three main goals: *eat more*; *make a friend*; *find passion and purpose in life*.

Softly, she says, "I did both of last week's assignments." One assignment was to eat at least two slices of pepperoni pizza, her favorite food. The other was to join an online Meetup group for cat lovers. Meow, her cat, is her closest friend.

Together, we look at her workbook. In pale lavender ink, she's written, "How difficult it is to click 'Join,' but . . . drum roll . . . I did it. And I will not unclick!"

"Congratulations." I smile with real pride. "How might your life change through the group?"

"I might . . ." She hesitates ". . . meet a kindred spirit."

I nod my head and stare discreetly at Rothko's *No. 14* above her head: my first and favorite Rothko. Before my aneurysm I knew nothing about him. In fact, I knew barely anything about visual art. I wasn't so awful that I said things like, "With her finger paint, my two-year-old niece could do better than Jackson Pollock." But I came close.

In order to stop the bleeding in my brain, I underwent neurosurgery. Things were rocky for a while. I forgot plans. I forgot things people said to me. I was terrified I'd never again be able to help my clients. My inattentiveness to Jeff was eroding our relationship.

But I recovered. I remembered my coachees' needs and wishes, and I resumed work. I showed up on time and at the right place for dinner with friends. I meant it when I congratulated Jeff on a new logo or website design.

To celebrate my recovery, he and I took a short vacation to San Francisco. No matter where we went or what we did, hopping on and off cable cars, tasting the goods at wineries, strolling the Golden Gate Bridge, he complained of chest and stomach pains. "I'm having a heart attack," he whined on a windy day as we rode the ferry to Alcatraz. "Or maybe I have Crohn's. Or celiac."

"It's heartburn from the Mexican food we had for lunch." I felt impatient, as I often did when his hypochondria reared its head. Still, I attempted a smile. He'd recently saved my life, and I owed him big time.

Grimacing, he clutched his stomach while I gazed at the water.

The next day he woke up feeling better: "Let's go to the modern art museum."

Although I didn't look forward to being bored for hours inside a stuffy museum, I nodded enthusiastically.

The moment I saw Rothko's *No. 14* on the wall of San Francisco's MOMA, I felt anything but bored. *No. 14* exploded in front of my eyes. Colors were stacked together but not stagnant. Reds, oranges, blues, and purples were simultaneously radiant and dark. They leapt, jumped, and swirled off the canvas, directly into my heart. *No. 14* was intense and stylized. It was life. It was death. It was me. I clutched Jeff's hand. "This is the best painting I've ever seen."

"Cool," he said, looking at me quizzically.

Later that evening in our hotel room, I went online and learned that Rothko had committed suicide. He'd been found dead in a pool of blood on the floor of his Bowery studio. He'd hacked deeply into his arms and shoulders with a knife, as if intending the dark red blood surrounding him to be his final work of art.

Where had his pain come from? Had his creativity dried up? Had he longed for even greater acclaim? Was his childhood so bad he couldn't "move forward"?

If you think of your brain as a balloon that's completely stretched out, an aneurysm is the weak spot in the balloon. When mine burst, it felt like someone was stabbing me over and over. Afterward, everyone said how lucky I was not to have died, gone into a coma, or suffered permanent brain damage.

I *am* lucky: My eyelids don't droop; my face doesn't sag. I look like a healthy forty-five-year-old who exercises and eats well. Nevertheless, I've memorized the statistics: brain aneurysms are fatal in about 40 percent of cases. Women have them way more often than men. Of those who survive, about 66 percent suffer some permanent neurological deficit. Four out of seven have lifelong disabilities. How lucky am I, really?

Coachee #1 writes down her single goal for the following week: "*I will attend an 'In Real Life' meeting of the cat lovers group.*" Wide eyed, she looks at me. "But what will I say to the people there?"

"What might you do to bond with them?"

"Share photos of Meow?"

"And?" I prompt.

"Ask to see photos of *their* cats."

I never tell clients what to do. Life coaching is about asking questions that lead to solutions. "Is there any way you can reward yourself for your accomplishments?"

Her voice is meek. "A vanilla cupcake?"

"Perfect," I say, shaking her hand, my end-of-session ritual with all my coachees. I rise from the recliner. Standing tall in the center of my living room, I do yoga breathing and stare at *No. 14*. Its colors wash over and soothe me.

You're a walking time bomb. I repeat this before my session with Coachees #2 and #3, a married couple. They look alike, with round faces and curly hair. Their shared goals are to improve their wilting marriage and to save their small printing business.

Their relationship is too familiar, too reminiscent of mine with Jeff. The wife, #2, is impatient with #3. Even more irritable than usual this morning, she snaps at #3, "You're never proactive about anything!"

Involuntarily, I'm brought back to when I used to tell Jeff repeatedly that he needed to commit to our relationship. "We've been together long enough. It's time to move in together!"

#2 and #3 have no idea that they bring up uncomfortable feelings for me. #2 doesn't know how annoyed I am when she constantly interrupts #3, the way I used to do with Jeff. All I show them is my energy, warmth, and desire to help. I never reveal my impatience.

#1 doesn't know that if she blows off the cat lovers group, a part of me will want to throttle her.

None of my coachees know that Jeff, the love of my life, left me. They don't know about my aneurysm. Or my personal mantra. Or the poor odds that I'll lead a long life. Or that the reason I have so many Rothko prints isn't because I love abstract expressionism but because his art reminds me of my brain's brutal betrayal.

#2 has achieved her weekly goal. She's compiled a list of constructive actions and phrases to use to better communicate with #3. She rakes her fingers through her fluffy hair as she reads aloud from her notes: "I promise to take a deep breath and ask myself what I'm feeling before I speak. And not to raise my voice. And not to threaten divorce."

#3 has not met his goal of cold-calling two potential new clients. Sheepishly, he looks down at the floor.

#2 stops fiddling with her hair. She frowns and places her hands primly on her lap. "I won't divorce you for not calling them."

The three of us agree that this is a start. We close by discussing potential "New Moves," including checking in daily with each other about their feelings. We shake hands. I close the door.

Inhaling deeply, I gaze once more at Rothko's *No. 14*, focusing on a bold splash of orange. I remember the orange Popsicles I loved as a child. My mother, who so rarely paid attention to me, bought them by the dozen and stored them in our freezer.

I check my voice mail. Coachee #4 has left one of her typically breathy, stoned-sounding messages: "I'm so sorry, can't come today . . . unavoidable conflict."

I'm working hard to be less judgmental of #4. But whenever she calls herself a "poet," I can't help but mentally insert the word "wannabe."

#4 smokes a lot of weed and hates her job as a special education teacher at a private school. "All those entitled parents expecting me to perform miracles," she complains each time we meet.

It drives me crazy that in three months of working together, she's yet to write a single line of poetry. I long to say, "Just write a damn haiku!"

Calming myself, I nibble at the baby carrots I placed earlier on my kitchen counter in a brightly colored ceramic bowl. I bought the bowl during a vacation to Mexico with Jeff early in our relationship.

Above the counter hangs Rothko's *No. 16*, moody and shadowy in shades of red, brown, and black.

During my first meeting with #4, I asked her, "What are you passionate about?"

"Writing poetry."

"What do you avoid?"

"People who don't take me seriously as a poet."

"What's holding you back from writing poetry?"

"People who don't appreciate my poetry."

"Take a deep breath and close your eyes," I suggested. "Visualize where you would like to be in a year."

"Writing poetry full time on a Greek island."

I wanted to scream.

It's just as well #4 has canceled today. Munching on carrots, I look at my cell phone. Jeff's Facebook and Instagram pages are set to private. It's been two years since I've seen or spoken with him. It kills me not to know what he's doing. Has he gone bald and grown a beard? Gotten married and had a kid? Moved into a SoHo loft to rekindle his Warholian fantasies? Developed a real illness, as he'd always feared?

The final straw, the nail in the coffin of my relationship with Jeff—the reason he left me—was that I did something no life coach in her right mind would ever recommend to anyone.

I called his mother.

I said, "Hi, Myra, I'm calling to ask you a favor."

Jeff had already told me that Myra didn't like me. When I demanded to know why, he sighed. "Well, for one thing, she calls your career '*meshugganah*.' She says, 'You live, you die, who the hell needs a coach for that?'"

Despite knowing this, I asked, "Myra, would you help convince Jeff to move in with me?"

"You've *got* to be kidding." She hung up.

Why, oh why, had I called her? There were so many things Jeff and I could have done to "find our truths" as a couple and eventually move in together and get married. We could have done yoga and meditated together. We could have seen a life coach, maybe the famous one with the podcast. We could have seen a traditional shrink and rehashed our miserable childhoods, blah blah blah, had that been necessary to "empower" ourselves.

Today will be my first meeting with Coachee #5.

For a hedge fund CEO, his voice over the phone was surprisingly timid. "I dread public speaking," he told me. "I sweat. I feel paralyzed. I take Prozac every morning and Trazodone every night."

After the call, I googled him. He'd inherited the company from his father and his grandfather before him. Judging from their Wiki entries, neither of them had ever had a problem with public speaking.

"You're a walking time bomb." I repeat this to myself just seconds before #5 enters. His suit sags on his large frame. His hair is unkempt. He slumps into the sofa.

Tipping back ever-so-slightly in my recliner, I ask the same questions of him that I asked of #4 during our first meeting. "What are you passionate about?"

"Nothing."

I lean forward to better hear him. "What do you avoid?"

"Public speaking."

"What's holding you back from your goals?"

"Trying to fill the footsteps of my father and grandfather."

A few minutes later, while #5 is in the bathroom, I gaze at another Rothko. This one has a name, not a number: *White Center*. Shimmering whites, yellows, and pinks make it light and buoyant. It fills me with hope—hope that Aneurysm #2 will never come, and hope that one day soon I'll be able to let go of my memories of Jeff, who wants nothing to do with me.

#5 returns from the bathroom. We agree to set just one immediate goal. Once a day for the following week, he will stand in front of a mirror and read aloud the Gettysburg Address.

"I think I can do this." His voice is stronger than when he arrived.

We shake hands.

#5 is my final coachee of the day. I glance at my cell phone. There's a group chat from my friends confirming my birthday celebration tonight.

There's also a voice mail. Undoubtedly, it will be a coachee rescheduling, canceling, or desperately needing to speak with me *this very instant*.

Instead, it is Jeff's voice that I hear: "I've missed you. Can we talk? I shouldn't have walked out on you the way I did. I really miss you."

His words are music and poetry combined. My heart races; then it soars. I'll call him as soon as I calm myself with a cup of chamomile tea. I need to be "fully present" when we speak. I promise myself I won't interrupt him. I will listen patiently, even if he complains about some imaginary ailment.

But the instant I finish pouring my tea, I know it's too late. Not even Jeff can save me this time. My neck stiffens. My vision blurs. I feel faint. The pain behind my eyes is a thousand times worse than it was five years ago.

I sink to my knees, knowing that I've lived the best life I could. I wasn't selfless—not by a long shot—but I really did try to help others live the best lives *they* could.

One last time, I repeat my mantra: *You're a walking time bomb.* I take in the beauty of the Rothkos surrounding me. Their colors embrace me. I feel embraced by Jeff. I understand that no matter who you are—life coach, therapist, stoner poet, hedge fund CEO, or famous artist—this moment will come for you.

As I slip away from the world and the world slips away from me, I also understand with every fiber of my being that it is never *meshugganah* to try to do good—however imperfectly—in the very brief time we are given.

It may not be the most original epiphany in the world.

But it doesn't have to be.

Christa Faust *is an author of award-winning crime novels, media tie-ins, and comics. She has worked in the Times Square peep booths as a professional dominatrix and in the adult film industry both behind and in front of the cameras for more than a decade. She currently lives and writes in Los Angeles.*

Adirondacks by Helen Frankenthaler

GARNETS

BY CHRISTA FAUST

She said her name was Sara. No *h*. She tossed off the "no *h*" line as though she'd been saying it forever, but there was something a little too studied in her casual delivery that made me doubt she'd been born with that name. Girl after my own heart.

I told her my name was Cam. That's not the name I was born with either, but it was Danni's nickname for me. Short for Camelot, punchline of a convoluted private joke that seemed so cool when we were kids. I'd been planning to use a different alias, like maybe the one I'd used to rent this car, but Cam just popped out. Shows where my head was at.

It was a big risk, picking up Little Miss Sara-No-*h*. Like an end-of-everything kind of risk. But I've always had a problem with impulse control. How do you think I got to be in this situation in the first place?

The sun was just coming up when I saw her standing alone at the far end of the parking lot of a rest area just outside Johnsberg, the Adirondack town where I grew up. It was looking to be one of those dreary gray autumn days that's a big disappointment to the leaf-peepers and she was looking chilly, her chin tucked down into the collar of her ugly puffer jacket. Her wild, dirty hair was acid green with mousy roots. She had a backpack decorated with crooked patches and Sharpie doodles. She was a big girl, tall and thick. Strong legs. My type, but way too young. Bad-idea young.

I stopped anyway. Flicked my cigarette butt out the window and asked if she needed a lift.

Of course she did.

She went around the back of the car and rapped on the trunk lid, wanting to put her backpack inside.

"No!" I almost shouted. Then, embarrassed by that reaction, I tried to make a joke out of it as she got into the passenger side. "Hitchhiking 101, kid. Always keep your stuff close enough to grab in case you have to bug out at a moment's notice."

"Are you telling me I'm gonna need to bug out to get away from you?" She flashed a teasing smirk as she wedged her backpack between her boots.

I came up with all kinds of cool, witty responses later on, but at that point I just said, "You never know."

Which was actually the truest answer I could have given. Story of my life.

We didn't talk much after we exchanged names. She didn't even ask where I was going. If she had a phone, she never took it out. She had a kind of uncanny stillness about her that I've never seen before or since. Not zoned out like a junkie, just quiet and alert. Like a bird of prey.

"I heard you can find garnets around here," she finally said. "Is that true?"

"That's not a garnet, stupid," Danni said, *twenty-six years ago. "That's just rust on a rock."*

For a second, my heart stopped. Was she a cop? Did she know?

It didn't seem possible. She was just a kid. Sure, she had the same blue eyes as Danni, but lots of people have blue eyes. Frank Sinatra. Fairuza Balk. Jeffrey fucking Dahmer. Doesn't mean anything.

"It's my birthstone," Sara said. "Garnet."

I nodded, sneaking a glance at her. She was looking out the window at the passing scenery. She was beautiful in that way that young people are before the world roughs them up. But also keen, like a brand-new knife.

Still a really bad idea, but one that was getting harder to shake.

"What about you?" she asked.

"What about me what?"

"What's your birthstone?"

I shrugged. "No idea."

"Well, when's your birthday?"

"June," I said too quickly, before I realized it would have been smarter to lie.

"Pearl." Again, that smirk. "Doesn't suit you. Moonstone's better. More mysterious."

"I'm not mysterious," I said. "I'm just a curmudgeon."

"You're too young to be a curmudgeon. How old are you? Thirty?"

"Forty-two." Another quickie glance. This time she was looking right at me. I looked away. "You?"

"Eighteen," she said, like it was no big deal.

I hoped she wasn't lying but didn't really care. There was an unspoken gravity between us now that made whatever might happen feel inevitable. I couldn't tell if I wanted to fuck her or confess to her. Both, probably.

Neither one of us said anything else after that. Didn't need to. We rode together in this hot, electric silence while I debated changing course and heading off in a new and different direction. A motel, maybe. Canada? California? Anywhere else.

I didn't. I turned into the overgrown dirt parking area near the head of Danni's trail just like I'd planned. Only I didn't plan on Sara.

She was all over me before I'd even killed the motor, predator-playful and impossible to resist. Her mouth tasted like fast food and she needed a shower, but I didn't care. I was instantly smitten by the way she took control, putting my hands where she wanted them and pinning me down with those sharp blue eyes. Kissing my breath away.

"Slap me," I whispered when she finally let me come up for air.

She looked at me with her head cocked, sizing me up. This was where most of my depressingly infrequent sexual encounters usually went off the rails. Most women just don't have it in them.

She did.

I hardly thought of Danni at all.

Nobody knew about the game. Our parents thought we were hiking, a healthy, normal hobby for healthy, normal girls.

It started when we were kids. Of course, it was Danni's idea. We'd been best friends since second grade, and I'd always been her slave, even before the game was invented.

She was pretty, popular and smart. I wasn't. Well, not the kind of smart that made you popular, anyway.

When she went missing in the summer of 1992, she got even more popular.

After all, she was the perfect victim. The girl next door. Wispy blond bob, pink lip gloss, chunky sweater. Big tits, but not too slutty. A nice girl.

She was not a nice girl. Which is why I was so in love, so tangled up in her. Still am, to be honest.

The game started off with her pretending to be some kind of queen and me her loyal servant. Sometimes I was a knight. Sometimes I was a ladies' maid. Sometimes, my favorite times, I was a prisoner of war. It wasn't exactly sexual at first, though it wasn't exactly not-sexual either. Being subjugated by her in various ways flooded my conflicted body with feelings I was too young to understand. I collected garnets for her from the icy creeks on Gore Mountain, and she rewarded me by spitting in my face and telling me it wasn't enough. *I* wasn't enough.

I couldn't get enough.

Later, when we were older and could no longer pretend what we were doing was just an innocent game, things got way more complicated. I had my first orgasm grinding against her hiking boot, and I was sure I was going to die from it. Meanwhile, she was dating boys and hanging out at the mall and being a normal teenager who would never press the point of a knife against the soft spot under another girl's ear while she was getting head.

Around that time was when she started threatening to expose me as a disgusting lesbo pervert if I ever told anyone about the game. She took Polaroids of me, splayed open and laying in the dirt at her feet, and said she was going to sell them to guys to jack off to. I still have those photos.

You probably think she was abusive, don't you? You're probably thinking I'm this poor little victim, but that's not how it was at all. I didn't kill her because she hurt me. I killed her because she decided she didn't want to hurt me anymore.

Don't act all shocked, like you didn't see that coming a mile away. What, did you think this was some kind of love story? Although, when you think about it, I guess it kind of is.

"I was gonna rob you," Sara said as we lay sprawled half-naked and tangled together in the back seat. "Steal your car. Maybe kill you if you fought back. I've done it lots of times. But, I don't know. I just didn't want to this time."

"Lots of times, huh?"

She looked away, sheepish.

"Well, two times. Anyway, those guys totally deserved it."

"I'll bet they did," I said. "Thing is, I do too. Though probably not for the same reason."

"Why would you say that?" she asked.

"Put your shirt back on," I said, "and I'll show you something."

I hit the button to pop the trunk and then got out of the car. Sara got out of her side and came around the back.

"Whoa!" she said, wrinkling her nose. "Who is she?"

I lit a cigarette to counteract the smell, took a drag and then handed it to her.

"This podcast lady," I said. "She seemed nice and everything, but . . ."

Sara smoked in silence, her face unreadable. I wondered if I'd made a terrible mistake but figured I'd just steer into the skid, like I always do. If I crashed, I crashed.

"Do you know about the Danielle Embry case?" I asked.

"Missing girl back in the nineties?" Sara handed the cigarette back to me. "Body was never found. Didn't they do one of those cold case TV shows about her? They said it was that Hudson Falls Killer, the one who liked blondes."

"That's one theory," I replied.

The podcast lady was named Eugenia Pike. I'm still not sure if that's a terrible name or an awesome one. She was in her fifties, with lots of springy gray ringlets surrounding a triangular, catlike face. She had the style and demeanor of a favorite teacher or a children's librarian. Friendly, but not above shushing you if she needed to. For some reason, I thought she would be wearing glasses, but she wasn't. Her dark eyes missed nothing. She was trouble and I knew it, but I agreed to let her into my apartment anyway.

She wasn't the first person who wanted to interview me about Danni. I normally said no, but she was relentless. I knew she wasn't going to go away, so I figured I'd just toss her a few false leads about Danni's various boyfriends and bemoan the lack of "closure." Maybe cry a little.

She wasn't having it.

She asked if she could record our conversation, but I could see by her expression that she was telling, not asking. She let me talk a little first, let me say all the things I had planned to say about this one guy who collected knives and how I once heard this other guy threaten to "make her sorry" if she broke up with him. I was gearing up for the crying part when she slapped an eight-by-ten photo on the kitchen table between us.

"Is this you?" she asked.

It was a beautiful photo. A hawk soaring across the face of a rocky cliff. Warm sunset light like everything was dipped in honey. Almost postcard perfect, the kind of thing you'd see in an ad for an Adirondack vacation, only the composition was a little off. The bird was too far over toward the right of the frame. There was probably a better shot on the same roll, one snapped a few seconds earlier.

"I don't understand," I said, even though I already knew in my gut where this was going. I recognized that cliff face like I recognize my own body. It was our favorite place. A secret place.

"I don't want to do this anymore," Danni said. *"I'm over it."*

Eugenia took out a little round magnifying doodad like photographers use and set it down on the top left corner of the photo.

"Look closer," she said.

I looked up at her and then down at the photo. My heart was pounding in my ears as I leaned down to put my eye against the magnifier.

Standing on the edge of the cliff, two tiny, blurry figures. One blonde, one brunette. The brunette had one arm raised high above her head.

Of course, it was me.

"Look, a garnet," I said, *ignoring Danni, wanting to pretend I didn't hear her say she didn't want me anymore.*

"That's not a garnet, stupid," Danni said. *"That's just rust on a rock."*

But there had been garnets, hundreds of them, deep red droplets glistening in the slanted amber light from the setting sun. And when my arm got tired from smashing that rock down again and again, I used my boot to push her convulsing body over the cliff's edge.

"The photographer is named Emmett Landers," she told me. "He shot over a hundred photos of different birds near the Lower Catback cliff face the day Danielle Embry disappeared. This is the only one in which these two figures are clearly visible."

"But I still don't understand why you would think that's me," I said, trying to keep my hands open and my breathing slow.

"Emmett Landers was my favorite suspect for years," she said. "Even though he had been ruled out by police and written off by pretty much everyone else online. When he died back in February, his daughter just wanted to get rid of all the boxes of slides and negatives piled up in his garage. Sorting through them was a huge undertaking, but so worth it."

She pulled out another photo and set it on top of the first. This was a photo of a fat little sparrow holding a piece of grass in its beak, standing on the ground near the back end of a parked car.

"You told police you were home sick with the flu the day she disappeared. There was no reason to doubt you at the time. But . . ." She tapped the photo. She was clearly getting off on this. "That's your car, isn't it?"

Of course it was. It was a beat-up old Malibu that my father had given me as a present for my sixteenth birthday. It was nobody's dream car, but he bought it totaled and fixed it up for me himself. I loved that car. The little bird was in focus and the car was out, but you could still make out the numbers on the license plate.

My drag queen neighbor picked that moment to crank up the loud, awful pop music she'd been driving me nuts with every night for months. I could have kissed her.

"Sorry," I said, shrugging like I meant the music.

That wasn't what I meant.

"So you killed this lady because she found out you killed that girl?" Sara said. Not freaking out or anything, just stating the facts.

"Right," I said, stubbing out the cigarette against the bumper. I was about to flick it away when I thought twice about it and tucked the butt into the pocket of my jeans instead. "I mean, there were others, but those are the two that matter."

"So what's the plan?"

"Plan?" I frowned. I was never very good with plans.

I'd started off my road trip with this romantic notion that I would take the podcast lady up to our spot and pitch her body off the cliff so she could be with the girl she tried so hard to find. But it was a stupid, impractical idea. So stupid, I was too embarrassed to say it out loud. Not like there was anything smart about killing her in the first place. Or Danni, for that matter.

People on TV loved to breathlessly speculate about Danni's theoretical killer, to imagine him (it was always *him*) as this fiendishly clever criminal mastermind. I hate to break it to you, but in real life, I'm just a lucky fuckup. Or maybe not so lucky anymore.

"This a rental?" Sara asked.

I nodded.

"Fake name?"

"Yup. Stolen credit card too."

She shrugged and slammed the trunk.

"Fuck it," she said.

Did I mention she was a girl after my own heart? Of course I knew I'd get caught eventually, sooner rather than later. But in that moment, this beautiful young girl was looking at me with cruel blue eyes, and I didn't care. I had no fucks left to give.

"Funny," I said. "You were thinking you might have to kill me, and I was thinking I might have to kill you. But you know what? I don't want to either. Even now."

She smiled. She already knew I wouldn't.

"I can get us another car, no problem." she said. "You want to ride together for a little while?"

I knew this wasn't gonna end well. It couldn't. Nothing ever did.

"Yeah," I said anyway. "I do."

*Primarily an award-winning screenwriter (*Little Man Tate, Get Shorty, Out of Sight*) and writer-director (*The Lookout, A Walk Among the Tombstones, Godless*),* **Scott Frank** *is the author of the novel* Shaker, *a thriller set in earthquake-prone Los Angeles.*

Gertrude Vanderbilt Whitney by Robert Henri

HE CAME IN THROUGH THE BATHROOM WINDOW

BY SCOTT FRANK

Millard Mayhew had been hiding in plain sight for nearly two years when he went out his apartment window on the eighteenth floor of the Georgica Arms. His neighbors rarely saw or heard from him, so no one could say for sure whether Millard Mayhew had been pushed or jumped. And those on the ground who had the misfortune to witness the sixty-seven-year-old real estate developer hit the pavement headfirst from eighteen stories up were too busy trying to forget what they just saw to be of any help with such minor details.

The Georgica, a redbrick prewar pile that looked like every other redbrick prewar pile on the block, had fallen into disrepair when the latest owner, a shell company that, it would turn out, was formed by Millard Mayhew when he began buying buildings in Spanish Harlem and the Bronx a dozen years earlier, went bust. Bare wires hung from broken fixtures in the hallways, the elevators rattled and shook when they worked at all, while hot water was rare to nonexistent and only a small fraction of the radiators actually radiated anything in the winter beyond a loud metallic clamoring, usually in the middle of the night. Just a week before, a fourth-floor window broke free of its rotting frame and shattered on the sidewalk when a cat jumped onto the sill and leaned against it. Luckily, unlike its negligent landlord, the cat lived.

There were sirens seemingly within seconds of Millard Mayhew pancaking on the sidewalk, and, now, somehow out of nowhere, an off-duty fireman materialized and began covering the human puddle with a blue tarp, the plastic sheet generously provided by J's Hardware Store located on the ground floor of 221 next door. Hovering over the late Mr. Mayhew, the young fireman struggled with the thick plastic packaging for a few endless moments, before awkwardly unfurling what seemed to be the infinitely folded plastic sheet, and finally putting the nightmare to bed. Mayhew would be one with that spot for another three hours. It would be nearly eighteen hours more before anyone bothered to look inside his left shoe, where Mayhew had hidden a map. But, then, why would they have?

Max and Cheryl Batzer from across the hall in 18F would later claim they heard Mayhew arguing with someone the night before he went out the window. They assumed he had been talking on the phone, as the Batzers couldn't hear the other side of the quarrel, but investigators would discover that Mayhew, fully embracing the concept of "off the grid," had no phone.

Like everyone else, the Batzers knew very little about their neighbor in 18G other than that he seemed to have a rather extensive art collection. The day Mayhew moved in, they stood at their door and watched through a cloudy peephole as a seemingly endless number of archival crates were brought one after another from the service elevator to the small one-bedroom apartment. On the rare occasion they left their unit at the same time as Mayhew did his, the Batzers glimpsed the crates stacked floor to ceiling in the small space. Recently, however, they noticed Mayhew began taking them *out* one by one. Sometimes several times a day. And on the last occasion they bumped into Mayhew and were able to glimpse inside the apartment, there remained just a single painting by the window and nothing more. Not a speck of furniture.

Just an ornately framed canvas leaning against the wall containing, in the few seconds they had before Mayhew shut the door, the painted figure of a woman. A few days later, Mayhew would cart that one off, too.

Detectives had first assumed that Mayhew had been selling off his collection piece by piece to pay off his myriad debts. But upon digging further, they found that instead of selling anything, he was *hiding* everything in his various properties around the country. So unwilling was he to part with any of his precious works to pay his debts—the bulk of which, it should be noted, were owed to one Stevie Badame of Bayonne, New Jersey, for a "bridge loan"—he fled his eight-room co-op in the Carlysle and went into hiding at the Georgica.

On the day of his death, authorities found nothing in the apartment beyond a sleeping bag, a loaf of Wonder Bread, a toothbrush, and an unopened three-pack of Fruit of the Loom briefs.

Millard Mayhew was obviously a desperate man, but there were whispers from his former circle about a lover. More than a lover, an *obsession*. It made sense that Mayhew, a man who vigorously fed his reputation of never doing anything halfway, might have been consumed by a woman.

His wife had left him a dozen years earlier, and the balding, sagging pear of a real estate tycoon had frequently been seen with a variety of young, gorgeous women at various functions around the city. Each of them was variously introduced by Millard Mayhew as "working on her PhD in Economics at Stanford" or "running a nonprofit for recently released offenders," but all were clearly paid by the hour. So when Millard Mayhew breathlessly confided to a friend over lunch of sweetbreads and lobster salad at Café Boulud that he was for the first time "totally overcome with genuine passion," people in his circle began playing society's favorite guessing game of "Who Is She?"

At roughly the same moment Millard Mayhew took his fatal tumble, hundreds of miles away, in a dark mini mansion off the coast of South Carolina, another man was falling. Kyle O'Keefe, or "Okeedopey," as the guards at Raiford had liked to call him, was dragging a two-hundred-pound SentrySafe from a hall closet into the center of the living room in order to better get at it with his blowtorch. The safe still had the Sam's Club price tag on it, which should have been a dead giveaway, but Kyle wasn't one to sweat the small details. As soon as he saw the black lead box, he began pulling it across what was once upon a time a lacquered maple floor toward what the online brochure described as "The Great Room."

The floor was covered with dirt, broken glass, and various varieties of rodent shit, making it hard to see just what made it so great, but, more important, making it even harder to see the four-foot hole in the center of the room. One could argue that the dirt, broken glass, and rodent shit were all further signs that Kyle somehow missed. Most of the furniture had already been stolen months ago. Anyone in their right mind would have taken one look at the place and turned right around. In fact, Kyle was on his way out the door when he noticed the closet, opened it, and couldn't believe his good fortune. Though, in hindsight—hindsight being not that far off—he would amend that particular phrasing.

So it was that Kyle had just managed to muscle the safe into the center of the great room floor when he—along with the nearly two-hundred-pound box—fell through it.

Del used to say, *It's not the fall that'll kill you, it's the sudden stop at the end.* That was one of his favorites. Or . . . *How many drops you 'spose are in that water tower just yonder the barbwire? One big one!* When he wasn't shoving Kyle's head in the toilet or stealing his commissary, Del could be a real riot.

Kyle wasn't sure how long he'd been lying on the floor when he awoke, flat on his back, held in place by something that felt like a molten harpoon. A thin spear of rusted iron had pierced his spine and continued on its way through the soft tissue to where the glistening red end of what Kyle unhappily determined was a piece of rebar protruded from his side. Numb from top to bottom, Kyle felt simultaneously the heat coming off the spear and the cold rush of shock. He figured pain would come later as the shock wore off, or he was paralyzed and it didn't matter. Either way, he wasn't going anywhere anytime soon.

Afraid to look at his legs, he stared straight up at the hole in the floor while he collected his thoughts. A fawn nosed its way to the edge and peered down at him. For a second, Kyle thought he might still be unconscious. It was a strange sight to be sure, this wild animal casually moving about the house above him. But the stranger thing was that Kyle could smell it from down below. Even though it was dark, he could see the texture of its wiry brown coat, could even see the ticks and pieces of grass that were embedded there. And if that wasn't enough, he was certain he could hear its heart beat. Not just hear it but *feel* it.

Kyle tried to move and screamed, every splintered bone in his body screaming right along with him. It took him several more minutes to finally work up the courage to examine his legs. He could feel his toes in the right, a good sign. But the left was numb from the knee down. The safe, lying atop his flattened shin, most likely the cause—the door hanging open, having never been locked in the first place. The only thing inside was the manual, still taped to the top of the box. A warranty card from SentrySafe Co. lay on the floor a few feet away.

Kyle decided that he would either have to come up with some slow and no doubt incredibly painful way to drag his ass out of there, or wait for someone to come along and find him. Neither option sounded promising. He couldn't see much of his current location. But based on the brochure he had printed from an old website, he determined that he was currently skewered to the floor of the "finished storm basement." The basement didn't look all that finished and was currently piled high with garbage and assorted junk that previous, more discerning looters had declared not worth the effort. A few feet away, to his right, was a broken statue of what looked to Kyle like two naked cherubs leg wrestling in front of a painting Kyle couldn't quite make out through the clutter—beyond two green eyes staring out through the dark.

Kyle had first heard about Daufuskie Island from a diver named Garret Olsen at Snake & Jake's Christmas Club Lounge in New Orleans. Garret, a muscular Swede with long blond hair held in a loose ponytail by a leather scrunchy, had been doing underwater welding in the gulf for a dozen years and would most likely know all the right people. Before prison, Kyle had most recently been a purchasing clerk on a rig off Galveston. He had come to Louisiana after striking out in Texas, no one wanting to hire a convicted check kiter and identity thief to handle their payroll and purchasing if they didn't have to. So there he was, spending the evening and the last of his money plying Garret with drinks in order to get a line on a job at BP, when the man told him about Daufuskie.

A dot off the coast of South Carolina, between Hilton Head and Savannah, the island had recently become the Sutter's Mill for looters of all stripes. According to Garret, some crooked developer from New York had partially built a resort in the Melrose section of the island that went bust after it was discovered that the financing was shaky at best, a full-blown Ponzi scheme at worst. A clubhouse and several dozen four-thousand-square-foot beach "cottages" had already been built when the Feds came knocking on the door of the model showroom a few blocks from Lincoln Center, on the Upper West Side. Many of these places had been furnished with open hands and were done to the nines, complete with expensive art and antiques, even copper cookware, to make it look as though people had already snapped them up. Expensive shoes and clothing hung in the closets. The developer and his mobbed-up partners, posing as owners, threw catered parties in the various homes for prospective buyers, telling their guests how much they loved living there and to go ahead, have a look around, but be sure to swing by the open bar first.

And now Garret was telling Kyle that all that stuff was *still out there*. That the cottages were still loaded with goodies such as lamps and brass fixtures and—if one had an eye for these things—even a valuable painting or two. And if that wasn't enough, a few years back, some rock star had bought and rehabbed an old church near Melrose as a vacation home that he apparently never used and was, therefore, *never there*. His place had to be for sure jammed full of all sorts of killer swag. It was all just waiting for someone to come and pick it up.

As Garret put it: *There's gold in them cottages.*

The only catch was getting there. There was no bridge from the mainland, nor was there a ferry. One got to Daufuskie Island by water taxi, which, for a burglar, was far from ideal. The looters, up until now, had been primarily kids going over on rubber Zodiacs and Jet Skis and coming back with whatever they could carry. The big stuff was untouched. Rumor had every sort of item worth stealing stowed in one cottage or another. All one had to do was get a decent-size boat, dock it at the clubhouse, jump into one of the many brand-new golf carts that were just sitting there, and go to work.

It was starting to sound a bit like some beach in Thailand Kyle had heard about. Or was that a movie? This insanely beautiful place that you had to jump off a waterfall to get to. But once you got there it was spectacular. Perfect. The girls were all topless (at least that's how Kyle remembered it), and everybody was fucking everybody else (as Kyle remembered it). Only catch, aside from the jumping off the waterfall part, was that the place was surrounded by murderous, Uzi-wielding pot growers. There's *always* a catch.

Kyle would learn that the Daufuskie situation was riddled with catches.

The only boat big enough that Kyle could rent was a thirty-five-foot Intrepid Center Console with a trio of three-hundred-horsepower outboard Yamaha engines that went for, if Kyle heard correctly, twelve hundred a day. The only boat Kyle could steal was a fourteen-foot Boston Whaler with a two-stroke engine that began having coughing fits ten minutes into the trip before finally running out of gas a few hundred feet from the Daufuskie shore. Kyle's first thought was to wait it out, that, eventually, he would just drift in to the beach, find some gas somewhere on the island for the trip home. He might possibly even find a better boat. But after an hour of waiting in the dark, keeping his eye on the few lights he could see on the island, he realized he was drifting *out*, not in. So he set his duffel full of tools atop a flotation cushion and swam for it, stumbling up onto the beach forty-five minutes later, exhausted, his clothing sandy and soaked through. At some point during the effort Kyle had lost his right shoe, so that, along with half his face, his right foot was covered with jellyfish stings.

He walked up and down the beach, but unable to find a proper access point in the dark, he finally had to haul his gear through the bushes for a good twenty minutes before he emerged onto what had once been a golf course. After a year of disuse, the lawn had been taken over by weeds, all of which had sharp stickers that found their way into Kyle's clothing, as well as ticks that Kyle could feel drilling into his already raw and exposed right foot.

The only thing worth anything in his life were his tools. They had been his grandfather's tools before he died a dozen years earlier of emphysema. Papa Jim, as he liked to be called, was always smiling, a cigarillo constantly nestled in the corner of his mouth. Kyle spent a month building a fence with him. And then a toolshed. And then a new room on the house for Kyle. Papa Jim felt that all of life's lessons could be taught through carpentry. That working with one's hands was the highest calling. So when he was old enough, Kyle worked in construction doing framing and rough carpentry throughout the Houston suburbs for five years until 2008, when the world fell in on itself. With few construction jobs to be had, Kyle enrolled in an online course in bookkeeping from the University of Phoenix and got a job with the oil company. It was steady work, but Kyle still owed fourteen grand to the UOP and was getting further and further behind. So when a purchasing agent named Tess explained over the phone in a voice that made Kyle dizzy how easy it would be for them to skim on a few transactions between their respective companies, Kyle found himself going along. If for no other reason than he wanted to meet Tess. Her company sold, among other things, the galvanized fittings and pipes that Kyle was authorized to purchase. She would knead her books so that the price on her end appeared to be less, but Kyle would pay the actual agreed-upon price, and they would split the difference. It was a match made in heaven.

The first and only time Kyle saw Tess was six months later, at their arraignment. A tiny Filipino woman in her seventies, Tess was facing her fourth conviction and third jail term. The DA agreed to deportation and dropped the charges while Kyle went off to Raiford.

What was he doing on Daufuskie? This was the act of a desperate man, and Kyle had never seen himself as desperate. Just slightly behind everyone else. Even so, he never gave up. Kyle *tried* harder than anyone. There was always another way through. Tonight he hoped would be a brief stop on the way. He didn't expect to get rich, just to buy some time, to buy some *air*, so he could breathe and think, for once, without running at the same time.

According to the brochure, a developer named Millard Mayhew had built the Melrose Resort as "a place for both dreamer and doer; wanderer and washashore." And while Kyle wasn't exactly sure what that meant, he decided that if he didn't find treasure, he would find himself. No matter what, he would come back from Daufuskie Island a changed man. It was exactly this sort of utter nonsense that had gotten Kyle into trouble his entire life. It was the credo of pretty much every petty thief since Adam and Eve first stole a piece of fruit.

If I do this one dumb thing, it will for sure lead to a better thing.

So Kyle soldiered on, breathing a sigh of relief when he came upon a dozen golf carts lined up in front of the abandoned clubhouse, the windows all boarded up or broken, the plywood spray-painted with tags, one of which—*fuck this fucking place*—gave Kyle a moment's pause as he climbed into the first cart.

The key had been left in the ignition, this apparent stroke of luck cheering Kyle for the first time since he had set out from the mainland. He would soon discover that *all* of the carts had their keys conveniently left in the ignition. Sadly, however, none of the electric vehicles had been charged in more than a year. After dutifully trying and failing to start each cart, Kyle accepted this new disappointment as he had all the other disappointments before, with his usual thoughtfulness. He wondered, *Maybe this is a sign?* But sadly, Kyle didn't linger on the idea too long and continued his search for booty.

The rock star didn't live far from the golf course. Kyle had only resumed his hike a few minutes earlier when he saw the old church steeple rising above the trees. He heard music inside and then voices. He got close and, sure enough, the house was full of people. It seemed the guy who was never there was there. Along with about fifty other people. A dog began to bark. A big one, from the sound of it.

Kyle moved on.

He kept walking until, *Eureka*, he came to the first of the four-thousand-square-foot "cottages." There were, of course, no lights on. The windows upstairs were all broken. The front door was gone, leaving in its place a rectangular mouth, wood splinters in the jam jutting down like broken teeth, seemingly hissing to anyone who passed, *Fuck this fucking place.*

Inside, Kyle found a total wreck. The home had been vandalized as well as looted. Someone even had piled a bunch of wood on the tile kitchen floor and made a fire. Kyle bent down and picked up a black lacquered spindle from the fire pit, noticed another half-burned piece with the gold leaf letters "nway" still readable. Someone or someones had dragged the rest of the piano nearby and had been apparently chopping it up as needed.

Kyle found similar destruction in the next three "cottages" he went into. None had contained anything remotely valuable. Even Kyle had to accept that the chances of coming away with anything valuable were getting pretty slim. He decided to check out one more place—if it was a bust, he would go find the water taxi and get off the island. Not only that, Kyle made up his mind right then and there that the minute he got back to the mainland, he'd get on a bus and go straight to Jacksonville, where he would enroll in a hair academy as his parole officer had suggested. A representative from JHA had come to Raiford to speak to those prisoners on their last thirty days at the bimonthly Convict Career Day. Listening to the presentation, Kyle thought the life of a barber seemed quiet and steady.

Her voice brought him back.

"Now don't you feel stupid."

Kyle felt a bright light burning his already numb cheek. Sunshine had found its way into an opening in the roof and down into the hole above and was now blinding him. He turned his head from the painful glare to see a woman staring at him from across the basement.

"It's been like that since they took out the chimney."

He looked up at the sun hovering right above the broken roof and immediately shut his eyes.

"Oh come on," she said. "It's not that bright."

He blinked to make sure that it was in fact a person he was now looking at.

"But then," she went on with a warm laugh, "apparently, neither are you."

The green eyes were familiar. But now he could see her entire face. Had she moved the statue? The little angels were behind her.

"This is a dream, isn't it?"

"If it is," she said, still smiling, "it's not a particularly nice one."

She was seated, well, "lounging" would be a better word for it, on a couch, or *divan* as Del would say. He would pat the lower bunk and say to Kyle, *Come join me on the divan.* She looked to be in her thirties, was wearing some sort of green pajamas and a dark blue robe. The light from upstairs coming off the diamonds on her fingers in green rays.

"Who are you?"

"You may call me Trudy or Gert or whatever you fancy."

He tried to sit up, and what felt like the sting of a thousand wasps hit in his side. He remembered the rebar and his impalement and tried to calm his breathing. Again, he didn't dare look down at his legs, as he could no longer feel either one.

"You've really done it to yourself, haven't you?"

He may have lost sensation in his legs, but his other senses had somehow continued to sharpen since the fall. He could, for example, easily make out the red lipstick. The Greek nose, the sharp chin. Her short hair parted so that, to Kyle's mind, the exposed skin on her forehead formed the shape of a heart. He smelled strong perfume.

"Are you going to help me?" he asked. "Or . . ." He paused, part of his brain telling him that this woman couldn't possibly be real, but another part of him was utterly convinced that she was.

"I wonder," he started again, "if you could help me lift this safe?"

"Why would I?"

"I think I broke my leg."

"Broke it?" And there was the laugh again. "Crushed the fucker is more like it. Probably your pelvis, too. And your back."

"There's something sticking through me."

"No doubt a piece of rebar from the old fireplace. Looks like it went in near your fourth lumbar and is now sticking out just above your appendix."

"Are you a doctor?"

"Sculptress."

"Oh . . ."

"I know my anatomy."

"Okay."

"The fireplace was the only nice thing about this fucking house."

He asked, "What fireplace?," and turned to look for it, forgetting how much it hurt to move, and started screaming.

She waited for him to finish before explaining, "There was *once* a fireplace, but thieves more able than yourself have stolen all the marble and granite."

"How?"

"One stone at a time."

He desperately wanted a glass of water.

"I'm really thirsty."

"I imagine you are."

"You think that you could maybe—"

"I could not."

She still hadn't moved, her arm still laid across the back of the divan. Wait, it couldn't be a divan, Kyle thought. They don't have a back. He knew this because he had ruined his grandmother Gayle's divan when he'd spent those six weeks lying on it. He had been only eleven, but he had thought for sure that he was going to die on that piece of furniture. That would have been a much better way to go than slowly bleeding out in a basement on some asshole-size island. But then, as his grandmother so loved to point out, no one dies from the measles anymore.

He looked at the purple blanket draped over the cushion beneath her and said, "I'm cold."

"I thought you were thirsty."

"I'm both."

"You're in shock."

"Can I have that blanket?"

"It's all yours," she said. "Come and get it."

Kyle could hear music now. It took him a moment to realize he was hearing the shindig at the rock star's house. That seemed impossible, but it was the same music. He just knew it.

"Kyle?"

He opened his eyes.

"Don't fall asleep."

"Who *are* you?"

"I've already told you."

"Do you live here?"

She found that hysterical. "Certainly not."

"Then why—?"

"I'm hiding from Millard," she said. "Or he's hiding from me. Sometimes I get confused."

"Millard?"

"Mayhew. He built this house. And the others."

"He brought you here?"

"Just the opposite," she said. "He *sent* me here."

"Because?"

"There're people in his family that were looking for me." She looked around. "His Uncle Sam won't ever find me *here*, that's for damn sure."

"Well," Kyle croaked, "I hope someone finds *me*." His throat felt raw; the dust and the mold down there weren't helping. And now, since he'd opened his eyes, the feeling in his leg was returning, and that feeling was all bad. What had begun when he drifted off to sleep as an itchy tingling was rapidly developing into a hot sensation, like he had woken to find his leg in the middle of a campfire and was unable to pull it free.

"I stole a boat," he said finally, to distract himself from his leg.

"Did you now?"

"Someone on the island could find it and go looking for who took it."

"Or someone could decide it simply broke loose in the storm and forget about it."

"There was a storm?"

"There's *always* a storm," she said. "Or worse."

"I must have been out for longer than I thought."

"Who's Dale?" she asked.

He looked at her. She crossed her legs.

"You kept saying, 'Dale, please leave me be,' or something like that."

"Del," he whispered.

"And who is Del?"

"My cellmate at Raiford."

"Cellmate," she said with renewed interest. "You were in prison?"

"Thirty-nine months."

"Well," she said. "I know what that's like." And her laugh filled the basement.

Kyle couldn't be certain when the rain began. He woke to the sound of raindrops hitting the floor all around him and became immediately preoccupied with capturing as much as he could in his mouth. Sadly, the location of the hole above, combined with the strong wind blowing through the wrecked house, conspired otherwise. Trudy's face, however, was beaded with water. The driving rain coming through a broken window somewhere upstairs at apparently just the right angle. She didn't seem to mind.

She said, "It won't be long now."

And it wasn't long before the house began to make a ghostlike wail that quickly grew to a full-on scream as the wind became a gale and blew through it. Despite being driven nearly sideways, the rain slowly filled the basement. Kyle watched with growing panic as the water began to rise, the corpses of dead rats and birds and all manner of other small animals and insects gently lifted from their hiding places and set free, the tide carrying them past Kyle one at a time for a final viewing, a waterlogged wake. For her part, Trudy sat there looking back at him.

"It's not such a big deal," she said. "Dying."

"You're not real."

"What am I, then?" she asked. "An imaginary friend? Someone offering you comfort in your last hours?"

"Why not?"

"Have you ever looked at a photograph of someone and felt them looking back at you. Felt them *really* looking back at you?"

"I don't know. Maybe." He was shivering beyond control now.

"Do you know what 'essence' means?"

"I don't really give a fuck."

She laughed. Kyle suddenly felt tired.

She whispered, somehow cutting through the noise of the storm, "It's your spirit, your nature, your soul."

"Okay," he said. "If you say so." It suddenly occurred to Kyle that everything he said could turn out to be his last words. He wasn't sure if he wanted *If you say so* to be his final utterance. Though it wasn't bad.

"Some people have a powerful essence." She wouldn't stop. But all the same, Kyle didn't want *Shut the fuck up* to be his last words either. So he let her continue.

"You look at them for just a second and then close your eyes, and they're still there. You can somehow still see them. Like when you look up at the sun for a second or two."

Kyle felt himself surrender. Felt his body cross a line that he somehow knew was significant.

"Kyle? Do you understand what I'm trying to tell you?"

"Not really."

Kyle hadn't meant to speak and reflexively added *oh shit* as he drifted off for what would be the last time.

The rock star had originally come to Daufuskie Island to hide from the press after his last sixteen-month world tour of cush rehab centers. It was a year earlier, before his third marriage broke up, that his twenty-six-year-old massage therapist and soon-to-be fourth wife told him about the place. She used to spend summers there. So it was that on his sixtieth birthday, they rented a house on Bloody Point to be alone and work on their "relationship" and to once more make a go of drying out. It wasn't long before it became clear that neither would happen, so the wife left and the rock star stayed behind.

He began to go for long hikes every morning to clear his head and look for pieces to use in his artwork. He had recently started making collages out of found objects, and the island was littered with goodies, from old horseshoe crab shells to doorknobs. It wasn't until a year later, when he bought the old church and converted it into a house, that he ventured wider and discovered the hidden treasures of Melrose. Almost immediately he started using old doors for his blank canvases, the abandoned houses being full of solid oak examples on which he could glue all sorts of found flotsam. The last piece he created had sold in the Pace Gallery in Chelsea for sixty thousand dollars.

So it was for the past year that the rock star and his three Rhodesian Ridgebacks combed through pretty much every empty house at least twice. He had purloined (in the name of art) everything there was to purloin. But on the morning after his sixty-second birthday party, he found himself with a dozen hungover houseguests clamoring to see these broken and entered monuments to Development Run Amok they had heard so much about.

The group gathered their designer backpacks and tote bags and marched through Melrose, scavenging whatever they could. There were still plenty of small treasures to be found—a spoon here, a mezuzah there, the odd doorknob or hinge.

The last house had been the rock star's favorite. It had taken him the better part of a year to get all the stones from the fireplace to his house. Once they were finally all in his possession, he had a Brazilian mason turn them into the octagonal fire pit they'd all been vaping around the night before. The Ridgebacks started barking almost the minute they got into the house. They were standing around a hole in the floor not far from where said fireplace had stood. The rock star carefully climbed down into the basement; it looked as though it had been flooded a million times over the years, this being the lowest point on the island.

The muddy space stunk of rot and mold. The dogs somehow found their way down and were on high alert. Rex, the biggest, dug in the mud around what appeared to be an old safe, now itself full of mud, and came up with a bone. And now Gunther and Una, the other two dogs, were digging and finding bones of their own. The scavengers came down after the rock star and kicked at the spot with their Blundstones and their Prada Climbers.

"Some animal," the rock star explained. "Must have got stuck down here."

"Poor thing," someone else said.

The rock star took a step deeper into the basement. He bent down and gently began clearing mud away from something else buried down there. He held up a painting and smiled.

"What is it?"

He turned the painting around so the others could see the canvas. They all began laughing. The image, whatever it had been once, was now just a dirty brown blur, the mold and water damage having collaborated on an entirely new subject.

"I like the frame," the rock star said. "It's weathered just right."

He then carefully pulled apart the wooden frame, the sides soft from the moisture giving way easily, and stuffed them into his knapsack. He took a last look at the canvas, considered keeping it for a moment, but then tossed it atop the pile of bones.

Someone outside was whooping and hollering, apparently celebrating some new discovery, and so the group moved on.

Tom Franklin, *from Dickinson, Alabama, is the author of three novels*—Hell at the Breech, Smonk, *and* Crooked Letter, Crooked Letter—*and* Poachers: Stories, *a collection.* Crooked Letter *won the UK's Gold Dagger Award and the* LA Times Award *for Mystery/Thriller. Franklin has won an Edgar Award (1999, Best Story) and a Guggenheim Fellowship. His most recent novel is* The Tilted World, *co-written with his wife, Beth Ann Fennelly. He teaches fiction writing at the University of Mississippi and lives in Oxford.*

This Much I Know by John Hull

ON LITTLE TERRY ROAD

BY TOM FRANKLIN

Bad days begin with phone calls, so when his cell rang at four A.M., Dibbs rolled over with dread. He felt in the sheets for the phone. He didn't remember getting into bed but knew it had to have been after two, when the bars closed. He also didn't remember driving home. The phone rang again, and he found it. "Yeah?"

"Lolo?"

Jesus. "Ferriday?"

"I'm in trouble," she said.

He swung his feet off the bed. "Where are you?"

"That Indian motel."

"Are you alone? Are you hurt?"

"Yeah. Alone but not hurt."

He stood, glad he'd slept in his clothes. The curtains were bright with moonlight and the room so cold he could see the captions of his breath. She was apologizing, saying she didn't know how late it was.

119

"It's okay," he said. "I'll be there in fifteen minutes. Don't move or call anybody."

He hung up. He lived alone in this old hunting cabin in the woods, the fireplace in the den the only heat, and not too long ago it had occurred to him that not one other person had been here since he'd moved in three years before. His job—he was a deputy sheriff—kept him in plenty of contact with lowlifes, which went a long way in lowering his estimation of his fellow human beings, and beside the other deputies and police officers he worked with, there really wasn't anybody else.

Except Ferriday.

He killed his lights as he pulled around the back of the motel. As usual, the parking lot was nearly empty, a couple of junky cars, probably migrant workers. He hoped Fouad, the owner, was asleep and wouldn't see his lights. Dibbs eased past a green El Camino and parked in front of Room 12. He got out of the pickup and wiped his palms on his jeans and went to the door.

She opened it before he knocked, wearing a Star Wars T-shirt and panties. She had mascara smudged below her eyes and a thumbnail bruise on her cheek, and her long, wet red hair was a rat's nest.

She said, "Hey."

He came in, and she closed the door. The room smelled like cigarettes. When he turned, she was hugging him, saying his name over and over. His own hands he kept in the air, unsure what to do with them, aware of her breasts against his stomach, gradually letting his arms fall to her back.

"What happened?" His voice was thick in her hair, which smelled of motel strawberry shampoo.

"I was out at Little Terry's—"

"Jesus, Fer. What were you doing there?" Though he knew. It was the kind of place you went looking for trouble. Residence of a fuckhead dealer named Terry Little that everybody called Little Terry. Usually with him was his cousin Spike, who Dibbs had arrested more than once. Last time, couple of months back, Spike was "spiked up," as he liked to say, and clocked Dibbs in the jaw, resisting arrest. Dibbs had tuned him up a bit after that while his partner turned away. Took it a little too far, couple of broken ribs. The sheriff didn't say it in words, but Dibbs knew he had to pull back.

"Where you been staying?" he asked. "When'd you get back?"

"I don't know. Couple of weeks?"

So long. Last he'd heard she was living in Santa Fe. She was into photography. This, a year ago. And now she was back? How had he not felt her in his bones?

"Tell me what happened," he said.

"I kept meaning to call you, but I needed to get myself sober first. I just wanted to go out there and get a little weed, you know?"

"What happened?"

She began to cry and pushed away from him and sat on the bed. He went and sat next to her and covered her long legs with a sheet and put his arm around her and began to untangle her hair. "Tell me."

She did, between bouts of crying. She wanted pot, but they told her they had some exceptionally clean crank and they wouldn't take no for an answer. They drank pink wine, smoked some pot. Then, somehow, she found herself in their dirty little kitchen, and they were snorting this yellow shit with rolled-up dollar bills. Then they were leading her into the bedroom and taking off her clothes. "I tried to stop them," she said, crying again.

"What happened?"

She took a breath. "They threw me on the bed, and then they started to argue about who went first."

"Spike and Terry?"

"Yeah." She said Spike pushed Little Terry, who was saying since it was his house, he got to go first, but Spike pushed him again and said bullshit. Ferriday had looked on the nightstand and seen a pistol and began to scooch toward it while Spike had Terry in a headlock and Terry was pounding Spike's back with his fist.

"I got the gun and checked was it loaded and it was—"

It had been Dibbs himself who had taught her to shoot, when she was seventeen.

"—and I got off the bed. They didn't even see me till I was nearly out the door. I had to get my clothes. Then they both let each other go and came for me. I raised the gun and shot Spike and then Terry started screaming and I shot him too."

She began to cry, silent, the bed shaking.

He said, "Shhhhh." It was Tuesday, he thought. That was good. It was after two A.M. Also good. The place would probably be deserted until midmorning, when the early crankheads started to stir. He leaned forward and took her shoulders in his hands and turned her.

"Are they dead, Ferriday?"

She shrugged and shook her head. "I just ran, Lo. I knew I had to call you, that you'd help me like you always do. Even though I'm not your responsibility."

If she wasn't his responsibility, then what was she? A question he'd been trying to answer for ten years. She was the daughter of the woman he used to live with. Dibbs had been dating Barbara for more than a year, and they'd been talking about getting married. Then, one night, Ferriday showed up. It was the first time he knew she existed. Barbara had had Ferriday when she was sixteen, and the girl had been raised by her father and her father's wife and rarely saw her mother. But she'd fought with her father and stepmother, and there she was, with two suitcases. And as gorgeous a girl as Dibbs had ever seen, ever prettier than Barbara, with her same legs and smooth skin and red hair. Of course they took her in, though Dibbs felt uncomfortable with a sixteen-year-old girl living in the same house, a girl not his daughter, or step-daughter, a girl he didn't know. He and Barbara got along fine, always had, but it began to trouble him that she'd never once mentioned having a daughter.

"Are they dead?" he asked again.

Ferriday pushed away from him and lay on the bed and covered her head with the pillow. "I don't know. I threw down the gun and ran."

"It was their gun."

The pillow nodded.

"You're sure."

Another nod.

He rose and went and turned off the light and looked out the window.

"They were asking about you," she said, her voice muffled.

"Me? How?"

"Saying wasn't we related. Seemed to know all about you. Asking did we ever fool around, stuff like that."

They hadn't. After Barbara's death, there had been all kinds of tension between him and Ferriday. Sexual was just one of them.

A car passed on the highway, and he watched until it was gone. He felt his body temperature rising; his face felt red and hot. "What else?"

"Asking was there any dirt on you. Anything they could use."

"Use how? What'd you tell 'em?"

"Nothing, there ain't nothing to tell, far as I know. What you got going on with them two?"

"We had a little go-round a while back. I'm sorry it caught you up." And glad, too, in some twisted way, because here she was. The thing about Ferriday, though, was that every way was twisted. It seemed all kinds of wrong, for example, how he felt about her. He was forty-four and she twenty-seven, for one thing. Not to mention that he'd once lived with her mother. "Nobody else was there?"

"No."

"Did you leave anything?"

"No, I got my purse."

"What about the gun?"

"I threw it down, I think."

He came back to the bed and sat down and looked squarely in her face. Her eyes were glazed; she was still high. She gave him a little trembly smile. In a way, this was them at their best, her needing him and him being needed.

"Stay here," he said. "Don't make any phone calls or text or let anybody in. I'll be back soon as I can."

She stood, and the sheet fell onto the floor. "Where you going?"

He picked up her car keys. "Your El Camino?"

"Belongs to a friend." When he gave her a look, she said, "I borrowed it, okay?"

He put the keys in his pocket. "It's something I want to ask you. When I get back."

She started toward him, but he slipped out the door before she could hug him again (during their last long goodbye, she'd picked his pocket). He got in his truck and started the engine and sat thinking about what he was going to do. What he was willing to do. He'd have to quit his job, for one thing, but that was okay with him. God knew this place could grind you up under its heel. They'd have to leave town, too, maybe the state. When he thought about it, Arkansas was the place he thought about going, the Ozarks. Maybe she'd stay with him if there were mountains.

By the time he turned off the four-lane, the heater had kicked in. He slowed and veered onto a two-lane and then, soon after, a smaller two-lane and then a dirt road known as Little Terry Road, where there had once been a barn in which the owner hanged himself. Dibbs turned off his lights and stopped a hundred yards from the house. He got his personal, unregistered Glock out of the glove compartment and worked its smooth action. His service weapon, a Glock identical to the one he held now, was under the seat. He stuck a pair of rubber gloves in his pocket and checked his ankle holster, the tiny .22 in its place. He left his jacket on the seat despite the temperature and stuck his Maglite in his back pocket and, pistol in hand, trotted down the road, his breath trailing in the cold. The house came into view lit up like Christmas, the whole night world lit further by a high white spotlight of a moon. You wanted darkness, a no-show moon, on nights like this.

There were three vehicles in front of the house, a new SUV with its windows lowered and a car and a truck. These last two looked abandoned, tires flat, weeds growing along the doors. He crept past, his shadow morphing beneath him in this weird moonstruck night. He noted an old shed ahead. He'd have to check it next.

The door to the house was ajar. He nudged the door, and a messy room swung into view. A naked man lay on his belly half in, half out of the room, not moving. Facedown. It was Spike. Ferriday said she'd shot them in the bedroom, so he must've been trying to crawl out. He didn't seem to be breathing, and there was a huge puddle of blood beneath him.

"Shit," Dibbs said, glancing behind him.

Here. Now. Here and now was his last chance to call for backup. Every step from this moment on would be the step of a criminal.

He took it, went forward and peered beyond Spike into the bedroom, where the floor was smeared in yet more blood, a yellow rug now turning brown. Careful not to bloody his boots, Dibbs stepped over Spike and into the room. Following the Glock, he moved into the corner; nothing behind the bed.

He went back into the front room. He scanned the floor, looked beneath the old sofa, the chairs, nothing. Beyond Spike's body, Dibbs noticed a bloody footprint—a man's sneaker, looked like—in the dark hall. He eased forward and saw another print in the kitchen in the back of the house and saw that the door was open and the screen door ajar. He pushed it open the rest of the way and eased down the steps into the night, darker back there because of the trees.

"Help!" a voice called.

Dibbs clicked on his Mag and followed its light into the woods. He was on a path, careful not to snag a thread of his clothing on a briar, careful where he stepped so he wouldn't leave a print. Going this slowly, this carefully, it took him a full two minutes to find where Little Terry lay.

He was passed out, lying flat on his back in the middle of the path that some part of Dibbs's brain understood would eventually lead to the river.

Dibbs's light showed that Little Terry's long johns shirt was heavy with blood, his jeans, too. Like his dead cousin Spike, Terry had bled a few gallons. Dibbs shone the light around the man, trying to see if he'd grabbed a pistol or a phone, but he didn't see anything. He came forward, the Glock ready, knelt, and, with the back of his hand, tapped Little Terry's pockets, feeling for the familiar weight of a handgun.

Nothing.

He stood and looked back toward the house, lights blinking through the dark trees. Where was the pistol? Ferriday said she'd dropped it. He made his way back and checked the shed. He came out and walked around, shone his light in the tall grass, into the interiors of the SUV and the junk cars next, a 1967 Thunderbird and an old Dodge Ram. Nothing, nobody.

Count yourself lucky, he thought. So far in a situation where a thousand elements could have gone wrong, none had. Yet. If only Little Terry would be dead when Dibbs went back . . .

He wasn't.

His eyes were open, squinting against Dibbs's light. He tried to lift a hand to shield his face but couldn't. He was young, early twenties, Caucasian, pimples on his cheeks and kind of a goatee thing around his mouth.

"Who's that?" he asked, in a voice stronger that Dibbs would've expected.

For a moment Dibbs considered not answering.

But he had questions of his own.

He lowered the light and came forward, the Glock loose in his right hand. "Hey, Terry."

In the darkness it took a moment for recognition to change Little Terry's face. People looked at you entirely differently when you wore the blue. Dibbs in his flannel shirt and jeans could be anybody.

"Thank God!" Terry said. "I never been so glad to see a fucking cop in my life."

"I heard y'all was looking for me."

"Not me, but Spike was."

"Well, here I am."

"You call 9-1-1?"

Dibbs took out his phone and looked at its bright face. No new calls.

"Thank god," Terry said. "That fucking bitch shot me."

Dibbs put the phone away. "What bitch?"

"Yeah, is the ambulance coming?"

"You didn't say who. You didn't say why."

"Why call the ambulance?"

"Why she shot you. Who she was."

"Does it matter? We can discuss it in the fucking hospital. Are they coming?"

"Let's talk now."

Little Terry gaped. He was clutching his stomach with both hands, his shirt soaked. "She came looking for crank. She's been coming the last few days, and we all been having fun. I was about passed out on the sofa when they woke me up yelling in the bedroom. Screaming at each other, him saying she was robbing him. Then she shot him, and then she came out and fucking shot me!"

"Ferriday"—Dibbs said the name out loud in the night like a hex spoken— "said y'all was fixing to rape her."

"Oh Jesus, Dibbs, that's a fucking lie! She's the one wanted to buy off us and didn't have any fucking money. She said she'd blow us both if we set her up."

"Did she?"

"Blow us? Hell yeah, she did. Like a pro."

Sad part was that Terry's version of the story was likely as true as Ferriday's. Now, though, it was becoming Dibbs's story. Or he was making it his. He knew Terry's past. Everybody did. Terry had a bad dad, sure, but so had Dibbs. Terry's file at the police station was full of things he'd done to people starting in his early teens. The couple on Second Avenue. That lady's dog that time.

How he threw that kid off the railroad trestle at Chance. Lately he'd been helping his cuz Spike distribute low-grade crystal meth.

Dibbs knew all of this and knew that Ferriday had had an even worse time. Who could blame a girl for acting the way she did when she'd been raised by a father who (it turned out) sexually abused her? Barbara had had no idea but tried to make it up to the poor girl, and Dibbs had tried, too, taking them to dinner, floundering, watching movies "as a family." That weekend of red-fishing at Gulf Shores. Crossing into Mississippi for the Neoshoba County Fair. The Lyle Lovett concert where Barbara and Ferriday danced and even Lyle noticed.

Barbara's aneurysm killed her as quickly as a bullet to the brain, the doctor said. Dibbs began to drink. Ferriday stayed in her room. For two months the two of them were a pair of ghosts haunting different rooms of the same house. He kept volunteering for nights, and she was a senior in high school. When she came into his room one night, about three months after Barbara's funeral, he was drunk. She slid into his bed and was kissing him and his hands filled with the weight of her but it wasn't Barbara's weight. It wasn't her smell. When he opened his eyes it was Ferriday, stoned out of her mind. He pushed her off and stumbled out of bed. She ran from the room and outside and was gone. The next day she'd called from an uncle's house, her father's older brother (a lie), and said she would be living there.

Terry's eyes had been closed for several minutes, his breathing shallow, and Dibbs hoped this might be it. For a while he'd been shivering; now he stopped. His eyes opened. "This wasn't my fault," he said. "I swear. Most of the times it is, you know. Most of the times I'm the one fucking up." He began to shiver again. "It's so cold. Can you at least get me a blanket?" He started to cry and repeat that he was cold. He promised he would do anything Dibbs wanted, he'd say whatever Dibbs wanted him to, he'd say that Spike tried to rape Ferriday if Dibbs would call 911, please, he was so fucking cold.

Then he said, softly, "I know why you murdering me. It's 'cause of Ferriday. You think you're gone save her, don't you?"

Maybe. Dibbs turned and went down the path toward the house, Little Terry calling after him. He walked to the edge of the woods and watched the house and considered turning off its lights and reconsidered. The less he touched, the better. He walked to the pickup truck, which was missing its tailgate, and sat on the edge. He lit a cigarette and adjusted his ankle holster. Terry still calling. The moon had moved, and he felt a little better concealed in this darkness, perhaps the way he would feel for the rest of his life. He'd crossed one line; now here he was looking at a whole other line. The question was, when would the lines stop?

He checked his watch. Five A.M. It had been quiet for a while, down there. Dibbs's cigarette had burned to the filter and he crushed it out on his boot toe, put it in his pocket, and went down the path to make sure Little Terry was dead.

He got back to the motel at dawn and knew before he turned the corner that the El Camino would be gone. He'd taken her keys, but she still had the knowledge he'd once taught her, hot-wiring a car.

The room was empty, too, of course, except for the smell of strawberry shampoo and cigarettes. He stood staring at the rumpled bed and then went in the bathroom. He rolled toilet paper around his fingers and knelt at the edge of the tub and cleaned the long red hairs she'd left, flushed them. He emptied the ashtray and took her little bag of garbage and went around the room rubbing away her fingerprints and trying not to think about how he had snapped on his rubber gloves and put his hand over Little Terry's mouth and nose, expecting a fight but all the fight gone, Little Terry's lips moving in silent words. It happened barely an hour ago, but Dibbs felt centuries removed and regarded the man he'd just been—hopeful at seeing Ferriday again—as the fool he was.

He sat on the bed. Sometime later this morning, somebody would go to Little Terry's house for a fix and find Spike dead. They'd steal shit first, cell phones, the television, maybe the gun Dibbs couldn't find, then eventually somebody would call 911. The crime scene would be contaminated as hell and there'd be a crowd at the door by the time Dibbs and his partner, Chaney, got there.

Dibbs rose from the bed and went to the window and looked out. A few big trucks trundling over the road, the sun beginning to redden the pavement. He needed to get to the station. He'd let Chaney drive the cruiser this morning. He was younger and liked it behind the wheel. Dibbs would suggest they get an early bite at Keller's on Highway 3. He wouldn't mention how close the place was from Little Terry Road, which, as everybody knew, was where you went if you wanted trouble.

Jane Hamilton *has written seven novels, including* The Book of Ruth, A Map of the World, *and* The Excellent Lombards. *Of her story, she notes: "The old biddies in Wood's DAR painting are so repressed and hostile and pleased with their positions, a person wants to laugh and cry at the same time. Wood must have gotten a lot of pleasure memorializing them. For my part, I enjoyed thinking about their entrenched bitterness and the bubble bursting a little bit."*

Daughters of Revolution by Grant Wood

SOMEDAY, A REVOLUTION

BY JANE HAMILTON

You can have no idea what concerned us that day. Was it happiness? you might hope. Could it possibly be joy? you might wonder. Nineteen hundred and forty-seven. April. We three I suppose were in our usual configuration before the meeting.

"Betty," Florence Bennet said to me. My name a little tune, the chilling high note of the first syllable, the drop to the low note of the second. An impressive range.

Florence always wore lace collars, the small clasp a berry with a stinging insect at her throat. I myself did not say good afternoon or utter her name. I may have nodded slightly, the gesture of a dignified woman, a woman of stature.

Ida Tribble was standing by, Ida with the single grown son in California, a banker, father of three. Ida's husband was long dead, time out of mind. She did not suffer from self-pity, good heavens no, even though her family one way or another had escaped her, Ida believing in herself before doing so was a commandment.

I had always been frightened in Iowa, let me say that now. The endless fields and sky, the hollow land. The eternity of that placid surface. Punctuated by the storms, of course, the ripping, the flattening, the rage blowing up out of nowhere, and then, as if nothing had occurred, the birds abruptly singing. When Louise, the daughter of a farmer, my husband's cousin, hanged herself in the barn, age nineteen, right before Easter, I looked at that brave girl in the casket and I thought, Now she will never have a husband. Never bear children. No longer get up day after day after day.

How long had Ida Tribble and Florence Bennet and I been attending DAR meetings in Iowa City together? We, pillars of our society for too many years to count; we three I'm sure felt permanent, quite as if we were the original daughters of the Revolution. Ida in fact boasted an ancestor who was one of the signatories of the Declaration of Independence. Florence Bennet's great-grandfather participated in the Boston Tea Party. Obadiah Taylor, my forebear, signed an oath of allegiance, my Obadiah a loyal rebel. Additionally, Mary Lockwood, a founding member, was my fourth cousin once removed, worth a small little something. But the signatory of the Declaration was the greatest distinction to hold, Ida Tribble the most revered member of our chapter.

"How, Betty," Ida said to me, after Florence had sung my name, "how is your Lawrence?" Her voice was not, and had never been, suitable for a lullaby. Her long fingers holding the teacup were itching to accuse. I knew instantly that even if Ida did not understand the particulars, she was alert, that pinched nose doing its sniffing.

I was a widow myself, no small feat to raise seven children alone, my husband, the surgeon, killed in an automobile accident when Lawrence was just six. Ida Tribble and I had never said one word about our widowhood, never privately admitted it as a hardship or—perhaps a release. It was the doctor, I confess, whom I sometimes blamed for our troubles, my poor boy without a father. No wonder Lawrence sought the company of older boys, no wonder he looked up to them.

"Lawrence," I said, smiling—I smiled—"has been accepted at St. Andrews Preparatory School. In Connecticut. He'll leave at the end of August."

Ida took a sip of tea. "Going so far away," she considered, "for his senior year?" Florence murmured, "A change of scene."

It struck me then in full that my fair-haired boy, brimming with health and vigor, was going to leave me. Florence Bennet, she of the low brow and the stinging broach and the floaty gaze, it was she who had in effect forced my boy to leave Iowa City when he was not yet college age. It was she who had written me a note, one line: *Lawrence is a scourge of humanity.* In black ink, in her fine, tight penmanship. I wish I had looked directly at Florence and said—what? What words could I possibly have uttered in Lawrence's defense?

Instead, it was Ida who spoke, Ida who said to Florence, "And your William?"

Yes, yes, I wanted then to cry, *let us not leave William out of it!* William, Florence's oldest child, was a dark-haired boy with a flush in his cheek, a slender, blue-eyed lad with black lashes. A year ahead of Lawrence in school. He had always sung the tenor solos at the concerts, such a voice, a shivering in your veins, in your marrow when he opened his mouth. *Where'er you walk, cool gales shall fan the glade.* Florence and her husband, a grocer, and their plain twin daughters sat up front in the auditorium, as if they had a right.

"My William," Florence said firmly, "has decided on Oberlin College. From his many choices." She quickly added, "The conservatory at Oberlin."

How would Ida react to the Presbyterian college that had long admitted both women and Negros? And yet surely no one could argue against a conservatory for a boy with William's gifts. She passed no judgment on the matter, saying, rather, "The two fine friends—William and Lawrence—will most certainly miss each other."

There seemed to be nothing in her tone, her comment oddly neutral. It was as if, I later thought, she had a razor that was unexpectedly dull to lance the boil. Or, more likely, she preferred to take her time, to draw out her pleasure. Florence was looking elsewhere. I believe I again smiled. Ida took a sip of her tea, her eyes shut hard, as if the gratification of Lipton was difficult to bear. That Florence and I might have regarded ourselves as one force did not occur to us. Imagine our doing so. That we could not admit to our fellowship is a sorry fact. As it was, we were like two girls standing before the headmistress, both of us plotting against not a common variety of evil but each other.

Florence turned to me and said in a simpering way, "Lawrence has so very many, many—*fine* friends."

On the whole I blame myself, make no mistake. How, I often wonder, does a character form, from whence comes a person's proclivities? Perhaps desires develop not simply from one phone call, the tragedy announced, the father dead, but also because of many small indecencies. Little Lawrence, ten years old, being sent to the pharmacy downtown to pick up the girls' supplies for their monthly visitor, the red wagon filled with box after box of sanitary napkins. Six older sisters often in bed with their hot water bottles. Someone had to pull the wagon up the hill, and the help were otherwise occupied. Although my Lawrence was always cheerful, he may have suffered a humiliation I chose to ignore. Six daughters—a mother can never rest with daughters; a mother must not indulge in high spirits, head up, keeping watch, nose to the grindstone, an impossible posture. One of my girls married a Jew, another one a man with hair in braids who blew up buildings in the 1960s. Seven children, no husband, the two maids who were themselves an affliction. My oldest daughter once asked me if I'd been happy even once in all my life; she asked this with a sneer on her face.

At the meeting, taking our seats, I would have liked to put Florence's eyes out. For taking my boy from me, for her note, and maybe—why not?—on general principle. Never would I forget how Lawrence was my comfort. I made that vow later. My son and I were at our best in the parlor precisely every day at five, ancient Prue serving us bourbon old-fashioneds. The age of fifteen was not too young to begin that civilizing habit, especially for a brilliant, charming, cultivated, hardworking boy like Lawrence. A boy who was a brilliant conversationalist, who I never imagined would give me a moments trouble. My entrepreneurial son stayed out of high school with my permission one or two days a week to write essays for university students, the boy set up at the card table in the living room with his typewriting machine and stacks of library books. Hour by hour he wrote lively, incisive papers on every subject you could name, from Hesiod to Herbert Hoover. His fingers on the keys, the light tapping, the ding of the carriage, his own sonata. Of course he sometimes had to dampen his interest and capacity, doing what he could to aim for a B or even a C, as the customer required. "You old dope," he'd laugh as he typed. The labor was in my estimation more of an education than he was receiving from the high school history teacher, Mr. Clarke. I will only say that Mr. Clarke, a man with a sunken frame and wild hair, was not an example for my Lawrence, not a worthy mentor.

Oh, to be able to return to that day of the meeting, the three of us sitting in the second row of the hall, Ida speaking about her son, the banker who had come through the war admirably, her son in command of his great wealth. Truly, I would wish, were I on wings, that I could care nothing for Ida Tribble and her judgment, care not a whit about Florence's unwillingness to see what she herself had made. In some other life could that have been for me a moment of resolute happiness? To know the worth of a thing, to see clearly, and maybe the revelation leaves charity in its wake, or maybe it does not. But to see in the light. Florence as a girl might at one time have had some softness in her face and in her mind; that was not impossible. She always wore her hair tightly over her ears, as if she did not want to hear anything unpleasant, or maybe any speech at all. Say I could return without caring if I were part of the garden club, the historical society, the DAR, that I could do without my standing in the city. Say a woman could return without anything that mattered to her, and yet retain the desire for meaning.

I had heard the filthy rumors—not from Florence but from ancient Prue, the maid who somehow could see into every corner, every darkness. And when I told Lawrence, when I intimated what I'd heard, and when he sobbed, I knew the filth was true. I sent him first to speak to Father Michael at the First Episcopal of Iowa City. I happen to know that William Bennet also was sent to Father, as if anyone could upbraid the angelic voice, the voice that was the boy. Father's severe warning had, I'm afraid, no effect on Lawrence. Father saying, quite rightly, of course, that young men of his sort shall go directly to hell.

It's possible, though, that I was not as worried about Lawrence's soul as I might have been. It was his reputation that I took to prayer over, never mine, no, but his. I, Betty Grant, widow of the late doctor, president of the Iowa City Graded School Board, and member of the DAR, Betty Grant felt that with strength and vigilance, with proper management of the situation, keeping Ida Tribble firmly in my sight, and having some small power over Florence Bennet, Betty Grant would surely remain in her place. But Lawrence, a young man with his whole life ahead of him! Who could he be? How would he move through the world? Was it possible, as Florence had suggested, that too many people, too many fine friends, loved Lawrence, verifying what I'd always known, that it is far worse to be loved by too many rather than by none?

After the fruitless visit to Father Michael, I sent Lawrence to Dr. Jenkins, a well-regarded psychologist at the university. Do you know what the doctor said to my son? As if he were a duke, as if he were that removed from the lower aristocracy, he said, "Lawrence, you must simply learn to be more discreet." In that time, and in that place, he said so. There is, for a mother, no advice more fearsome.

The meeting began. Before the main speaker, about whom I recall nothing, there was a short discussion about whether the fair-skinned Negro, Lucille Weathersby, might be allowed to accompany one of our newer members, Mrs. Albert Henner, to our annual tea. Whether Miss Weathersby had proof of her lineage—there were, after all, slaves who joined the Patriot Army, and on some occasions there was documentation—most of us were nonetheless fixed in our standards.

I was sitting between my two old friends, giving little consideration to Miss Weathersby and her wish to be among us. I was thinking of Lawrence, of the firmness of his freshly shaven cheek, of his silky light hair and the clarity of his hazel eyes. The gaiety of his laughter, the way he threw back his head, rewarding his friends for their wit. He often went on double dates with James Landau, the captain of the football team. After the girls, chaste, powerful with restraint, were dropped off at their homes—no, I could not think of what had been reported about those boys in James's car. The automobile, the back seat, the front seat apparently were places of upholstered opportunity. It would later be said that Lawrence, industrious as ever, had serviced every single boy on the football team. But I could not—I would not—believe it. How, and when, and did they line up outside of the Ford Coupe, each boy—

Lawrence, allow me to say, years and years later, wrote a book about the time when he finally arrived in New York City, a young man excited to participate in the culture, as he called it. And how dismayed he was by the foppish behavior of the men he met in taverns. It turned out that his ideal, he wrote, were the men of Iowa City, not those limp-wristed, lisping creatures prowling the East Village. Where, he wondered, in all of Manhattan, were the boys on the team? Those lovely, strong boys who would go on to be the captains of industry, men with dutiful wives and many handsome children. My Lawrence also wrote about how at St. Andrews, the preparatory school he'd been banished to his senior year, how every student had a single room, and there, in his punishment, he experienced loving friendships with boys. Often he slept with a fellow student all night long, their arms and legs entwined. He exulted: *What use I made of my exile. If Mother could have seen me then.* It was at St. Andrews that he learned about real relationships, he wrote, about sustained tenderness. As if he had never experienced such a thing! Regret, I believe, Ida Tribble, trumps anger and bitterness. Well before my children were grown I understood that there would not be enough time in all of eternity to do my weeping.

That day at the meeting, to have seen ahead, to have known that my boy would marry a beautiful and accomplished woman. William Bennet never married; William, devoted to his career at the San Francisco Opera, dead sometime in the 1980s. Lawrence would have four children, three grandchildren, and great-grandchildren, too. Lawrence, a beloved professor of English literature, so many students grateful to him.

What would seeing ahead have afforded me? I don't know. Would I have spoken fulsomely from outside of my time? No, that is not possible. And after all, how much of a view can a mother endure? To see my fresh-faced boy so terribly old, with a husband, finally, two husbands in the marriage. Man and man on their lanai in St. Petersburg, drinking freshly squeezed orange juice with champagne, toasting their marriage of twenty-five years. Their veined legs hairless, those bald legs. Most old people, no matter their leanings, no matter a noble life or a dissipated one, are not attractive. God does not reward even the virtuous at age eighty-five with lovely legs. Would the sight of Lawrence on his lanai, would that amazement have felled me?

It was Ida Tribble who stood that day in the meeting, Ida dabbing her nose with a handkerchief. She said, "As much as it pains me to say this, I must report—I'm afraid I must report that some members' families do not reflect the ideals of our organization."

I realized, with a start, that she was speaking about me. And possibly about Florence, too. About Lawrence. About William, the boy who, when he opened his mouth to sing, made most bitter old women recall some small, beautiful thing. I shut my eyes. Because I did not wish to see all those women straining to look at me. William Bennet: I thought about his hair, his lashes, his mouth, a boy who bore no resemblance to his floaty-eyed mother. I pictured Lawrence, his more robust frame, his hearty flesh. The boys in my mind's eye shielded me from all the women in the hall. They seemed to say, *Pay no attention to them. Watch us, why don't you, in the wooded park by the river. Grant us that courtesy—* yes, they used the word "courtesy" about the world going up in flames.

It was clear to me that they knew they'd find each other in the thicket, each entering from a different direction. Ah, but there they were, suddenly on the same path. It was William who first touched Lawrence's face. How I wished Florence could see behind my closed eyes, William making that first bold move. Lawrence was saying something that made the boy laugh, Lawrence irreverent even when he felt the moment was sacred. They couldn't help but admire the beauty of each other's faces; in that regard each was like any young lover. William traced Lawrence's finely etched lips and then he gently slipped one long, slender finger into my son's mouth. He removed it slowly, and then with a degree of urgency it was once again between Lawrence's lips.

"Some members," Ida Tribble repeated.

I believe sitting in my chair I felt a shudder of joy that even now I cannot explain. Although I was not thinking about Lucille Weathersby's hope to come to our tea, to participate in our democracy, the Negro was suddenly with the boys, the three of them in the woods by the river, Lucille singing in a dusky voice. I thought, Let Lucille become a member of our venerable chapter. Let her grow thin and pinched, sipping her tea. Let everyone be a member, every child, man, and woman who loves liberty. Let them all stand in judgment. I believe I might have laughed. I do recall knowing I must leave the room. I went, pocketbook in hand, through the foyer, finding myself out the door, admiring the innocence of the daffodils. We were the Daughters of the Revolution, but perhaps, I thought, we were the mothers of the revolution, too. I didn't have any idea what that thought meant, and yet it was with me. I wondered, had I spoken out loud inside the hall? No, no, I couldn't have made that nonsensical announcement.

Ida Tribble and Florence Bennet, we can't know what we've made. We can't know either the ways in which the world will work on our children, our sons and daughters, who are a mystery to us. It is better not to know them, and yet—to imagine, even for the briefest moment—what joy is theirs—

Barry N. Malzberg *is known primarily as a science fiction writer but has written seventeen novels in the category of the criminous, notably three collaborations with Mystery Writers of America Grand Master Bill Pronzini. He notes that he was "the first winner of the John W. Campbell Memorial Award for Best Science Fiction Novel of the year 1973. That was a long time ago, folks."*

River Front by George Bellows

RIVERFRONT

BY **BARRY N. MALZBERG**

ook here, Bellows: you never learned from where she came, from what she came. Here is the simple and compromising truth: you never knew her name or anything about her beyond the horrid evidence of the painting. No, Bellows, all that you knew at the end was the *Riverfront No. 1*, that damned landscape from which she must have emerged.

"I am her," she said. "That woman at the lower right. I am holding my baby. We have awakened to find ourselves in this terrible place, and you have put us here."

He had wanted to be a realist of some kind, maybe as Seurat in *La Grande Jatte* he had wanted to be some kind of a satirist. After the woman, all of that was lost. After the woman, he drifted past landscape into the fierce and brutal world of the stags at Sharkey's, cruelty, confrontation, pain inflicted by men on men in a more casual and brutal fashion. Dead at forty-two, George Bellows, and glad to be out of it.

For here was the unbearable truth: He had prefigured Terezin, Treblinka. Maddonick, Dachau, Auschwitz. The Riverfront was a resettlement camp, and the bathers and witnesses were the process. Bellows was no fabulist, no visionary, no keeper of the spells of darkness, just a working artist, a social creature, a kept jester, but there it was, and the blue landscape materializing carried an apprehension of doom. Of what doom he could not be sure, but he was learning, learning.

Kearns had never wanted to take on Firpo. Jack was out of condition, semi-retired, flogged by the draft dodger scandal (which was no scandal, just a manifestation of common sense), and if Kearns had had his way, he would have frozen the title, lasted there as long as he could, and called them thieves when they took it away. But Jack had his principles, such as they were, the money was good and they could not avoid the fight. Bellows was not concerned with any of the politics; he was not concerned with Dempsey, who was rough trade, he did not give a damn about the Wild Bull, but in the years after River Site, with its terrible implication, he had found himself drifting toward the ring, that place where the origins were clear, the rules applicable and men who did not hate one another forced themselves into the postures of hate. So he was there, three rows behind the press, a good setting, copped for him by the broker. Firpo was not intimidated, Dempsey was unprepared, the knockdowns began within seconds of the opening bell and his view was unobstructed.

For there was a clarity to this carnage. Unlike the other that had haunted him out of landscape. There was this about the ring: it was explicit, under-standable, unstoppable, and when Firpo seemed finished, when it seemed that he had taken the last fall, he had not, emerging from the floor on a late count to put Dempsey over the ropes and into the first row of reporters.

Everyone was astonished. From this angle Bellows could see the terror on Dempsey's face, the way in which the terror had quickly leached from aston-ishment, and watching the boxer struggling against the reporters who were trying to lift him back to the ring, Bellows came to understand what he had not been able to learn from the woman or his own portrait of the pier. It was a vision apprehended.

There she is, upper right, the one of the only women in this tumultuous, straggling representation of weekend inhabitants. She is holding a baby, the only infant in this scene, and like her, the face is hazy, expressionless. The painting itself is an oddly degraded or replicated version of Seurat's *A Sunday on La Grande Jatte*. The pier adjoins a crowded scene, a tumble of men and boys in bathing attire poised on the edges of the pier. The work had been painted in what must have been a frenzy of rage, conscious or not, poured on the canvas in a kind of savagery, the precision of the portrait not Seurat's pointillism but rendered through a kind of savage discipline. Not the pointillism, no, but rather a cartoon spread of the figures.

Looking at it later, he felt the construction (he could think of it only that way) ravaged him. These New Yorkers on the East River were destitute or close to it, seeking a kind of freedom and ease that Seurat's celebrants might have known, but that was in another country and Seurat was dead, cut off young long ago. Bellows had planned it to be the first of a series to be folded somehow into a canon. Thus he had called it *Riverfront No. 1* as the first of a series, even if he had no way of seeing past this to other works. At the upper left of the painting he placed a gray smokestack, industrial waste then and a surrounding haze of hopelessness.

What he would not know is that this could be a bleak anticipation of Dachau or perhaps that children's camp, Terezin, glimpsed more than two decades before the coronation. Would he know this? Did he paint in some abyss where time itself had conjoined? There is no way to know. Bellows was dead more than a decade before any of that happened. The woman was not Annelies Frank. She was not born until 1929. She died twenty years after Bellows.

The mysterious woman behind the painting might have told them this, but she had nothing to say beyond presenting him with a photograph. That gray photograph showed a flat sprawl of bodies. There, some were atop one another, others sprawled to the side.

When he first saw the photograph, Bellows said, "This is not at all the kind of thing I do."

"It is what you will do now."

"I am not the artist you want. It is too horrible."

"You must do this. You will be paid. Do you need me to sit for you?"

"That woman is holding a baby. Is that yours?"

"I will bring the baby."

Beneath his discomfort was the beginning of a deep anger. Something terrible was being asked of him, something beyond his means. But there was something behind this, something beyond any capacity to understand. That must have been what drove him to sport. In sport, the ambiguity was of a different kind. Dempsey might have found a way back to the ring on his own, but then again maybe he would not have. But it was a simple mystery with only two answers. What he was putting on that canvas, however, had no answer.

She objected to the study. He had worked furiously, but the image of the woman was suppressed. The baby hung unsupported, suspended in the empty air. It was a symbol, he told her. A symbol of abandonment. And the woman was not recognizable. He had differentiated her as dramatically as he could, rendered her obese and, behind the blurred features, disfigured.

"That is not me," she said. "That looks nothing like me at all. And if I am not there to hold the baby, she will fall."

"No, she will not. It is mystical." The child is not born yet, he wanted to say. The child will not be born for another decade and a half. She will grow to hide in an attic, and then she will be taken and exterminated. But he could not say this. There was no way that he could possibly speak that.

The woman cursed him. Her words were terrible. and under their spell Bellows felt himself shrinking to the proportions of the men in his painting. He was small, helpless before the river of her fury.

"If I do this," he said, "then it will be real. Then it will happen." He knew this was true.

And knew that there was no way out. There was no way out of this. Whatever he did for the peripety of the century, it was too late.

At the base of the origin story there is another legend. Mozart's K. 626, his *Requiem*, was commissioned by a mysterious stranger seeking a setting of the Catholic Requiem Mass for an unknown patron. This Requiem, Mozart came to understand, was to be his own, but he had come to that realization only when Bellows's patron did not return. He completed the work anyway.

Shuffling, shuffling decades later toward the smokestack, the thing that had been Bellows, now reincarnate, now a Jew, knew toward the end that he must have seen this before. Before *Stag at Sharkey's*. Before Dempsey heaving outside the ring, he must have grasped this hilarious, unspeakable event. Who was he, really? What might he have otherwise been? Instead of a society painter, a celebrant?

Mengele's finger had pointed toward him and then to the right. It is beyond my comprehension, he thought.

At least Annelies is not here. Is she?

A prank for the ages.

Warren Moore *is Professor of English at Newberry College in Newberry, South Carolina, and a repeat offender in Lawrence Block's anthologies, having appeared most recently in* At Home in the Dark. *His 2013 "heavy metal noir" novel,* Broken Glass Waltzes, *was reissued in 2017 by Down & Out Books. He lives in Newberry with his wife, is fond of root beer and his daughter (not necessarily in that order), and recently found his car keys.*

Homage to "Les Fauves" by Warren S. Moore, Jr.

SILVER AT LAKESIDE

BY WARREN MOORE

I t was sunset, and patches of red shone on the lake, while a cloud hung silver blue above it and the darkening woods across the water. Had Eric Matheson's father been there, he might have called the lake magenta, but to Eric, it was just red. Eric's father had painted, never as well as he would have wanted, but better, Eric knew, than he could have ever done, and his father knew colors.

When Eric took a six-week art course in eighth grade (during a set of revolving classes called the "exploratory class"), they had been told to buy a set of watercolors from a local shop. Nothing fancy—toys, really, the sort you might find at Gold Circle or Kresge's near the stationery section. (Neither store was around anymore, Eric knew, but he supposed there would probably be a stationery section in the big boxes that replaced them.) And the other kids brought them in—lozenges of paint glued into indentations in a tin, each lozenge labeled with the name of its corresponding color. Most kids brought in tins of eight or sixteen colors. One girl brought in a box of sixty-four—she had said she wanted to study art at the vocational school next year, but she wound up in the same college prep classes as Eric.

Eric's father gave him a set from his studio, saying he preferred acrylics, but he figured watercolors were probably easier to clean in an eighth-grade classroom. The plastic box had a label that read, "Grumbacher," and it was filled with twelve tubes of color, like travel-size containers of toothpaste. The box also contained little trays for the mixing of different paints—both Eric's father and Mr. Wilson, the art teacher, had said that the colors in the tins were just starting points, that artists always mixed the colors themselves. The other kids would wet their brushes, dragging them across one lozenge and then another, finding colors by trial and error—mostly error. But Eric had liked the purity and saturation of the colors in his set the night before he brought them to class, especially the one in the tube marked "Cobalt Blue," and he resolved to try to sneak it into something before the term ended.

When class had begun the next day, Mr. Wilson told them to get out their paints. There was a mix of clatters as the other students got out their tins of paints, and hinges squeaked as they opened the sets. Eric noticed that Jerry Bryant (who got free lunches, smoked in the back of the bus, and only had an eight-color set) had a little spot in his tin where he could place the brush when he was done.

Eric opened his box and arranged the tubes on the table. "What are those?" Jerry asked.

"Paints."

"Why aren't they like everyone else's?"

"They're just packed differently, is all."

"You're such a weirdo, Eric." Jerry waved to the teacher. "Mr. Wilson! Is Eric supposed to have this kind of paint?" And as Wilson approached, Jerry grabbed a tube from Eric's set and laughed. "This says 'Hooker's Green'! Hookers! You gonna paint dirty pictures, Eric?"

"It's just the name of the color," Eric said. "My dad told me."

By this time, Mr. Wilson had come over and looked at the scene. He frowned at Jerry, who shut up (but only for the moment—for the following week, when Eric walked in the hallway or waited in the lunch line, he heard first Jerry, and eventually the other kids, mumbling about "hookers," "the weird kid," and "dirty pictures" and then laughing). Wilson said, "Eric, you don't need paints of this quality. Why did you bring them?"

"They're some my dad had. When I said I needed paints for class, he gave them to me."

"Well, they're very nice—but they're expensive." (Which got him a dirty look from Jerry and a chair shoved into his way in the cafeteria later.)

"My dad gave them to me." Eric paused. "He paints." Eric wanted to go on, to talk about his dad having taught art, having had shows in galleries, and having moonlighted painting murals on vans before moving the family to new jobs and new schools, but he didn't think it would make a difference, and the other kids were already giving him the hairy eyeball. So he didn't say any of that.

"He must," said Mr. Wilson. "But since you have them, you may as well use them." And he passed out large sheets of paper and had the students use the brushes and plain water to coat it before beginning what he called a graded wash—bands of strong color at the paper's top, fading as the students moved the brushes horizontally across the sheet, moving down a brushwidth at a time. "Don't add more paint," Mr. Wilson said. "Just refresh it with water when you need to."

By the sixth or seventh pass Eric made, he was simply adding more clear water to the paper. Maybe he hadn't used enough paint to start with. He reached with the brush to the blob he had squirted from the blue and yellow tubes, but Mr. Wilson saw him and said, "No, Eric—let it fade. I know you have those nice paints, but you don't have to use them all the time."

"Show-off," Jerry mumbled, and later, making his way out of the classroom, a foot had shot out and tripped him. The paper rubbed across his forearm as he caught himself on the doorframe, leaving smears on the paper and on his right sleeve. His mother asked what had happened as she gathered the laundry, but Eric didn't say.

The next day, Eric didn't bring his paints. He told Mr. Wilson he had simply forgotten and left them at home. "That's a zero for the day, Eric," Mr. Wilson said. But Eric did well enough in the other units—one- and two-point perspective, etching, a penciled landscape of a barn on a hill—that he made the A he was expected to make and then never drew anything else again. From time to time in the following years, he saw his father's paintings around the house or at the house of a family friend and wondered at how a brushstroke here or there could produce a detail, or the suggestion of one. And sometimes, when Eric doodled, he drew the same barn on the same hill that he had imagined forty years before.

The sun had set a little lower as Eric looked across the lake again, but the lake was still red, and a slightly silver mist was at the edge of the woods, like an echo of the cloud that lingered overhead. It was finally autumn, but some of the trees had held their green even as others had gone to brown. Not too much longer until winter.

What would you do, he thought, *if you were stuck here, at this lake's edge, and winter coming on?* Eric wasn't sure, but he was pretty sure the answer wouldn't be pleasant. All things considered, it was just as well that his car was waiting for him and that soon enough he'd be in it and returning to Kate and the girls, to the papers that needed grading and the next revision of the faculty policies manual.

Again, he thought of his father. When he was younger—in grade school, before they had moved from Tennessee to Kentucky and the art class—he had bought a *Boy Scout Handbook* from the late fifties or early sixties for fifty cents at a garage sale and read it, memorizing details about earning merit badges, about resting with your feet above your head to keep from getting stiff during a hike, about using a tourniquet only when the choice was between a life and a limb. There was also a section about strange new feelings and bodily changes, but that part wouldn't make sense for a few more years, and he read that segment without particularly processing it.

And when he turned eleven, he asked his folks if he could join his local troop. They said yes, and his father was especially excited. He hadn't volunteered to be Scoutmaster—the troop already had a fine one who had served for several years—but when he brought Eric to meetings, he lent a hand, and when it was time for hikes or camping trips, he was always eager to help and to share what he had learned from backpacking with his friends over the years.

So when it was time for the Scout Winter Camporee at the local reservation by a Corps of Engineers' lake, Eric and his dad had shown up at the troop's sponsoring church by six that Saturday morning with the other Scouts and a few dads, loaded equipment into the Scoutmaster's van, and made the half-hour drive down the interstate to the camp.

It had been a few campouts earlier when Eric had realized that he didn't really *like* camping. Maybe it was the bug spray, or the reminders not to touch the side of the tent in the rain, or the fact that they were always supposed to be "honing their skills," as Mr. Shears, the Scoutmaster, put it, identifying leaves or making structures from Scout magazines and pamphlets ("A Cherokee Kitchen!") out of tree branches and endless loops of binder's twine. Eric had done well enough to earn merit badges in things like Reading, Scholarship, First Aid, and Journalism—*indoor* merit badges—but once they got outdoors, it didn't go nearly as well.

It had just been one campout earlier when Eric, having washed the troop's dishes after dinner, asked Mr. Shears how he should dry them.

"Just air-dry them," Shears said. Eric wasn't sure what that meant—his mom did the dishes at home or loaded them into the dishwasher. Did Mr. Shears mean something like the electric hand-dryers in gas station bathrooms, or like the blow-dryer his mom used before going to work at the Fotomat? Did they *have* those at campgrounds?

So Eric asked, "Where is the air I'm supposed to use?" *He* thought it was a reasonable question. Mr. Shears thought it was the funniest thing he'd ever heard. He pointed Eric toward bags made of netting. Put the dishes in the bags and hang the bags from the tree limbs. *There* was the air. But he couldn't stop laughing, and when Eric's dad came back to the campsite with some of the boys who had gone on a hike, he told him about Eric's having wondered *where the air was.*

But here they were again, and the skill Eric chose to hone was that of trying to look busy without getting in the way of anyone actually likely to accomplish anything. He picked up things, carried stuff from here to there, and tried to do as he was told and be a good listener. Listening—that, he could do.

And the day moved into evening and then night, and Eric crawled into the two-man tent his dad took to the Smokies, adjusted his sleeping bag on one of the rolled-up foam mats he and his dad had brought—lighter than a blow-up air mattress, easier to use, and never leaking. The campfire was still burning—magenta light and gray smoke in the troop's open ground between the darkened trees. But Eric had said he didn't really feel good and headed to the tent. He wasn't lying—he *didn't* feel good; "A Scout Is Trustworthy!" But lying in the tent, and hearing the other boys and the leaders talking, and seeing the fire's glow through the tent's orange sidewall all seemed to remind him how he was in a Wrong Place, another place where he didn't fit. Another gift his father had that he didn't.

He was still awake when his father came into the tent, but he pretended to sleep. He could smell the Camel cigarettes his dad smoked even over the woodsmoke from outside. "Eric," his father said, "I know you're awake." After a pause, he continued. "What's the matter?"

And Eric couldn't answer—he didn't have the words then. He didn't know how to say that he knew he wasn't where he belonged, that the other kids seemed happy and he knew he wasn't, that he didn't know why he couldn't be happy doing the things other kids did, and that while he could remember entire articles from *Mad* magazine or Jonathan Winters routines from his dad's albums, he was never going to be anything other than the clumsy Poindexter who didn't have sense enough to know where the *air* was. And it was cold—not like the cold of a Jack London story (he had read all those, but this was just a lousy campground in Tennessee, for Pete's sake. He didn't curse, even in his head: "Keep myself physically strong, mentally awake, and morally straight.")—but just cold enough to remind him that he was someplace he didn't like being and that the next morning would only be more reminders that he wasn't a very good Scout. He didn't put all that together then, so he simply said, "I don't know."

"Do you want to go home?" He *did*, but at the same time, he was even more miserable at not being the kind of boy he read about in *Boys' Life* magazine every month (although even then, he turned to the comics and joke pages first). And this was something he was doing with his dad, and something that boys were *supposed* to do, and to like, and to do with their sons one day. But Eric didn't like it at all, not even a little bit, and at the same time, he didn't want to make his dad sad, so again: "I don't know."

"You don't have to be here," his father said. "How about if I take you home? I'll have to come back in the morning to help Mr. Shears, but I'll just say you weren't feeling good. And you aren't, are you?"

"No!" Eric wanted to say, "I *don't* want to go! I want to be the Scout of the Month, to be a Patrol Leader, to Eagle, to become an Arrowman." One of the older kids had made it to Order of the Arrow at summer camp months earlier. He wore the patch on his jacket. Eric had a jacket, with patches from the campouts and events he had attended, but the Arrowmen were as good as it got.

But instead he said, "Okay." And he stuffed his things into his backpack, and walked with his dad to the Vega in which they had followed Mr. Shears's van, and put the backpack in the way back of the car, behind the patch. His dad went to Mr. Shears's tent to tell him what was going on. Eric thought he heard the words "cold feet . . . literally," and his dad came back, and they went back to the interstate toward home.

"I'm sorry," Eric said.

"For what?"

"For letting you down."

"You haven't," he said. "We do this stuff because you said you wanted to do it. If you don't want to sometimes, that's okay too."

But Eric knew better, and when they got their patches for the Winter Camporee, he told his dad that he didn't want it sewn on his jacket.

"Why not? You *went.*"

"Yeah, but I didn't stay." And a couple of months later, his father got the new job, and they moved to Kentucky, and he started eighth grade there, and had his exploratory art class. Years later, in grad school, he talked to other boys who had done Scouts, Eagles and, yes, Arrowmen. "I was in Scouts for a while," he would say, "but we moved after I made First Class, and I just didn't pick it up again." Again, it was true, but he wondered. The family camped in the fall, driving five hours to the Smokies and using a pop-up camper, but Eric never really liked that either, and these days he told people that his idea of roughing it was when the concierge spoke broken English. It got a laugh—he knew how to be funny.

It was getting later, but Eric was still standing in the parking lot as the sun slipped lower and the mist continued to rise from the warm lake water into the cooling air.

His father had died eight years earlier. It had happened quickly, while Eric was on a summer break with Kate and the girls. Rose was twelve, and Annie was nine, and Eric was forty-three. By the time the EMTs had made it to the house, there was nothing that could be done. So they turned around, dropped the girls off with Kate's parents, and went north to take care of what everyone called "the arrangements." That's how he put it on Facebook: "Information on the arrangements will be forthcoming."

And as "the arrangements" were unfolding, he heard the same things over and over—his father was a good man, and good at so many things. The computers by which he made his living (Eric had tried those in college but had chosen history instead), the paintings and drawings and prints, the advice he gave to people in the neighborhood about everything from car repair to how to cook a country ham. How he seemed to know all about a lot and something about everything. A woman Eric's age—a first-grade teacher now, like Kate—had told him that when they were teens and her parents had split up, she went to his dad just to talk about being a teenager. She said she owed him a great deal.

"A lot of people did," Eric said.

Over and over, people told Eric that his father had been a smart man, a wise man, a talented man, a *good* man. And Eric knew all that to be true—he had grown up with him, hadn't he?—but it was nice to hear it anyway. And then when it was time for the funeral, he and Kate and the girls took roses from the arrangement the college had sent and dropped them into the hole next to his mother's grave from years before, onto the top of the vault that contained the casket.

A few days later, Eric and Kate were sitting in their living room, wondering how they were going to get his dad's house emptied and ready for sale. And suddenly, Kate said, "You know, not long ago—when we were up there for Christmas?—your dad was downstairs reading and the girls and I were watching TV. Out of the blue, he said he was glad that you had done something with your life, that you found something you love and were good enough at doing to provide for your family."

"He did?"

"Yeah."

And Eric remembered eleven years earlier, when Rose was a toddler and Annie wasn't even born yet. He had worked different entry-level jobs after college, none of which really managed either to pay all the bills in any given month or even to feel as though he had done anything that mattered. So as the months had passed from Rose's birth to toddlerhood, Kate and Eric decided they might as well be poor while the kid was too young to notice, and he applied to a few graduate programs. One of them came through, and so they loaded a van and drove to a university where Eric could try to do something new. His father had followed along to help with the move in—not much older than Eric was now, but strong as a damned ox.

As they were taking a break, Eric's father lit a cigarette—generics now, as Camels were too expensive—and said, "Son, this is a pretty bold move you're pulling here."

Eric's eyebrows rose. "You think?"

"Yeah. Remember when you came home from school that one weekend and told your mom and me that you were tired of the computer thing and wanted to do history?"

"Yeah," Eric said. "I was scared to death of what y'all would think."

"I can't really speak for your mom, but what I thought was 'It's about fucking time that someone in this family had the balls to do what they wanted to do.' And now you're doing it again."

"I hadn't thought of it that way, Dad. Thanks." And Eric's dad finished his cigarette, pointed at the cornfield behind the university's graduate apartments, and said that when the corn came down, there would be nothing between the playground and the North Pole but about three trees and some reindeer, and they got back to unpacking boxes. His dad dropped the cigarette butt on the pavement, the end glowing against the sidewalk until he stepped on it and ground it out.

The sun disappeared, and Eric heard a hum as the lights in the parking lot beside the lake switched on. He turned away from the water and walked back to his car. He wondered how long he had carried the weight of his father's talents—not his expectations, but Eric's own expectations of those expectations. Even now, as a father himself, he knew that all he wanted for the girls was that they be happy. And he knew that was all his father had wanted for him.

It was easy to forget that, sometimes, to linger instead on the ways in which he could see himself not measuring up to his father. It was much harder to remember the other moments—not because there were fewer of them, there weren't, but simply because that was who Eric was, and likely who he would always be. But when he could remember, those memories pushed through the others like his headlights through the mist drifting onto the parking lot.

And with the sun down at last, Eric Matheson followed his headlights past the darkened lakeside woods to his wife, to his daughters, and to home. Behind him, his taillights shone red, or perhaps magenta.

Micah Nathan *is a novelist and short story writer. He can't believe it took him this long to discover Daniel Morper.*

Light at the Crossing by Daniel Morper

GET HIM

BY MICAH NATHAN

We begin on a train, as these stories often do: a train headed west to San Francisco, passing through Colorado, filled with passengers who lean their heads against the windows and stare out into the scraggy blur, some of them wearing a troubled expression, some of them asleep, some of them with that bovine placidity particular to the morphined or the long-traveled. The conductor has taken off his hat and sits alone; the slowing train will roust him, but until then he dozes, chin to chest, hands in his lap.

A few seats down a young man stretches his arms and lets them butterfly so that his hands clasp behind his neck, and this pose seems to fit, so he sits back and crosses one leg over his knee. He takes stock. His name is Quinn Diederich, and he hasn't slept in nearly two days. The fatigue doesn't bother him. He's hungry, but he doesn't want any food. His bag sits nearby, in it a week's worth of clothes, a silver brooch from his grandmother, and his father's old service pistol. Quinn has fired a gun maybe five times in his entire life.

His father insisted he take it along; a counterpoint, Quinn believes, to the silver brooch.

Quinn's boots are polished, with clean laces. At the hotel in Herrin he'd starched his shirt and pants before boarding and since then he's monitored his movements such that the creases still hold, though he's prepared himself for the possibility that by the time he disembarks in La Veta, Elizabeth will see him and know, at a glance, that he's exhausted. Not that it would matter much—he could shave and put on a fresh suit and Elizabeth would still know he hadn't slept or eaten. She sees through the things most people stop at. It's the best explanation for why she said yes when he proposed, though the ring might also have helped; he smiles at this private joke.

He found the ring nearly one year ago to the day. He'd been worrying about money and feeling sorry for himself when he saw it sparkling in the middle of a sidewalk crack, a gold band topped with a diamond the size and relative shape of a wild strawberry, and he seized it like it had been stolen from him and he'd been looking for it his whole life. The ring seemed like Elizabeth's size; turned out it was. He'd kept the ring in his fist the entire walk home, looking over his shoulder to see if anyone followed, and he slept with it under his pillow until the day of the proposal, when, on bended knee and with sweat pouring down his sides like he was on the receiving end of a dentist's drill, he asked Elizabeth Rose Stock to marry him.

That night they made love in the woods behind his parents' house. Just there on a blanket in the mossy dirt, among the beetles and mushrooms. The moon fat and bright, slatting through the pines and striping Elizabeth's chest, her eyes as dark as the churned soil, her red hair spread out like midnight flame. Quinn swore he saw things crawling over her: ants and millipedes; coiling worms; a spider in the hollow of her collarbones. Either she didn't feel them or she didn't care. It's because of how much she loves getting fucked, Quinn told himself. His sweet Elizabeth just opening herself up to him.

Distant jealousies stirred then as they stir now—he stares out the window at a passing town and remembers when he was thirteen; when the sun, not the moon, had striped the butter-tan flat chest of Mary Glanton. He and Mary had walked a mile through the forest to the swimming hole. She'd said she didn't feel like having lunch at Quinn's house if his father was home, and Quinn decided to not ask anything about all that; instead, he warned her about wearing a bathing top through the woods, what with all the horseflies, but she waved him off and said horseflies didn't like her because she was too bitter. They swam together and talked schoolyard gossip. Mary confessed she had a thing for Lucas Pike. Quinn told her he had a thing for Veronica Monroe, and Mary said Veronica knew he had a thing for her because of how he was always staring.

"I don't know when I'm staring," Quinn said. "I just find that I am."

Mary smiled. "Veronica says you look like a dog on a hot day, with your mouth hanging open and your tongue waggling."

"My tongue doesn't waggle."

"She says it does."

"Yeah, well, she's lying."

"I believe her. I seen you staring at me."

Quinn turned away to hide his blush.

"Not the same way you stare at Veronica," Mary said, "but I seen you staring."

Quinn kicked to the edge of the swimming hole. He thought he would stay there awhile, feeling the reeds poking his back, giving him something to concentrate on other than his embarrassment. A dragonfly buzzed a leaf right in front of him. He held out his finger, and the dragonfly landed on the tip.

"You playing with bugs again?" Mary said.

Quinn shrugged.

"You know I could say something to Veronica for you, if you want."

He shook his head.

"Come on," Mary said, swimming closer. "What if I told her you want to walk her home from school? And that you promise to stop staring?"

The dragonfly blurred its wings but stayed put. Mary swam close enough that Quinn could hear her breathing hard; the water was cold and starting to make them shiver.

She went on. "What if I told her you wanted to kiss her?"

"You wouldn't."

"I would."

Quinn turned to her. "Then I'd—"

Mary splashed him, and the water got into his eyes and went up his nose. There she was, grinning at him, waiting for him to stop coughing while on her forehead squatted the biggest horsefly he'd ever seen—it looked like a giant black olive with legs. Quinn lunged, smacking her forehead. She cried out. Her leg brushed up against his, warm and slick. They splashed each other; they play-wrestled; he grabbed her head and held her under, ignoring how she kicked and clawed, and once she stopped, he figured she was just pretending so he held her down a little while longer. Then he pulled her from the water onto the bank.

Mary's eyes stared, and green-flecked water trickled from a nostril. He told her to stop fooling. Quit trying to scare me, he said. Still she stared. He realized her top had come off. It was his first time seeing a girl bare-chested. He made himself look away, waiting until the shadows grew long, inching his body closer to hers until they touched, like a kind of flirtation. Then he found himself dragging her into the forest's edge, where under slatted shadows he removed her shorts.

Duckweed clung to her underwear. He probed with his fingers, then brought his fingers to his nose: pond water and musk. He got onto his side and pressed himself against her cold, wet back, just sort of rubbed awhile until he got bored. He remembered not knowing how to proceed, whether this was a test or an approbation of some kind. Thinking of his place among the hierarchy of things. Mary had scratched his arms and they stung, but the stinging was pleasant. He wondered if the blood would draw horseflies. Then he dragged her from the forest's edge and into the swimming hole where she floated, her hair blossoming out like questing tendrils, and as the sun set, he walked back through the woods.

Now he's on a train to La Veta to meet Elizabeth's parents, and later in the week there will be a small wedding. Part of him believes Mary Glanton led him to Elizabeth, that she may also have led him to finding that ring, and that this will be compensation for the life Mary couldn't live. He catches his half reflection in the window—the crescent of his face with a single eye staring both at himself and at the sunset-washed plains. The sun bows behind a mountain, but its beams shoot overhead like raised arms. Everything gold and green. Stands of pine. Farmhouses. A dark silo. Quinn allows himself to close his eyes.

At a rooming house in La Veta, Bob Widdowfield sits on the edge of his bed. If he had a cigarette, he'd light up, but he's been trying to quit for a few months. Bob strokes his mustache. He coughs, and it makes him nostalgic. He wonders if the corner store that he passed by is still open, but then he sees his boots all the way on the other side of the room, and he looks down at his pale bare legs, at his neatly folded pants on the side chair, and at the half bottle of Corby's waiting on the nightstand. Not a bad night, considering.

He unwraps a fresh pack of cards and lays them out in rows on the coverlet and loses a few rounds of Solitaire; by then the Corby's is gone. Now Bob Widdowfield is slightly drunk, what he likes to call "half-plonked," that sweet spot between trying to get drunk and thinking you haven't nearly had enough. Bob quits Solitaire and stands on one leg, arms out to the side, eyes closed. Then he puts on his boots and grabs his wallet.

The corner store is clean and well-lit; a young man stands hunched behind the counter, looking at a magazine with the sort of confused intensity Bob equates with people who cannot read. Bob grabs a pack of Old Gold. The young man rings him up.

"Too hot for you?" the young man says.

"What's that?" Bob says.

"I said 'too hot for you'?"

"I know what you said; I just don't know what you mean."

The young man tries to hide his smile. "Nothin'."

Bob walks out into the warm night, lighting a cigarette along the way. The land is like a fence on all sides—beyond the rows of houses and shops it's just dark plains and darker mountains. There's no mystery here. It's not a question of *what* or *why* but of *how*, and even then the means are straightforward: Bob brought his K-38 for the job, along with a backup Winchester that felt a little silly even as he packed it because from what he knew of the Quinn kid—and he knew enough—at most he'd have on him a knife, and it'd only be a knife for peeling apples.

Quinn is thirty-five with no record of any kind. Looks about as intimidating as a glass of milk; skim, at that. The photo showed a young man with dusty-blond hair and close-set eyes; Bob thought he was the kind of kid nobody remembers at class reunions. Born in Herrin, Illinois, and lived there his entire life, working in the mining offices where his father was one of the managers. Met a girl named Elizabeth Stock from La Veta, Colorado, they dated for a year, and three days ago Quinn put in for vacation and left for La Veta, where he was to get married. Why La Veta and not Herrin, no one could say.

Regardless. Big Will Glanton had reached Bob through the usual channels, and they met in Chicago. Bob had been on his way back to Los Angeles from a Michigan job. Big Will brought along the photograph and the cash. The story told itself well: Will Glanton's fourteen-year-old daughter Mary was found naked and drowned in a swimming hole not far from the Diederich home. That had been in 1933; Will's wife, Susan, drank herself to death five years later. From Big Will's telling, everyone had their suspects—most thought a Negro drifter named Walker had done it, especially since Walker went missing a few weeks after they found Mary's body—but there was nothing that could be done.

Big Will had seen the scratches himself, the day after Mary didn't return home, when the police brought in thirteen-year-old Quinn and asked if he knew anything about Mary's disappearance and he sat there calmly and just said *No sir.* The scratches all over his arms were from a fight he'd had with a bobcat the day before; he told the police he'd killed it and left it in the woods behind his house, and when the police searched the spot they found the bobcat.

Will found it too. He didn't claim to be an expert of dead bobcats, but he did know that animals in general don't rot so quickly as that bobcat seemed to have, and that feline claw marks were usually needle-wide and ran deep. Quinn's arms looked as though he'd been gouged with fingernails. And the boy could look at everyone in the eye except him. Also, Big Will just knew. He did. He knew it like he sometimes knew what his wife was going to say before she said it. Like he knew what sort of mood his daughter was going to wake up in. *Familiarity is the best psychic,* Will told Bob. Will always had a strange feeling around Quinn, like the boy carried secrets beyond his years.

So Big Will waited until Quinn got older, and by then he found he was too tired to do what needed to be done. Or maybe not just tired. Revenge wouldn't bring back Mary. It would ruin Quinn's parents, who were by all accounts decent people, even if the father seemed to have passed down some of his strangeness to his son. And if by some wild chance it turned out Quinn hadn't killed his daughter, what then? Would he be able to live with himself knowing he'd brought about an innocent man's death? So he started drinking more and sleeping more, and that got him through the remaining years until he heard Quinn was set to marry a pretty girl from out of town, and when he saw the photo and the pretty girl's resemblance to Mary, well, that did it. I mean, that *did it*.

"I have my preferred methods," Bob said to Big Will. "If you want it done in a specific way it'll cost you double, on account of my inconvenience, and that assumes your way can be done. I don't go for anything fancy."

"What would be considered fancy?" Big Will said.

"I've heard all kinds. Anvils dropped. Exploding pens. A box of cobras. One guy asked for scaphism."

"Never heard of it."

"From ancient Persia. The intended is stripped down, strapped to a canoe, force-fed milk and honey until he's set to burst, then coated in the same mixture of milk and honey and left floating in the middle of a pond. Nature does what it does. Which is to say over the course of a week the intended becomes food for flies."

"I don't need fancy."

"Anything else?"

"Nope."

"Think carefully, now. After this we won't speak again."

Will took his advice. After a while he said, "Your fee is more than I was led to believe."

"Done this before, have you?"

"God no."

"Then what led you to believe my fee would be anything other than what it is?"

"Common sense."

"There's nothing common about my business. Not much sense in it, neither."

"I just figured with Quinn being who he is and you being you—"

"You mean to say it should be easy."

"I suppose so."

Bob sipped his whiskey. "You ever been to La Veta?"

"Nope."

"Neither have I, but I know what towns like La Veta are like. They're filled with misery, and their misery is contagious, so I roll my suffering into the cost. How does that sound?"

"A bit esoteric."

"Maybe you should find yourself another means."

Will's hands clenched into fists. "I just need it done."

Now Bob has another long drag off his cigarette and flicks it away. He tips his hat at an older gentleman walking with the clumsy grace of a drunk trying to not appear so. The older gentleman tips his hat back.

"Nice ladies tonight," the older gentleman says. "Good moods all around."

Bob touches the cigarette pack in his shirt pocket but thinks better of it. "Where's that?" Bob says.

"Second to last on the left. Ask for Eloise. Tell her Mapleton sent you." The older gentleman gives Bob a queer look before continuing on.

It's twilight in the dining car, and Quinn has bought a glass of port for a woman named Chloe. The two of them sit across from each other, unmistakably not a couple by the way Chloe keeps herself turned to the window. Quinn mirrors her. Chloe keeps joking that if her husband saw them, he'd throw not just one fit but several concurrently; Quinn's response is a hands-up pose, as if she need only say the word and he'll not only switch seats but jump from the moving train if necessary. Chloe is on her way to San Francisco, where her husband, John, waits. She tells Quinn they've been apart for six months while John secures work out there. They moved from Aurora, where Chloe was a school teacher.

Chloe is pretty in the way Quinn likes, a common sort of pretty, unassuming and kind, good for a few decades before motherhood and gravity do what they do; but even then, Quinn thinks, that adage about your heart giving you the face you deserve keeps them so that even in old age you could look and know that at one time they were better than average. The pretty little schoolteacher with the nice legs? Sure. Fertile as a virgin field. All sorts of late-night splendors beneath her dirndl dress. Quinn imagines a final romp, but he knows it won't be with this one; it makes him respect her, and he likes respecting her. He drinks the rest of his Scotch, and she asks how he met Elizabeth.

"She and her family were just passing through Herrin," Quinn says, "on their way to New York for the summer. As it happened I was at lunch, and when she walked into the diner with her parents I just knew. I mean, I *knew* it. She wore a dress like yours. And this sounds funny, but it was her *voice* that did me in. I don't know how else to put it. I walked past their table and heard her ordering lunch, and I imagined myself hearing that voice every night before bed, every morning over coffee. I never wanted anything so bad as I wanted that. I sent her a note through the waitress. We wrote letters back and forth all summer."

"You found love," Chloe says.

"We did."

"It's romantic."

"You think so? My father finds the circumstances odd, but that's his way."

"What do you mean?"

"He wanted me to marry a girl from Herrin, preferably one of their friends' daughters." He pauses. "Thing is, my reputation is such that no girl worth having would ever have me. Not in Herrin, at least."

Chloe blushes a little. "I'm afraid to ask what type of reputation you're referring to."

"Oh, it's nothing like that." Quinn feels he's already said too much. "I had some trouble in my youth."

"I see."

"Though nothing that rose to the level of criminal."

"Of course not."

But his remark has scared her a little—he senses it—and the spell, however minor it was, breaks. He finds himself jogging one knee up and down. Sweat begins to dew along his hairline. He can't believe how fast it's all happening; suddenly he can't breathe. He loosens his collar.

"Are you all right?" she asks.

"I've had too much to drink," he says, forcing a smile. "Here I went and ordered Scotch to make you think I was the kind of man who can handle his Scotch."

And this works because she laughs, hand to mouth. "I hope Elizabeth doesn't blame me for your foolishness."

"Elizabeth knows my foolishness precedes having met you."

She laughs again. Quinn laughs with her, enjoying the irony that he did order Scotch to impress and that he is now more drunk than he expected, but rather than feeling sick, he feels deliciously *safe*, purged of a toxin; it's as though Chloe's laughter drew venom from a snakebite. He calls over the porter and says something about hair of the dog and orders another Scotch. The second Scotch disappears quicker than the first.

"I know I did wrong," Quinn says, answering his own thoughts. He watches the passing dark. Chloe sips her wine. "And I know it's a debt I'll never settle," he continues. "Because there's no ledger. No way to figure its appraisal."

Chloe's eyes are bright and wide.

"My father has his debts, but he just lets them lie. I envy him for it." Quinn scratches at his scalp. "There was one time I came home early from school and my father was piling wood in the shed, or at least that's what I thought, but when I went around back to find him, the shed door was open and he was in there and he wasn't alone. And I don't think the person he was in there with was necessarily happy to be taking part. In fact, I'm certain they were not." He tips back his glass and licks a final drop. "I'm talking in riddles, but I think you know what I'm getting at. If you don't, then you're more innocent than you look. Though you don't look half as innocent as you think." He winks at her. "Do you really consider it *romantic*, the way Elizabeth and I found love?"

"I do. Very much so."

"My father doesn't like her. I think because she sees through the things most people stop at."

"I'm sure he means well."

He sits back. He's surprised that the groan escaping him sounds a lot like his father. Chloe—bless her—senses his descent into drunken melancholy. She takes a chance on something poetic and says, "Maybe it's time to consider your debt settled."

Quinn stares. His eyes moisten, and that's all he lets them do.

The whorehouse has creaking floorboards and bare walls, the fireplace filled with vases of dried flowers. Most of the doors have been removed, with blankets hung instead. Eloise takes Bob to the last room at the end of the hall, and as she's unpinning her hair she smiles with genuine amusement and says, "I've seen plenty, but I've never seen a man leave his pants at home."

Bob looks down at his bare legs and cowboy boots. "I'd be lying if I said it was intentional."

"I like your style."

"You like them humble, then."

She shakes her hair down. "The humble ones are often gentler."

"Oh, I'll be gentle," Bob says, yanking off his boots. "I'm too tired for anything else."

After they finish, Eloise says she doesn't mind resting on the bed with him, in the dark. Bob finds himself talking to her in lieu of having another drink. There's nothing good that ever happens in places like La Veta, he says. Small towns are evil and always have been, stretching back to the Roman outposts that killed tax collectors and gave themselves over to the barbarians at first chance. I'd rather sleep in a Los Angeles gutter than sleep in the finest bed La Veta has to offer. And I've slept in my share of Los Angeles gutters. If I were born in La Veta, the minute I knew how to crawl, I'd make straight for sunrise and not stop until I reached civilization, and if I didn't reach civilization, then I'd let the wolves eat me. Feet first or whatever.

I don't know how you do it, Eloise. I really don't. I'm not assuming you're anything special, and you probably aren't, but at least you have some ambition and you can carry on a conversation, which is more than I can say about the livestock that passes for humans around here. I'll give you an example: I asked for a bed at the rooming house, and the one-eyed proprietor—who incidentally has more eyes than he has teeth—told me he could only accept exact change for the bed because they don't carry any spare change on account of theft. Now the bed costs seventy-two cents; I gave him seventy-five cents. That's three cents change, which I told him they should have because I counted four taken beds and that he should have plenty of change left over.

The proprietor looked at me like I'd fucked his grandma right there in front of him. I said do you follow my math? He said math ain't got nothing to do with it, we put all money into the safe, and I said well if you put the money in then you can take some of the money out, and he said no, it goes into a slot and every morning I bring whatever we have to the bank. To which I said and who opens the safe? To which he responded that would be me, the proprietor. So I said then why can't you just open the safe now? To which he said because of house rules. And I said do you make the house rules? And he said yes. And I said then I suppose you can make exceptions whenever you see fit, and he said exceptions to the rules are a thief's best friend. At that point I was done. Just *done*. I said I'll pay for the bed and you can keep the change.

But that one-eyed son of a bitch said no, if we keep too much money in the safe then thieves get word. I asked him: who the fuck are these thieves that they know how much money you have in the safe? He said I think they have an inside man. I said why the fuck would they have an inside man in some shit-pot rooming house in La Veta? He said, if this shit-pot rooming house isn't good enough for you, you're welcome to sleep elsewhere. Eloise, I swear it was all I could do to keep myself from making his head into a finger bowl. Instead, I bought a bottle of Corby's and gave him exact change from it.

Eloise starts snoring. Bob says into the dark, so I suppose a freebie is out of the question.

The next morning, Bob parks his car in the back of the depot and waits inside, leafing through a newspaper but not reading any of it, his hat pulled low, his pants—yes, he's now wearing them—still warm from his walk during sunrise when the sun cut like a scythe across the plains and he could already smell the dew burning off the buffalo grass. The K-38 is tucked into his waistband, loaded with his preferred hollow points; the bullets will open like umbrellas once inside their target, never passing clean through, never hitting anything on the other side. If there's something like a safe bullet, Bob thinks, the hollow point is it, even though it does to flesh and bone and vessel what plows do to snow.

The most he's had to fire into a single target was three. Lenny Watford, a former pro boxer who'd beaten his wife so badly she lost hearing in one ear and walked with a permanent limp. For good measure Len had also raped her with a broomstick and snapped it off inside. That's not what the contract was for, though; Len had cheated the wrong guy. A real estate deal or something like that. Bob didn't pay attention to the reasons, though every client wanted to explain the reasons. He didn't need any reasons. He found the whole concept of reasons not only irrelevant but absurd. Although he had made Len's death slower than was his custom—a load of birdshot in the Winchester from about twelve feet, spattered directly into Len's face, leaving him blinded, mewling, and choking on his own blood.

The depot agent announces the California Zephyr arriving as scheduled. Bob folds the newspaper under his arm, gets a cup of coffee, wanders outside, and stands under the eave. He uses the newspaper as a visor and looks down the tracks, where he sees a distant headlight quivering in the heat. He hears wind shifting through the grass. He counted three people inside the depot: the agent, a black kid with a push broom, and a young red-haired woman, pretty in an unassuming way, sitting at the end of a bench. She wears a simple dress; her knees are tight together, and her hands rest on top.

He brings the coffee to his lips but doesn't drink it. He wants a cigarette, but when he searches his pockets for matches, he remembers he left them in his room, so he slips back inside and asks the black kid for a light, and the black kid props the push broom against a bench and goes to the office, returning with a whole book. Bob tries tipping him, but the black kid waves him off, saying he'll take a cigarette if he can spare one, so Bob gives him a cigarette.

The train sounds its horn, closer now. Bob drops the coffee in the trash. He returns to his place under the eave. He switches the newspaper to his left arm. The train resembles a giant black beetle, carapaced and shimmering. Bob unfolds the photo from his pocket and gives it a long look. As the train slows to the platform, Bob pretends to read the folded newspaper. Quinn is the only passenger to disembark; the young woman in the simple dress rushes past Bob, and for a moment he thinks he's been ambushed, but no, she's no threat, she's only interested in Quinn, her legs scissoring gracefully under her dress. As the train pulls away, Bob walks up to Quinn and draws his gun at hip level. Quinn sees the gun, and the young woman sees it too; before they can say anything, Bob shakes his head. Then Bob motions for them to start walking, and he herds them to behind the depot, where his car sits alone, the engine running.

"Right there'll do," Bob says.

The young woman turns to face him, but Quinn keeps his gaze toward the rising sun. He drops his bag.

"I have money," the young woman says. "I have a diamond ring—"

"That ring isn't yours to give," Quinn says. He closes his eyes for a moment but then makes himself open them wide, and as he's staring into the sun, Bob fires a hollow point into the back of his head.

Bob gets in his car. He pulls past Quinn's body where Elizabeth now kneels, her hands pressed to the ruin of Quinn's skull. Bob rolls down his window.

"He murdered a girl," Bob says. "Fourteen years old."

She looks up, a few tears cutting the dust on her face. "He told me every-thing," she says, and she stands, holding out the ring. "That's a real diamond and real gold. Five hundred dollars' worth."

"What am I supposed to do with it?"

"Take it as payment."

"For what?"

"Quinn's father. Pete Diederich. Lives in Herrin, Illinois."

"What's your problem with him?"

"Does it matter?"

Bob looks at her bloodied hand. The train horn blares far away.

"I have my preferred methods," he says. "If you want it done in a specific way it'll cost you double, assuming your way can be done."

She shrugs.

"Anything else? Think carefully, now. After this we won't speak again."

But she just stares at him, a strand of red hair quivering across her forehead. Her dress ruffles in the wind. Quinn's head now lies in a dark circle. Bob takes the ring, wipes it on his pants, slips it into his pocket, and starts driving east.

After publishing her twenty-first novel, Shell Game, **Sara Paretsky** *has learned that for writers, as for Navy SEALs, the only easy day is yesterday.*

Baptism in Kansas by John Steuart Curry

BAPTISM IN KANSAS

BY SARA PARETSKY

Yes, we'll gather at the river, the beautiful, the beautiful river. . . ."

When she'd shut the window twenty minutes ago, they'd been singing, "Throw out the lifeline," with the same ragged tunelessness. Sophia couldn't stand the hymns, nor the loud, lackluster singing. Most of all, she couldn't stand the tent revival on her land. She wanted to stay inside with the curtains drawn, but the heat was too heavy to leave the windows shut.

A bonfire on the far side of the tent gave her a shadow play of the figures inside, the preacher waving his arms in an orgy of rhetoric, the sinners going forward to kneel in an ecstasy of self-abasement.

This was the fourth night of a six-night revival. Attendance had been small the first night, but the preacher had passed out leaflets in all the surrounding towns, and each night more people pulled up in Model Ts or horse-wagons. Sophia had tried to get Lawyer Greeley to force the tent to move onto the Schapen property—after all, it was Rufus Schapen who'd given them permission to set up.

Lawyer Greeley had patted her hand. "Miz Tremont, they're not doing you any harm, and they're bringing comfort to a lot of people. Why don't you just let that sleeping dog lie? They'll be gone in a week."

"You try sleeping with a hundred hysterical people on your land, lighting a bonfire in the middle of a drought," she'd snapped. "And it's high time Rufus Schapen learned that this is not his land to do with as he wishes. I'm not sure I want him to inherit it when the time comes. After all, Amos has nephews who would care for the land."

"Maybe this isn't the best time to make a decision like that," Greeley said. "Tempers are already high enough in the county. Let's wait for cooler weather and cooler minds."

The conversation still rankled. Women had the vote now, but men like Lawyer Greeley talked to her as if she were a child, not the person who had made this farm go almost on her own for most of its existence. She was rehearsing the grievance in her mind, wondering what she could do to force Rufus to move out of the house, when she caught sight of a slim silhouette rising and kneeling in the tent.

Georgie. If she was in the tent meeting, she had only gone to torment Rufus. Ever since she'd arrived on the farm six weeks ago, she'd been looking for ways to amuse herself; taunting Rufus was one of her favorites. Not that drinking and bareback riding on Sophia's cart horses didn't also entertain her. Rufus rose time and again to her bait, but her arrest had definitely been the last straw. If Sophia hadn't heard the shouting and come running, Rufus might well have beaten Georgie past recovery.

Sophia walked out of the house, wondering if she should go into the tent to remove the girl, but she stopped halfway across the yard. The silhouette with the bobbed hair had disappeared. She must have realized the crowd would think she was a true penitent, carried away by the Holy Spirit. They might try to put a white robe on her and carry her away to be baptized.

Perhaps it wasn't Georgie, anyway: her cousin wasn't the only young woman in Douglas County to bob her hair and paint her lips.

Sophia's own hair hung to her waist when she unpinned it. Even though it had gone gray, it was still thick and heavy, hair that Amos used to wrap around his hands to pull her toward him. He'd been dead so many years now she'd almost forgotten those nights.

"Yes, we'll gather at the river, that flows by the throne of God."

Sophia turned back to the house, away from the singing. The Kaw River was so low that you could walk across it on the sandbars, but no one wanted to; the mud stank of rotting fish.

She husbanded her well and rainwater carefully, bathing sparingly, washing clothes every second week instead of every week. The deep wells were for watering the stock and keeping some of the wheat and corn crops from dying. She used water from dishwashing and laundry on her truck garden, and the Grellier farm was doing better than many, but it was a hard summer for all of them; Sophia couldn't blame her neighbors for calling on Jesus for help. She just didn't want them calling from her property.

"I don't know how you've borne it all these years." Her cousin Fanny had shuddered melodramatically when she came down for breakfast on her first morning at the farm. "Still using kerosene lamps and a coal stove, milking a cow with your own hands, and look at your skin—it's tanned like leather."

"The heat is unbearable," Georgina moaned, appearing at the table in a silk chemise.

Rufus's face turned mahogany under his sunburn. "Get some clothes on. You may think you've come to an Indian reservation, but this is a civilized farm. You don't sit at my dinner table in your undergarments."

"He's right," Fanny decreed. "You have a family reputation to uphold out here; don't get off on the wrong foot."

Georgina shrugged and poured herself a cup of coffee. "Pottery mugs. How quaint. Tell me you're not eating dinner at eleven in the morning, Cousin Sophia, not when it's barely breakfast time. I'd like an egg and some toast. And if you have an orange or grapefruit?"

Sophia gave a tight smile. "We ate breakfast while you were still in bed, Georgina. Dinner is our midday meal on the farm, but you can make yourself an egg—they're in the larder, that door to your right off the kitchen."

"Dinner before noon? I *am* in the wilds of America. Coffee is fine, thank you, Cousin Sophia. But I prefer to be called Georgie, not Georgina."

"Slang and nicknames are unbecoming of a young lady, Georgina," Fanny said.

Georgie smiled brightly. "If I'm to be 'Georgina,' then you must be called 'Frances.'"

"Since to you, I am your grandmother, my first name doesn't come into the equation. Sophia, would you pour me more coffee?"

After a long pause, while Georgie stirred cream around in her mug, Rufus slammed down his knife and fork and headed back to the fields.

Sophia watched him leave without a word. She certainly was annoyed with Georgie, but it was really her son-in-law, claiming it was *his* dinner table, that set her teeth on edge. The farmhouse and the land were Sophia's, and she had the documents to prove it, locked prudently in a box at the bank, the key hidden on a hook behind the old coal stove, but Rufus kept thinking the farm as good as belonged to him. He took for granted that her acres would pass to him when Sophia died. Give him his due, he worked the land as carefully as if it were, indeed, his, but what her beloved Anna had ever seen in that soulless lump, Sophia had never fathomed.

Fanny and her granddaughter were the first members of the Entwistle family to come west since Sophia's mama, Anna Entwistle Grellier, and her husband, Frederic, had emigrated in 1858 to undo the chains of the bondsmen and bring Kansas free into the union. Sophia had been ten then, an only child: all her younger siblings had died before the age of five.

"The Lord has called him home," her grandmother Entwistle said at baby Frederic's funeral the year before they left for Kansas Territory.

"It is not by the will of any god that my son died," her father had replied in his accented English, his eyes bright with tears over baby Frederic's coffin. He was a freethinker and was outraged that Mama's family organized a Christian funeral over his objections.

He and Mama differed on Jesus, but they agreed on the need to free the bondsmen. They answered the call from the anti-slavery society in Lawrence for a teacher in their school for children of all races. Even Indian children were welcome there.

All the Entwistle clan were anti-slavery, but none of them was willing to join Mama and Frederic in the perilous journey west. Mama's brothers worked for Grandfather in the bank; they couldn't possibly abandon their heavy responsibilities.

Sophia herself had been furious at leaving Boston. Grandmother invited Mama and Papa to leave Sophia with them, in the white ruffled bed where Mama herself had slept as a girl, but her parents would not give her up.

It took Fanny and Georgina little more than a day to travel by train from Boston to Lawrence. In 1858, the journey took more than six long, hard weeks. Sophia and her parents rode by train to Cleveland and then by wagon to St. Louis, where they transferred all their belongings, including Mama's piano, to a steamboat on the Missouri River for the week's journey to Kansas City

They waited in Kansas City for another two weeks, the time it took for an armed escort to assemble and accompany them past the slavers who controlled access into Kansas Territory. While they waited, Mama gave birth to her third baby boy.

The baby died on the two-day wagon ride from Kansas City to Lawrence. Little Joseph, going into the wilderness, his grave was one of the first dug in the new town. With Mama weak and grieving, and Papa unable to deal with anything practical, it fell to Sophia to find the ferryman and give him a precious dollar to load and unload their goods and carry them to Lawrence.

Six miles from Lawrence, they'd crossed the Wakarusa River on another ferry, but once on the other side the wagon had splashed through water almost all the way to the town. The wagon driver told her and Papa to walk alongside the wagon, as he did, to spare the oxen: they were in wetlands, with water too shallow for a ferry, but muddy and a strain for the animals. At one point the water rose to Sophia's waist; Papa picked her up and carried her for a time so as not to add her slight weight to the suffering beasts.

Too much water, not enough, that was the story of Kansas—drought, floods, drought, locusts, blizzards—everything that nature could send to destroy the human spirit had descended on them. Neither of her parents knew anything about farming, and Papa wasn't interested: he cared only about his school. The homestead they'd laid a claim to Sophia and Mama learned to care for, with the help of neighbors.

Sophia always assumed she would return to Boston as soon as she was old enough to live without parental decree. But then Papa was murdered by border ruffians during the Civil War, and she and Mama took over the school and still tried to run the farm, and then the Tremonts arrived from New York State with enough money to set up a ten-thousand-acre bonanza farm.

Young Amos Tremont helped Sophia, the Grellier farm began to succeed, they married, had one child who lived to adulthood and married Rufus

Schapen. And now—Amos was dead, their daughter and her baby long dead in childbirth, and it was just Sophia and Rufus. She wished it were just Sophia.

Sophia had recently joined the Congregational Church as a place to find companionship away from her son-in-law, and she was happy to drive the horses into town every Sunday. Rufus didn't like the Congregationalists; he found them cold and unfeeling, lacking in the genuine Spirit that he found in tent revivals. This was the church her mother and grandparents had belonged to; she always made a silent apology to Papa during the sermon, wondering if his freethinking ideas were wrong and he was actually with Jesus in heaven. Not sure of her own ideas on the subject.

It was in the midst of Sophia's loneliness that Fanny wrote: her granddaughter needed a change from Boston; could she spend the summer in the country with Sophia?

Rufus objected: a city girl on the farm, no doubt spoiled, the last thing they needed, but Sophia had written back at once to welcome Georgina. A young girl around the place was just what she needed to revive her spirits. She did caution her cousin that the amenities Georgina was doubtless used to in Boston would be sadly lacking.

"And if we are to feed her for three months, then a dollar a week in board would be welcome."

She and Fanny used to spend every Sunday together at Grandfather Entwistle's tall, narrow house on Beacon Hill. They'd fought, played, shared the white ruffled bed on Sunday nights, and then, when they were eleven, they were suddenly torn apart. They had written letters at first, the stilted letters of children:

> Every thing here is covered with dirt and we must wash our own close in tubs there are no servants. The work is hard, but we are setting free the bondsman. We see Indyans every day and rackoons and sometimes wolfs.

She did not add that they barely had food to eat, especially since Papa was a vegetarian who would not allow murdered birds to be cooked in his house. Indeed, without the barrel of supplies Grandmother Entwistle sent them, they might well have starved to death. "Write nothing to excite pity," Mama said, editing her letter before she mailed it. "We are here for a high moral purpose, and we should be envied, not pitied for a few material lacks."

As time passed, the cousins' correspondence dwindled. They sent each other news of their marriages, of their parents' deaths, of the birth of their children and then grandchildren. Sophia had been vaguely aware of Georgie's birth to Fanny's younger son, but time passed, and she hadn't realized the girl was now twenty years old.

She also didn't know that the Boston family was sending Georgie west not for her health but for the family's. She was cutting a wide swath in Boston nightlife that was raising questions at the bank where Entwistles had been a presence for almost a century. The final scandal, which resulted in a forced stay in a high-priced sanitarium in the Berkshires, caused the whole family to gather on Beacon Hill to discuss what to do with Georgie.

It was Fanny who suggested sending her to Kansas for the summer. She hadn't seen her dearest Sophia in sixty-five years; she'd bring her recalcitrant granddaughter west, catch up with Sophia, and then return in time to join the family at their summer compound in Nantucket.

Much as she scorned Sophia's primitive cooking and plumbing out loud, after a few days on the farm, Fanny wrote to her daughter-in-law in Boston that "it couldn't be better. Sophia doesn't own a car: she has a gasoline tractor for the farm, but still uses horses and a buggy to go into town. And the only man on the place besides the handyman is a hulking Caliban of a son-in-law of about fifty-five. Georgina will not have much opportunity to sow her wild oats here."

Georgie did not enjoy country life, at least, not life in the Kansas countryside. She described all the primitive plumbing, cooking, and work chores that she was expected to share in in extravagant letters to her chums back in Boston.

> Give this country back to the Indians. No sane person wants to live without a telephone or an automobile. They have motion pictures in town, but neither Sophia nor Rufus ever goes. Every dime is counted four times before it's spent, so we do nothing as frivolous as motion pictures. Once one of the neighbors had a barn dance and I was so desperate I actually went! My bobbed hair and painted lips caused quite a furor. Very entertaining.

Rufus made no pretense of welcoming Georgie. As he told Sophia almost every morning, Georgie was exactly the self-centered, frivolous brat he'd expected. One morning he came back from the fields to find her sunbathing on the grass in front of the house. She was wearing the same kind of bathing costume that everyone in her set in Boston wore.

"How dare you?" he thundered. "This is a Christian household. We don't lie around naked like heathens and Indians."

"Do you have a tape measure on you, Rufus? Are you hoping to join the modesty police?" Georgie grinned up at him. "They patrol the beaches and measure how much leg we're showing. My friend Susan Whitney had to pay a ten-dollar fine, but as you know, I don't have any money with me. You'll have to send the bill to my papa, who will be appropriately enraged."

Rufus's head seemed to swell. Sophia feared he might suffer a stroke and moved to silence Georgie, but too late: Rufus carried her inside. She went limp in his arms and made the job as hard as possible, but he dumped her on the parlor sofa and stomped back out to the yard.

After that, Georgie went out of her way to taunt him, dressing as skimpily as possible, jutting out her hip as she walked past him, leaning over him to offer to pour him fresh hot coffee, her cleavage practically in his nose, and laughing as he started to roar at her. She would skip out of his reach when he tried to hit her.

"She needs to go back to Boston," Rufus said to Sophia after four days of this behavior. "I'm going into town to buy her a ticket."

"Rufus, this is my house, and she's my cousin. She's welcome here this summer. Neither of us is used to having a young person around, but if it's that hard on you, why don't you go across the field and stay with your parents until Georgie goes back home in September?"

He looked at her in shock for a long minute, trying to absorb what his mother-in-law had just said. "You know I can't do that," he finally muttered before going out to the barn.

Rufus's parents farmed five hundred acres on land just to the north of Sophia's farm. His two unmarried sisters lived in the farmhouse with them, along with his younger brother, whose wife and three children were also crowded in. If Rufus moved to his parents' home, he'd sleep on the living room sofa and not have any privacy.

Sophia had let him stay on with her after Anna and the baby died, first out of pity for his grief, and later out of pity for the misery of the Schapen house. She saw now she'd made a colossal mistake in doing so: it would have been better to hire a farm manager to do the work that Rufus did than to have him thinking the house belonged to him.

She turned wearily to Georgie, who'd been in the parlor during her exchange with Rufus. "I thought coming out here would be a welcome break for me, but you want it to be a failure, don't you? You're trying to punish Fanny or your parents, but you're only turning me against you and not gaining anything for yourself."

Georgie was silent for a moment before saying, "Did Grandmother or any of the others tell you what my rest cure was supposed to heal me of?"

Sophia sat. "Nothing specific, no. Fanny—your grandmother—said they thought you were running wild. Were you?"

"Maybe. Probably. Dancing, speakeasies. Bad company." She spoke flippantly, but the tendons in her neck stood out.

"You fell in love with someone unsuitable?" Sophia suggested after another long silence.

"Not quite." Georgie smiled brightly. "Let's say some of the boys thought they knew what love was all about. My father thought a trip to the farm for the summer would be best for him, if not for me. Or for you."

"It will be what you make it to be, Georgie. But it's a farm, not a country resort." Sophia hesitated, trying to find the right words. "Rufus . . . is not an easy man. Baiting him is easy, but you don't gain from it. Pitch in with the chores. It will make the time pass more pleasantly."

"Slops and chickens." Georgie's bright smile became even tighter. "Of course, Cousin Sophia."

After that, she did pitch in to a certain degree. She'd been emptying her slop bucket from the start, because there was no one to do it for her. She'd refused point blank to learn to milk cows, but she did halfheartedly hunt for eggs, she dutifully spelled Sophia at the mangle on laundry days, and even tried, very inexpertly, to iron.

She still taunted Rufus, but in subtler ways that he found hard to pin down—no more sunbathing, no more appearing at breakfast in her chemise. If Rufus commented on the weather or the state of the crops, Georgie would clasp her hands and look at him soulfully and say, "So wise." At the end of the day, if he complained of fatigue, she would coo, "Big strong man, he needs his dinner and his sleep."

Rufus would react angrily, but there was nothing in her words to object to—it was the mockery in her eyes, which she revealed only to him. If he snapped at her, she would gaze at him even more soulfully and say a man needed a vent for his strong feelings.

One Sunday afternoon after church, Georgie walked two miles along the gravel roads to an Indian college southeast of town. She'd seen a notice in the *Douglas County Herald* that the students were holding a kind of powwow and wanted to see it.

She'd been hoping for naked dancing around a bonfire, war cries, body paint, and was disappointed by the tameness of the display. It's true the students wore buckskins, but the men and women were all completely clothed. The men's hair was cut short in the same style that European men used, the women's long hair pinned up in braids.

The students sang standard hymns of the kind Georgie had been hearing all her life in church in Boston. The dancing was sedate, nothing like the war dances she'd seen in motion pictures, let alone the Charleston, which Georgie had been dancing recently at home. After the dancing, the students served lemonade and cake that the young women had prepared in the school kitchen as part of their domestic skills training.

The white audience was small: the Europeans in the county had little interest in Indian life and culture. They had a vague sense that the Indian school was doing a good thing, civilizing the savages, and except for making sure that Indians, like the local colored population, didn't eat in their restaurants or sit next to them at the motion picture theaters, the Europeans didn't pay them much attention.

The *Douglas County Herald* had sent a reporter to cover the powwow, a bored young man who spied Georgie sitting on the grass, her legs drawn up under her so that her skirt covered her knees. With her bobbed hair and painted lips, Georgie would have stood out at any gathering, but here she was especially visible. Two of the young Indian men were talking to her, and she was laughing.

"I'm Arthur Jarvis from the *Herald*," the reporter said. "Looks like you're having a good time at the show."

"The boys and I were just talking," she said. "Will Garrison here from the Dakota people lent me the blanket his mother wove for his pony, but I'd better give it back. The pony races will start soon, and you need it, don't you?"

She looked up at one of the Indians, smiling in a way that implied intimacy. He put down a hand and helped her to her feet, flashing a return smile.

"Come with us, miss; we'll see you get the best view."

Jarvis trailed after the trio. He waited until the two Indians disappeared toward the school stables, leaving Georgie in the shade of a giant cottonwood, near the open field where the races were due to be run.

"I haven't seen you around here before," he said. "Where you from?"

"You want to do an interview with me?" she said.

"Sure, why not? Tell me your name and what brought you to the powwow today."

"Georgie Entwistle, and I came here on my own two feet." She looked down at them and added mournfully, "Don't think I'll ever get the dust and the scratches from the gravel off them, and they cost me eight dollars."

"You walked here in all this heat? You must really love the Indians, Miss Georgie. But you want to be careful not to love them too much."

"What's that supposed to mean?" she demanded. "They were just a couple of nice boys."

"They look like nice boys, but you know, they're this close to still being savages." Jarvis held his thumb and index finger up so that they almost touched.

"I've seen white boys who were even closer than that to being savages," Georgie said. "Don't you worry about it."

"Just the same, Miss Georgie, your reputation—"

"Is this an interview for a paper or for the modesty police?" she interrupted. "My reputation is none of your business, Mr. Reporter."

Other visitors began strolling up to the fence next to the field. The school superintendent, with his wife and daughters and a few select dignitaries, were escorted to benches that had been set up for them farther along the railing.

At the west end of the field, near the stables, Georgie saw the ponies line up. She couldn't make out her new acquaintances at this distance, but when the starting gun went off, she clapped and screamed as the ponies streaked past the crowd. One of the white women, who had met her at church with Sophia, tapped her reprovingly on the shoulder. Georgie moved away, Arthur Jarvis trailing after.

Ponies and riders grew small in the distance, then rounded a curve in the makeshift track and galloped back. The youths on horseback didn't make a sound, which disappointed Georgie: she had expected at least in the races she would get an experience of an authentic Indian war cry.

The riders pulled up in front of the superintendent. Georgie went over to watch the superintendent's wife give a blue ribbon to the winner; the red second-place ribbon went to her new friend, Will Garrison. When he saw her applauding, Garrison trotted over and handed her the ribbon. Sweat ran down his face into the bandanna he'd tied around his neck, but he grinned down at her happily.

"They'll all be drinking joy juice at the School House tonight," Jarvis said sourly as Garrison rode back to his classmates. "You know Indians love their joy juice."

"What is joy juice, Mr. Jarvis?" Georgie asked in the soulful voice she used on Rufus.

"I thought a girl like you knew all about things like that." Jarvis was still sour.

"Like what? Is that a special Indian beverage that they make here at the school? I'm from out east, where we don't have any Indians, so I don't know anything about their customs."

"Indians don't have any head for liquor, but they love to drink it."

"Oh." Georgie made her lips round with shock. "But with Prohibition—"

"Don't tell me that out east there aren't people who know how to bypass Prohibition." Jarvis looked at her suspiciously.

"Maybe they do." Georgie shrugged, as if she had never shared a flask with a group of Harvard men and their girls. "My family are descended from the Mayflower Puritans. We have an obligation to uphold moral standards." If she had heard her father and grandmother say that once, she'd heard it fifty thousand times, especially during the last year.

"I take it the School Yard is a place where Indians can get specially created liquor?" she added.

"School House," Jarvis corrected. "The sheriff raids it every now and then, but people keep coming back."

"The School House?" The superintendent's wife came over. "That place is an abomination in this county. I keep telling Mr. Macalaster that he needs to get it shut down. Our boys are too well-mannered to frequent it, but their parents and cousins, who lack their good fortune in education, become sadly inebriated.

"And you, young lady." She turned to Georgie. "Don't get too friendly with Will Garrison or his friends. It's not appropriate for our Indian boys to be seen with white girls."

The School House was seven miles from Sophia's farm. By the time she'd left the powwow, she'd managed to learn the exact location. Georgie waited until Rufus and Sophia were asleep and then tiptoed out of the house to the barn.

The horses that Sophia used to drive into town or for minor hauling around the farm weren't trained for riding, but they were placid animals. Georgie brought a blanket with her, filched earlier from Sophia's linen closet. She put a bridle on the horse, which he didn't like, but dried apples from Sophia's storeroom calmed him down while she adjusted the straps and climbed onto his back. He snorted uneasily but finally walked out of the barn and down to the road.

She didn't try to make him do anything fancy, just guided him toward the road she wanted, let him set the pace, let him nibble at the dusty weeds in the ditches. She saw the School House easily from a distance, a grim cube of a building, with lights flickering at the windows, and tied Sophia's horse a prudent four hundred yards away. As she walked up to the door, she saw the yard was full of cars, Model Ts, some of the new Model As, and even a Stutz Bearcat.

Georgie didn't have money for drinks, but she knew that was never a barrier. She also knew that some men would see a single woman in a speakeasy as someone who wanted their advances, but she was used to that as well.

In the back of the building was a metal box with cables running from it to the School House. It smelled of oil and hot metal, like the electric streetcars at home. Georgie stepped away from the smell but saw that the cables must be providing light to the speakeasy. Why couldn't Sophia install one of those? Then she could power the fans in her rooms all the time, instead of just when the stupid windmill put out enough energy.

Georgie walked around to the entrance, which was locked. She was used to that as well: there would be a special knock, a code word, but again, a young woman on her own would be let in without much bother.

While she waited for someone to answer her pounding on the door, she saw the words carved into the lintel: Kaw Valley District Four School House. A bar built into a school; that thought made Georgie laugh out loud. The door had a spyhole on the inside; whoever was looking through it saw Georgie laughing, head tilted back, and let her in, with a grin of his own.

"Share the joke, sister, and first drink's on the house." He pinched her bottom as she sidled past him. She knew the rules of the game, knew she was supposed to pout, pretend outrage, give him a playful slap. For some reason, she couldn't bring herself to do it tonight, pushing past him into the packed room.

Not much had been done to the schoolhouse when it was turned into a bar, but the cables from the generator out back powered the flickering electric lights. There was also a ceiling fan. One of the blades was bent, brushing against the ceiling slats as it turned.

From Arthur Jarvis's snide comment at the afternoon races, Georgie had thought the Indians she'd met would be here, drinking joy juice. She'd pinned Will Garrison's red ribbon to the brim of her hat and began poking and prodding her way through the mob looking for them. The only person she recognized was Jarvis himself. He'd drunk a fair amount already. When he saw her, he got unsteadily to his feet.

"It's Little Miss Mayflower, come to play Carrie Nation with the drunks. You going to give me your lecture on Pilgrim purity?"

Several drinkers stopped mid-swallow to guffaw.

"Buy me a drink, Mr. Reporter, and I'll lecture you personally."

Jarvis nodded at the bartender, a thickset man in an open-necked shirt. The bar itself was just a couple of slabs of wood laid over sawhorses. The bartender poured something into a heavy mug. Georgie took a swallow and made a face—it was a quick-brewed beer, thin and bitter.

She slapped the mug on the sawhorses. "We Pilgrims only drink gin."

"That'll cost you a kiss, Mayflower."

Jarvis put an arm around her and tried to kiss her, but she reached behind him for the mug she'd put down and poured it over his hair. The crowd loved it.

"Why'd you go and do that?" Jarvis pulled out a handkerchief and wiped his face.

"Why'd you go and do that, yourself?" Georgie said.

"If it had been your Indian friend, bet you'd have been cuddling right into his red arms," he said resentfully.

"Probably so," Georgie said. "We Mayflowers and the Indians go back three hundred years together."

"Then I guess you don't know those Indian boys have a curfew and everything and Superintendent Macalaster makes sure they spend their nights locked up in their school dormitory. But there are some redskins around here if you have Jesus power to raise the dead."

Jarvis pointed at a corner of the room where two men were slumped on the floor, the wall behind them keeping them from falling over completely. Their clothes were dirty, and someone had taken the bandanna one of them wore at his throat and tied it around his head, sticking in a piece of rubber tubing in lieu of a feather.

One of the men at the bar took over a mug of beer and shook them awake. "Hey, chief, wake up. Got a lady who says she knows your great-grandmother. Have a beer and talk to her." He poured the beer over the two men, to an uproar from the crowd.

Georgie pretended to laugh but turned her back. She had seen drunks before, more than once, but these two men looked so naked she found it unbearable.

She put down her drink and tried to push her way through the door. Over the noise of the drinkers and the clacking of the fan as its bent blade brushed the ceiling, Georgie heard a siren. She froze, looking for a back door, but there wasn't one. A moment later, a sheriff's deputy came in, accompanied by two revenue officers.

Georgie had had other bad days, but none of them had ever included a night in police custody. The county didn't have a women's prison, so the deputy locked Georgie in the sheriff's office overnight, with a matron to look after her. She told the matron that her cousin Sophia's horse was tied to a tree near the School House.

"He needs to be taken back to his stable. Can someone look after him? Please? It's too hot for an animal to be out this long. I don't even know if there's water within his reach."

"You should have thought of that before you took him bar crawling with you," the matron said.

However, the sheriff, when he came in at seven in the morning, sent a deputy out to the Grellier farm. The sheriff knew Sophia, he knew two of her dead husband's nephews. He didn't want her to lose a horse just because she had a drunk cousin visiting for the summer. He moved Georgie into the courtroom with the other arrestees and told her to wait until her cousin arrived to pay her fine.

"What if she doesn't come?" Georgie asked.

"Then you'll be assigned to a county crew to work off the fine," the sheriff said.

About twenty detainees waited in the courtroom with Georgie. Not everyone who'd been in the School House had been brought in. Arthur Jarvis, the *Douglas County Herald* reporter, was missing, Georgie noticed. The judge gave everyone a choice of a fine, thirty days in the county jail, or a week on a county work detail. At the end of the morning, only Georgie and the two Indian men remained.

At lunchtime, Will Garrison, the Dakota who had come in second in the pony races, arrived. He was covered with dust: he'd walked the two miles from the school to the police station to pay the fine for the two Indians.

When Georgie saw Garrison, she turned crimson with shame and huddled deep in her chair. She didn't look up, so she didn't know if he looked at her or not.

Around midafternoon, Sophia drove the buggy into town. Her lips were tight and white with rage, but she kept her temper to herself until they were on the road out of town. She was driving with only one horse.

"You stole my horse, you left him tied up near a busy road. What is the matter with you? You come from a good home; you never wanted for anything! Why are you acting in this fashion, doing everything you can to turn me, and Rufus, too, against you? I can't keep this from Fanny: that ten-dollar fine is a lot of money for me. Your father is going to have to pay me back. And then what will you do? Where else can you go?"

Georgie didn't try to say anything in her own defense; she didn't feel guilty about going to the speakeasy, but she wished she had never taken Sophia's horse.

"Is he—Is the horse hurt?" she asked timidly.

"One of the neighbors saw him when he was out mulching at five this morning. He brought him home, undamaged but tired, which is why we're driving one horse this afternoon."

Georgie's contrition over the horse wasn't as deep as her shame that Will Garrison had seen her in the courtroom. She kept that thought tucked away below her diaphragm—she certainly wasn't going to share it with Cousin Sophia.

When they reached the farm, Sophia said, "You go muck out the stable. You will make the care of these two horses your mission for the remainder of your time on the farm. I want the stalls spick-and-span, I want the horses' coats glossy, I want them to have the water and food they need. You will *never* ride them again. Do you hear me?"

Georgie nodded. "Yes, Cousin Sophia."

Sophia gave her a pair of men's overalls. Not Rufus's, which would have swamped Georgie, but a pair of her own. She ordered them from the Sears catalog to wear when she was doing farmwork herself.

Georgie thought the worst was past, but when she washed herself off under the outdoor pump after working the rest of the afternoon in the barn, Rufus was waiting for her, shaking the evening paper under her nose.

"How dare you? How dare you take advantage of my hospitality?"

Georgie just had time to see the headline—"Mayflower Descendant Descends to Public Drunkenness"—before Rufus slapped her head so hard she was knocked off her feet.

"Whore," he grunted. "Rutting, drunken whore."

He yanked her to her feet, but she wriggled away before he could strike her a second time. Standing just out of his arm's reach, Georgie pulled the top of her dress down under the overalls, flashing her breasts.

"You want these, don't you, Rufus? That's why you're so cranky all the time. You want them, and you know I'll never give them to you."

Rufus started after her, but before he reached her, Sophia appeared in the yard.

"I don't know what game you two are playing, but stop it at once."

Sophia's voice was even colder and angrier than when she'd lectured Georgie in the buggy. "The next time either of you behaves like this, you will both leave the farm, if I have to get the sheriff to remove you."

It was later that afternoon that the itinerant preacher appeared. He saw Rufus and got his permission to set up the tent on the Grellier property.

Georgie waited until Sophia and Rufus had gone to bed before reading the article in the *Herald*. As she read, her own temper rose: Jarvis hadn't mentioned that he had been as drunk as ten skunks. Instead, he made it sound as though he had merely gone to the School House as a reporter so he could let Douglas County know what went on inside its pure borders. And he'd spent a number of paragraphs on Georgie, the Mayflower Descendant in love with the Indians.

> Miss Entwistle consorted with some of the young bucks at our local Indian school after yesterday's powwow. Superintendent Macalester's wife tried to speak to her about the dangers intimacy between white girls and Indian boys holds for both races, but Miss Entwistle seems to think that her Puritan ancestors protect her from following normal behavioral conventions—as she demonstrated at the School House that same night. She ordered gin from the bemused bartender and made herself quite the spectacle for all the rowdies who usually frequent such a place.

Georgie tore the paper into spills and laid them in with the coals in the stove. When Sophia lit the fire in the morning to make Rufus his fried eggs, the story would go up in smoke. She lay in bed in her stuffy room but couldn't sleep. She wanted revenge on Arthur Jarvis but couldn't think of anything drastic or punitive enough.

Around dawn her thoughts shifted to Will Garrison at the Indian school. They had been flirting in a harmless way, not consorting, but she wondered if he was in trouble with the school because of Jarvis's story. She thought of writing to the superintendent's wife, or to the superintendent himself, but Mrs. Macalaster was a cold woman. She seemed to look down on the Indian students, and she definitely looked down on Georgie.

At five, she heard Rufus go out the kitchen door. She watched from the window as he went into the barn to do the morning milking, and then she heard Sophia go down the stairs to the kitchen. She smelled the smoke as the fire started. At least Jarvis's hateful words weren't in the house any longer.

There was a small table in the room where Georgie kept her toiletries and a pitcher and basin. She sat there to write a note to Will Garrison:

> Dear Mr. Garrison, I apologize for any trouble I may have brought into your life. I enjoyed meeting you at the powwow on Sunday

and thought you were a super rider. I am living on my cousin Sophia's farm, the Grellier farm, about two miles south of your school, near to Blue Mound. At the big crossroads between us and your school is a mailbox held into the ground with a couple of big rocks. If you would let me meet you to apologize in person, or if you would like me to return your red ribbon, leave a note for me under one of those rocks. Ever yours sincerely, Georgie Entwistle.

As soon as Rufus had headed to the fields where he and the handyman were haying, Georgie came down the stairs. Sophia was washing the breakfast dishes. She nodded at Georgie but didn't speak.

Georgie drank her coffee, ate a piece of toast with tomato preserves, put on her overalls to go out to the barn. The overalls had pockets; she slipped the letter into one of them and walked past the barn, grabbing one of the big straw hats that hung just inside the door as she passed. She made a detour across a field where she couldn't be seen from the house or from the quarter section Rufus was working.

The July heat was fierce, and she was sweating heavily under the straw hat, but when she took it off, the sun glare made her eyes ache. She went to the school's front door, forgetting that she wasn't in Boston, where her name and privilege got her past most barriers, forgetting that she was dressed like a farmhand.

"Go out to the barn, boy, if you have a message from the farmer." It was Mrs. Macalaster herself who answered the door.

Georgie bit back a laugh. The overalls and hat were a perfect disguise, even hiding her sex. She walked around the main building to the barn, where some of the Indian boys were pitching down hay for the ponies and cows. Will Garrison wasn't among them, but one of them took the letter from her and promised to give it to him. He eyed her narrowly; she was sure that, unlike the superintendent's wife, his keen hunter's instinct knew not just that she was a woman but that she was the woman who'd been at the powwow.

She scuttled away from the barn but stopped at a pump in the yard long enough to sluice her hot head and neck. Her overalls and the blouse she wore underneath them were dry by the time she got back to Sophia's barn.

She led the two horses out to a shady place in the enclosed field where Sophia usually left them for the day. The stalls were relatively clean from her previous day's work. She shoveled the manure into the compost area behind the barn, put out clean straw, and rinsed off her overalls under the pump in the yard.

She bypassed the kitchen when she came into the house: Rufus was at the table, eating cornbread and a fried pork chop. The hot food on the hot day made Georgie queasy. She took a cold bath, despite the interdiction from Sophia not to use water wantonly, and lay down to sleep.

Rufus went over to the revival tent after supper. He urged Sophia and Georgie to go with him.

"A good sermon that brought you to a sense of your sins would be the best thing you could do for your immortal soul," he said to Georgie.

"You have such a good sense of my sins, I expect Jesus will pay more attention to what you have to say about them than he will me," Georgie said.

Rufus glowered at her but left for the meeting without saying anything back. Georgie sat in the parlor with Sophia and watched her darn socks. Finally she went up to bed, waiting for Sophia to turn out the lamp in the parlor. After she heard her cousin climb the stairs, she slipped down the stairs in her stockinged feet and then out the back door.

The house was between her and the tent, but she could see bonfires shooting up flames and could hear the singing and some of the excited cries from the sinners. She walked to the mailbox she had described in her letter and lifted the rocks. No answer had come from Will Garrison.

As she walked back to the house, automobiles began coming toward her: the damned and the saved leaving the revival. She stumbled into the ditch to keep from being seen and tore her good silk stockings on the nettles.

Georgie went to the mailbox faithfully for three nights, and on the Thursday was rewarded: Garrison himself rose from the shadows.

Georgie wanted to say something bold, the kind of comment she was used to making to the boys she knew at home, but she felt embarrassed and unlike herself.

"You came yourself?" she finally blurted.

"I was leaving a note for you, but then I saw you walking down the road."

"They told me you have a curfew."

"Yes, but the window's open. It's not so hard to jump out. Harder, maybe, to jump back in."

"Are you in trouble because of me?" Her voice had gone up half a register, making her sound like a child. She hated it but couldn't seem to control it.

"In a small way," he said. "The superintendent knows that Indian boys are weak in the face of temptation and that a white woman is a powerful temptation. Almost as strong as drink. He and Mrs. Macalaster blame you for trying to lead me astray."

His voice was steady, and in the dark she couldn't tell if he was teasing or if he truly believed it. She felt her face grow hot.

"I didn't want to lead you astray," she said in her little-girl voice. "I wanted— My family in Boston sent me here because at home I—they didn't like how I acted. Too wild. And on my cousin Sophia's farm I have been so bored. I thought the powwow would be exciting."

"You hoped for wild Indians who would let you behave wildly. I can't be a wild person for you, Miss Entwistle."

"Georgie," she said.

"For Georgie, either." He turned to walk away.

"You looked happy galloping on your pony," she called after him. "Happy to be wild for a minute. And that's what I want, a minute to be happy."

He came back and put his hands on her shoulders. "Miss Georgie, for you this is a vacation or maybe it is a rest cure, but for me this is life. I am at this school, with all the rules that I find stupid, because I need to help my family. We are helpless against the white men. As Little Crow truly spoke, you keep coming with your guns and your own laws that you twist and turn for your own advantage. Do you know that the land where your cousin farms once was underwater and home to many thousand water birds? My family was driven here from lands to the north and the east, but we learned to live with those birds. Now you have drained the land and made it white people's farms. To help my family I cannot be wild. I must be the tamest of all tame Indians. My mother and my grandmother sent me here with that mission."

He bent and kissed her and turned and left.

When Georgie got back to the farm, the revival seemed to be at a fever pitch. She went into the tent. The smell of all the sweaty bodies, the smell of sex, the people bowing and kneeling and moaning, swept across her, and she began to shout and kneel and writhe with them. No cocaine and Charleston party had ever been this full of hot, raw emotion.

"Sister, what's your name, sister?" the preacher shouted at her.

"I'm a wild bird," she said. "Birdie is my name."

"Birdie, come forward, confess your sins to Jesus."

People gathered around her, chanting. "Confess, confess, confess to the Lord and be saved."

"I confess," she said. "I confess to wildness."

Georgie slept late the next morning. When she came down Rufus was crossing the yard to the kitchen; it was close to eleven, time for the fried chicken whose smell made Georgie sick, not hungry.

Sophia wished her good morning and reminded her that the horses needed to be cared for.

"Yes, cousin," Georgie said.

She swallowed her coffee and started to pull on the overalls that were hanging by the back door. She was stiff in every limb and almost fell over as she hoisted her legs into the heavy denim.

Rufus grabbed her forearm before she could go down the stairs to the yard. "You were in the tent last night, confessing the sin of wildness. Everyone wants to know, was that a mockery, or was it a true confession?"

Georgie pulled her arm free. "That's between me and Jesus, Cousin Rufus. None of your business."

"If it was genuine, and you've really repented your wildness, why did you call yourself 'Birdie'? Why not give them your real name?"

"Thanks to that reporter, everyone in your county knows my name. When I'm confessing to the Lord, he knows who I am, but your friends and neighbors don't have to. Now, if you'll excuse me, Cousin Rufus, your mother-in-law's horses need tending to."

"Just so you know, Georgina, if that was a true confession, if you've given your heart and soul to the Lord, we're having a group baptism here at the horse trough on Sunday afternoon."

"I'll keep that in mind."

Sophia had stood at the screen door listening, but she didn't comment. That had been Georgie in the tent last night. What was the girl up to? Ragging Rufus, going to Jesus, or something else? Sophia had seen those tent revivals; she knew the raw emotions that swept through them. They were like prairie fires—easy to start, impossible to control.

In fact, the fire was already spreading, a plume of smoke here, a lick of flames there, because there is always fire if there's smoke. One of the people driving away from the revival Thursday night had seen Will Garrison with his hands on Georgie's shoulders. Wild girl, wild Indian, she had come to Jesus, but he was a savage interfering with a white girl.

By Saturday afternoon, the story was all over the county. Men confronted Rufus that night in the tent.

What are you going to do about it, Rufus Schapen? Your own cousin, your own home, you going to let that savage get away with it?

As the meeting revved up in intensity, Rufus glared down the men around him. "Anyone can talk, but who can act? If I act, am I on my own, or are you with me?"

"With you!" they shouted eagerly.

They piled into their Model Ts and As, bringing Rufus into the lead car. They drove to the school, knocked down the door, found the dorm, found Will Garrison, and dragged him to the school yard. To a tree.

Georgie heard about it at the social hour after church the next morning. Indian boy hanged in the night. A lynching, but he'd been seen out on a county road with a white girl. Sidelong glances at Georgie, who said nothing. On the drive home, Sophia tried to talk to her about what had happened, but the girl had disappeared into a remote place, so deep inside herself that she seemed not to hear a word. She had turned a pasty white and gave off the smell of vomit. Sophia touched her forehead; it was cold, despite the hot day.

When they got to the house, Sophia told Rufus she did not want the baptism on her land, in her horse trough.

"No way to stop it, Mama Sophia," he grunted. "Don't even know who's fixing to come, couldn't get word to them if I wanted to. Got a white robe laid out on Georgie's bed for her. Wash yourself in the blood of the Lamb and your wild ways will come to an end."

Sophia helped Georgie up the stairs.

"You lie down; you stay in bed. I'm bringing you up a cup of tea, and then you sleep. Don't go out to that trough; don't make another public display of yourself. Please, Georgie."

Georgie might have heard her, hard to say. She took off her shoes and her silk stockings, though, and lay under the covers. Sophia put the white robe on a chair. The group baptism wasn't for another three hours; with luck, Georgie would sleep through it.

Sophia was worn herself and went to her bedroom to rest. As she hung her dress in the wardrobe, she watched Rufus cross the field to his parents' house. He knew she was angry about the Indian boy; he was hiding with his mother as he usually did when Sophia was angry. He'd be back at five, though, swelling with importance at the trough—*her* trough.

Afterward, Sophia asked herself why she'd left the robe in Georgie's room. Why she hadn't stayed with Georgie. Afterward, when the preacher showed up with his eager penitents, and preacher and penitents all screamed hysterically to see the body in the trough, weighted down with the heavy rock Georgie had carried up the road from the mailbox.

Afterward, when Lawyer Greeley refused to redo her will so she could leave the Grellier farm to the Indian school—*I can't let you do that, Miz Tremont. No, it's not because of what people will say. It's because Rufus can make a good case in court, overturn the will, eat up the value of the farm in lawsuits.*

Afterwards she looked at the farmhouse, gray, worn, as she herself was gray and worn. Her whole life given in service to a piece of land. She'd never danced the Charleston or inhaled cocaine or even drunk as much as a thimble of wine.

She looked at the tintype of her father and mother in pride of place on her mother's piano, the picture taken by an itinerant photographer four months before her father's murder.

"Are you with Jesus, Papa? Is there a heaven? Is there a Jesus, who cares that you were murdered and I grew up without a father? Does he care that somewhere there is a mother crying for a dead Indian boy? Did anything you or Mama or I did matter in the least bit?"

She took a splinter from the woodbox and set it alight, touched it to the kitchen table and kitchen curtains, moved to the parlor curtains, traveled on to the barn where the animals were in their stalls for the night. Led the puzzled cows and horses to the field, climbed to the loft, and set the hay on fire around her. Rufus, stumbling out of the house in his nightshirt, his feet and hands singed, saw her outlined in the opening to the loft, flames riding up her long hair to form a halo around her face.

The son of a mechanic and a librarian, weaned on too many comic books, Hammett novels, reruns of The Twilight Zone, *and experiences as a community organizer and delivering dog cages,* **Gary Phillips** *has published various crime fictions and toiled in TV. Among his work is co-writing the prose version of the classic Batman vs. Joker story,* The Killing Joke, *and the graphic novel* The Be-Bop Barbarians, *set in the 1950s, about friendships tested, the Red Scare, civil rights, and heartbreak.*

Why Not Use the "L"? by Reginald Marsh

A MATTER OF OPTIONS

BY GARY PHILLIPS

The young woman's tapered fingers deftly and deliberately turned the combination dial on the wall safe. Her eyes were closed, her head bent forward slightly as she concentrated on hearing the soft slip of the tumblers rotating into place through the hollow binaural of her electro-stethoscope, a one-of-a-kind gizmo.

Rosealee Newton was dressed differently than she had been the previous evening in this mansion out on the Peninsula. Last night she'd been in her maid's uniform, making sure to ferry fresh cocktails to the upper-crusters having themselves a hell of a time as elsewhere down-and-outers lined up at soup kitchens. The lady of the house, a widow who'd inherited a steel fortune, was demanding, but that wasn't unusual. Nor was fending off the grabby hands of a drunk, red-faced man in the kitchen who just wanted him "a little brown sugah is all."

The trick, as always, was to appease the incessant demands of the madam and be able to giggle like a dimwitted school girl at an entitled man's lewd joking while deflecting his unwanted advances.

"Shit," Newton's friend and fellow maid Ruby Teasdale had told her, "one time this gray boy makes a grab for my tits while he's cornered me in the pantry. But instead of backing up or acting all, you know, shy and whatnot, honey, I grabbed his johnson, hard like I was pulling back on a mule's tale." She grinned wolfishly at the memory. "Told him while I squeezed that dimple 'tween his legs to let's get to it out on the bushes. But he better not disappoint me 'cause my brother likes to use his knife.

"Sheeet," she repeated. "He damn near tripped over hisself getting the hell on up out of there after I let go." They'd both chuckled and had more of their beer.

Newton hadn't been so bold. Though she had been tempted to put down her unwanted Romeo with a kick to his privates and a right cross. But getting arrested and doing jail time, and maybe some enterprising plainclothes dick checking out her previous jobs out here and elsewhere, that wouldn't do—not at all. Still, she managed to stall him by agreeing to meet him later upstairs. It was important to string these birds along so they didn't get mad and storm off and get her fired. Most often lying to the employer that he saw the smart-mouth colored gal maid pilfering some silverware or dipping her hand in Miss Lady's purse.

Even in her maid's attire she hadn't come unprepared, and a few knockout drops in his next drink had him snoring in a chair.

She refocused on her current task; the wall safe was in the first-floor study here behind a set of shelves with squat bric-a-brac. At the touch of a hidden button, they swung open on hydraulics like a set of double doors. The second number, its wheel, notched into place.

She paused then, her eyes open, looking around, removing the stethoscope's eartips. No footsteps across the plush carpet, no rustle of clothes. Upstairs the widow, who liked a couple of strong nips of her peach brandy before bed, remained sleeping as far as Newton could tell. Putting the eartips back in, the thief resumed her work and soon had the Sargent & Greenleaf lock cracked, the door opening on silent hinges. The tight beam from her small flashlight revealed cash, twin jewel boxes and several gold bars. She almost whistled. Newton was pilfering all right, pilfering big time.

But she didn't get carried away, tamping down the thrill that always shot through her like a raw current at times like this. Focus and discipline, she reminded herself, as she put her gloves back on and transferred the cash into the messenger bag strapped across her torso. She didn't bother to assess the jewels in the two cases but simply popped them open and dumped their contents into her bag as well. The gold bars were too heavy to carry. She closed the safe's door on them, wiped her prints off the dial, and removed a rectangular, magnetized metal box from the door that the stethoscope was attached to. This she also put in the bag and pushed the bifurcated shelf back together, the whole of it clicking into place. She padded across the study and was about to step out through the French doors, the ones she'd jimmied open to gain entry.

She froze. The wide beam of a flashlight was cutting across the grounds, and she heard feet crunch dry leaves. She stepped back in, quiet as a mouse, crouching down and closing but not latching the door.

Outside an older man in baggy pants and a weathered jacket walked a rather large dark-haired dog, a Great Dane. Newton figured he had to be some sort of groundskeeper who probably lived onsite. Neither keeper nor dog had been around yesterday. The two stopped, the big dog's nose bent to the ground as he sniffed, detecting her foreign scent. The dog looked up toward the study.

"What is it, boy?" the groundskeeper said. "Is it that tomcat again?" He patted the dog's flank.

It was evident to Newton that the animal was nothing but muscle and teeth. The dog tugged on its leash, eager to follow the smell that didn't belong. It hadn't started barking yet. The dog was now at the glass, sniffing and butting its snout against the pane.

"Okay, boy," the groundskeeper said, more edge in his voice this time. "What is it?" His flashlight came up, a sweep of a triangle of light into the shadows of the study. The door opened to the prodding of the dog's nose.

"Oh, no," he whispered.

Newton stepped into the light, close to the man and beast.

The startled older man gaped at the image of this woman in dark gray workingman's pants and a zippered collarless tunic. A same-colored silky cloth covering the lower part of her face like a Wild West road bandit completed the rogue look.

"You . . . you're the Satin Fox," he stammered.

The Great Dane was barking and snarling and had risen on its powerful hind legs.

"Get her, Othello, get her," he commanded the dog, letting the leash go.

Othello leapt into the room, bursting the windowed doors wide apart. Newton had expected this and prayed she could carry off her next few moves without those teeth of Othello's snacking on her leg. Like a matador, she spun out of the charging dog's way. She'd grabbed one of the plaster pieces off the shelf and brought it down on the base of the dog's neck as he went past. This stunned the Dane, and he went flat on his stomach, his legs splayed out from his mighty body.

"Othello!" the older man bellowed, stumbling forward, trying to club Newton with his flashlight.

Newton easily blocked his blow with her forearm and shoved him aside. She was out in the garden and sprinting toward a section of brick wall that bordered the property. The dog had recovered and was galloping after her. Newton crashed through underbrush, a path she'd walked last night, familiarizing herself with ruts and other ways she could trip. Now she made it to where her knotted rope hung from the top of the wall and leapt up to get her hands around the line. The dog was also off the ground, and his jaws closed hard on air as she swung her legs up, his muzzle grazing her backside as his arc brought him back to the earth.

"Sweet mother," she said.

Lights came on in the lady's bedroom. The Great Dane barking and leaping, claws raking brick, jaws opening and closing. Newton clambered up quickly, her heart thudding in her throat. She took a moment to get centered at the top of the wall, then jumped down to the grass on the other side and took off running again. Out here, the homes of the well-off were spaced far apart, with patches of wooded areas and open ground between the estates. She ascended into a hilly area, got to the wall of another large spread and pressed against it. She could hear the tinkling of cocktail glasses and laughter drift down to her from the other side.

Another nighttime function meant more colored help. There were a handful of butler and maid services in the city that provided staff for these kind of soirees out here. Newton was familiar with them, having hired out to several in the past. Her plan was to blend in later, when the workers would be clustered around the bus stops, those who hadn't carpooled in someone's jalopy, on their way to the trains that invariably returned them to O'Goshen, the black section of New Zenith. As the Peninsula was its own municipality, formerly Cape Egg, the loaded had taxed themselves to add the after-hours bus runs to ensure the servants got out of town before sunup.

On a few previous jobs, she'd made sure to have a maid's uniform stashed to get into and become invisible. But she didn't have one with her tonight, so that meant improvising. She pulled off her watch cap and used it to remove the powder she'd coated her face with. When the Satin Fox had been spotted, as she had tonight, with her nose covered and only her green eyes and brows exposed, she was believed to be a white woman. That's what Newton wanted them to believe. Though with or without makeup, would they let themselves believe that a black woman was capable of these sorts of thefts?

Pushing aside such speculations, Newton climbed up the wall and took a gander, keeping her head low. There were a few inhabiting the area, drinks in hand and chatting in a lush landscape fragrant with floral aromas and an array of topiary in shapes ranging from eagles, tigers, and elephants to mythological creatures like griffins. Newton descended and crept to another spot along the wall, went back up and this time over. She dropped down behind a large hedge sculpted in the form of a leopard about to pounce.

Briefly she considered grabbing one of these rich dames, dragging her behind this overdone bush and knocking her out in order to get into her clothes. But she'd stick out like a sore thumb. She could try to do the same to one of the servers, but that poor woman would catch hell afterward, so that was out.

Newton had no choice but to gain entry to the massive Tudor-style mansion and hope to find the appropriate clothes. She knew it wasn't unheard of for the well-heeled to keep a uniform or two on hand just in case. It helped too that this was a big place where she could move around undetected. Staying amid the greenery lining the wall, Newton got closer, thankful there was now enough of a chill in the air that most were back indoors, though there were French doors open to the outside. At the corner of the house, partially hidden by a Roman-style column, she used her grapple and line and climbed up to the second floor and a small balcony there. The window before her looked in on a gloomy room of some size. The sash was locked, but there was enough give between that and the window frame for her to use her flat pick to unlatch it. In she went.

"Oh, sweetheart," came a shudder of enjoyment from a woman.

Newton's eyes went wide, and she glanced over at the bed that she could now make out somewhat as her eyes adjusted to the dark. The four-poster was occupied with a tangle of nude arms and legs, the bodies they were attached to swishing about on silken sheets. She stood stock-still; apparently the sound of her raising and then lowering the window had gone unnoticed given the moans and grunts emanating to her left. She sunk to the floor and began belly-crawling her way out of there.

"Yeah, oh yeah, that's it," she heard the man declare. "Right there."

"Baby, you're the cat's pajamas," another male voice said, laughing throatily.

Newton halted momentarily, her mouth open in shock. It was two men and a woman in the bed. These damn silver spooners. She kept going and was worming past a plush chair festooned with their clothes when she paused again amid another round of grunts and moans. Taking a chance, she got out her flashlight. Cuffing her hand over the front, Newton snapped on the beam to probe the clothing with the light and occasionally removing her hand. Regarding the woman's attire, there was a Basque beret, a black turtleneck and stylish women's wide-legged wool slacks. But no dress or skirt.

At a recent dinner party she'd worked—before knocking the place over later, having also cased the joint—Newton had overheard women talking about the pants craze the actress Marlene Dietrich had started. Several of the woman there had been dressed accordingly. She took the pants with her and got to the door, which was slightly ajar. She looked back over her shoulder to see the three backlit by a window behind them as if they were now a living tableau, fitting one to the other in some fashion—pleasuring one another in the process. Newton shook her head and opened the door a few degrees more and eased out into a dimly lit hallway. Given how the three were chugging at it like locomotives, whatever movement any one of them might have detected wasn't foremost in their mind.

She walked along, paintings of stern-faced white men and even sterner white women hung on the walls. The cat burglar tried not to imagine their judgmental eyes following her. Somewhere downstairs, a piano was being played, the sound rising up to her level like invisible smoke. At a corner where there was an exquisite-looking vase on a round table, she got out of her workingman's pants and into the fashionable ones, using her belt to cinch them at the waist.

A little snug in the butt, she grinned as she felt back there. Newton folded up her pants and put them under the table. Her altered getup looked odd, but at least she wasn't a dead giveaway like in the other pair. On the lookout for the backstairs that the servants would use to go to the kitchen and possibly a maid's quarters, she came to a dead end and a staircase leading farther up.

A strong odor she recognized greeted her, and she sniffed the air to make sure. Sure enough, a different kind of vice was being indulged upstairs. Newton turned to leave, but footfalls on the second-floor thick carpet alerted her to others approaching.

"Shit," she muttered, and dashed upward. But at the top there was no hallway, only a landing and an impressive, ornately carved wooden door. "Double shit," she said. Having no choice, she pushed open the door to the sweet, clinging smell of opium vapors. The Greco-Roman-designed interior was lit by candlelight. Men and women lounged on divans, loveseats or big cushions, smoking opium pipes or staring at the ceiling in the grip of a many-tentacled narcotic bliss. There was a pedal harp off to one side, but nobody was plucking its strings. And nobody paid her any attention as Newton went farther in.

The door remained closed. Newton imagined the ones she'd heard approaching might have joined the other three or found their own room to cavort in. She prowled about, breathing though her mouth to avoid contamination. She had to remain sharp. She began making a beeline toward the rear corner she supposed would let her out and down onto the back of the mansion and near the kitchen. Passing a settee with a matronly type sprawled on it, the woman reached out and put her hand on Newton's knee. Her eyes lidded half-open.

"Who are you, you divine bronze creature?"

Newton laughed nervously. She recognized this woman as someone who'd been at one of the functions she'd worked not too long ago. But surely this woman didn't remember her? The features of the help merely dissolved one into the other, didn't they?

"I'm just a seeker," she said, intending to move on.

The woman's hand was now rubbing the inside of her thigh. "Really, you mustn't go. I simply must indulge your time. Have a seat and let's get to know one another, my dear."

Newton looked around, a slow panic stretching her nerves. If she blew this woman off, might she raise a ruckus? Better to humor her for a few moments, then be on her way.

"Oh," said a new voice.

Newton stared at a maid who'd appeared, carrying a silver tray with a crystal decanter and several matching glasses on it. The matron still had her hand on Newton's inner thigh, and the older woman grinned at the maid.

"Isn't she gorgeous?"

"Yes, ma'am," the maid said, a crooked smile on her face. "She with you?"

"I hope so," came the reply.

"Excuse me one second," Newton said, taking the woman's hand and patting it. She stepped closer to the maid, folded twenties in her hand. "This is a hundred for you to forget you've seen me."

"Where the hell would you get a hundred 'cept robbing these here fine white folks?" She whispered as Newton had, eyeing the messenger bag draped around her.

"That's exactly where I got it," Newton affirmed.

"Okay then," the maid said, taking the money.

Newton produced two more twenties. "Is there another way out of here beside the front door?"

There was a compact service kitchen on this floor and a passage to it from the makeshift opium den that didn't involve Newton having to be back in the upstairs hallways. The maid with the tray distracted the matron as the thief made it downstairs from the secondary kitchen to a rear area alcove that led to the master kitchen. There was a maid and butler in there on a smoke break, grousing about the usual, and Newton waited for them to finish and leave. She knew from the lady with the tray that there were no extra uniforms to be had. She exited through a side door that beyond a row of hedges let out onto an expanse of smooth pavement where numerous fancy cars were parked. The models included Duesenbergs, Pierce-Arrows and LaSalles. The chauffeurs of these vehicles in their livery leaned against them or clustered together to talk and smoke, and a few played cards at folding tables with lit lanterns in the center. As Newton turned to head the other way, a cop stepped into view in the near distance, his flashlight aimed at the ground as he looked around. Back into the kitchen she went.

"If I could have your attention, please," a man's voice boomed from the front of the house. Newton went to the swing door of the kitchen and pushed it open a hair to hear better.

Several members of the Cape Egg police force stood in the marble foyer. Their sergeant, a square-faced man with a crooked nose, had tucked his cap under an arm to show his deference to the ones who paid his salary. He spoke: "We don't mean to interrupt the festivities, but we are on the hunt for the woman known as the Satin Fox."

Murmurs of excitement rippled among the gathered. A lubricated woman holding a martini glass in one hand and a cigarette in an ivory holder in the other asked, "And what makes you think she's here, Officer? Come to rob us blind?"

"We're just trying to be thorough, ma'am. We're checking out the homes in the area, as she was chased from the Gordon estate down in the flats."

More excitement animated the gathered. A man standing on the lower part of the staircase said, "Is there a reward for this Satin Fox? She burgled a friend of mine not too long ago."

"Not so far, sir," the sergeant answered.

"Well, I'll put up five thousand for this jewel-hungry Jezebel," the one on the stairs said.

"I'll match it," said a heavyset man with a cigar.

"Huh," sneered the woman with the cigarette holder. "If it were a man, you'd be thrilled at the boldness of the Fox. But make it a woman, and you want to slap her down. Keep her in her place. Well I say," she began, twisting about, her glass raised, "fifteen thousand to anyone who helps her escape."

Boos and hoorays broke out as the knot of partygoers tried to talk over one another.

"Maybe she'll put on blackface and sneak out among the help," someone quipped.

The arguing transformed into two distinct camps, with some men in the "save the Satin Fox" camp, though more than one for a lascivious reason rather than for advancing the suffragette cause. The cops tried to restore order, but the guests, fueled on illegal hooch, illicit drugs and the fun of it all, would have none of that. Soon many of them were out on the grounds, yelling things like, "Here, foxy, foxy," and "Come to Mama, you little fox you." Many of the women had their furs around their shoulders. They laughed and stumbled over each other, and several descended the hilltop with hastily made torches or flashlights. They knocked on the doors of other mansions, in some cases rousing the slumbering occupants.

She'd have no better chance to blow than now, Newton reflected. Crouched low, she snaked her way among the parked cars. The drivers were watching and enjoying a bunch of tight swanksters cavorting about. Except one. He'd been relieving himself behind a shrub and stepped out just as Newton crept past. But like the other chauffeurs, he'd overhead the talk about the reward.

"Where you headed, gal?" he demanded. "How come you ain't in uniform?" He pointed at her, noting the bag. "What you got there?" He snapped his fingers. "Say, I bet you're working for that Fox girl, ain't you? No one would suspect a shine partner." He'd lost five dollars at the card game. But now he was going to earn more than a thousand times what he estimated. He was a good-size man, and he wrapped her in a bear hug, he behind her. The barrel-chested man lifted her off the ground effortlessly.

"Got you." He didn't call out to the others, because he didn't want to have to share the money. "Now you can stop struggling, girly; I used to wrassle. You just relax, and soon this will all be over."

"Yeah, and what do you plan to do with me?"

He regarded his employer's car, a sleek boattail Duesenberg Speedster. There was room for two in that trunk. "I'ma put the sleeper hold on you. You won't feel a thing."

He pressed his blunt fingers to a thatch of nerves where her neck intersected her shoulder blade, and black pinwheels went off behind her eyes. She better do something quick. He was carrying her toward the car.

Newton couldn't get her arms free, but she managed to plunge her hand into her equipment bag as a dark blanket smothered her head. She gritted her teeth and grabbed several loose diamonds in there and flung the stones on the ground ahead of them, their facets twinkling in the moonlight like falling stars.

"Hey, what?" She started at the sound of the stones hitting the pavement. He slipped on a couple of the bigger ones and went over backward, landing hard. His grip loosened, and Newton rolled away. The other drivers were still some yards away, watching the smart set weave down the hill.

"You gonna pay for that, you scheming black bitch."

As he sought to rise, she kicked him on the point of his chin. "Shut up," she said.

He went over but hardly out on his side. He started to curse her again, and she brought the business end of the electro-stethoscope down on his skull with a decided crack. He wobbled some in the position he was in, and twice more she struck him on his head to put him under. The gadget was broken, but she put it back in the bag so as not to leave it behind.

Breathing heavy, still woozy, Newton didn't have time to spare to look for her thrown diamonds. She got her hands under the big man's armpits and dragged him to the Duesenberg. She got the keys out of his pocket and, desperation clearing her head, muscled him into the trunk. The car was blocked front and back by other vehicles, so she couldn't just drive away. She got in with him and closed the lid. It was cozy in there but doable. She used her flashlight and shook some of her knockout drops into his slack mouth, which she forced open. She'd purposely left the keys in the ignition.

It was nearly two hours later, according to her radium-dial, emerald-encrusted Elgin wristwatch, and the tired-out revelers returned. Newton heard the voices of those trudging back after their outing. They were gleeful, the story of the great human fox hunt to be recounted for months to come. It was nearly two in the morning. Soon thereafter Newton could make out the car's owner questioning the other drivers where his had gone. He got increasingly angry at no one knowing where his man was to be found. Then came a *thunk* against the trunk lid, and Newton was determined to pop out when it was opened, swinging for the fences like Josh Gibson. But the trunk wasn't unlocked; rather, she heard the sound of vomiting and figured that was the car's owner. He must have propped himself against his car, then got sick. Perhaps he'd stayed behind to drink when the others went off, she speculated with a smile. At any rate, she heard more voices and footfalls, car doors opening and closing and engines coming to life. Finally the Duesenberg got rolling. But not too far down the road, the ride got bumpy and the car listed to one side. It was a flat. The big car pulled over, and the engine shut off.

Newton tensed. The spare tire was mounted on the outside toward the front of the car on the driver's side. But the lug wrench and jack were inside the trunk. She considered jumping out swinging the wrench but decided to play this differently. The lid came open, and for the third time that night, a face showed surprise at seeing her. He was a young, ruggedly handsome colored man dressed in a black suit and starched white shirt open at the collar, his tie having been removed. She assumed he must have been butlering at the party and had been pressed into doing double duty and driving the drunk white man home. Seemingly terrified, he took a few steps back as Rosealee Newton stepped out.

"Good lawd," he said, blinking hard at her.

"I know how this looks," she began, "but let's work together here, okay?"

He pointed at her, his mouth open, shoulders stooped. "You're that der Satin Fox them white folks was lookin' fer. Only you ain't white, is you?"

Newton glanced behind her to see the car's owner's head to one side on the back seat, snoring away.

"I can pay you to get me back to town," she said.

"Yeah, how much you figurin', gurl? Seems to me da law wants you bad." A ring momentarily glinted on his finger as he gestured.

"And seems to me you ought to drop the act."

He stared at her for a beat; then, standing straight, his face taking on a shrewd cast, he smiled bemusedly. "How'd you make me?" The country had gone out of his voice.

"The Howard University class ring you're wearing."

He nodded appreciatively. "Pleased to meet you."

She cocked her head. "You just happen to be the one to drive this man home?"

The college man held his hands wide. "I volunteered. That and the extra twenty for the effort."

Newton sensed there was more to him. But times were tough, and he wasn't the first educated person having to resort to menial labor to eat.

"We best get that tire fixed," he said. "Unless you want a cop stopping by and having to explain the unconscious white man in the trunk."

"You noticed that, did you?"

"Uh-huh."

A diamond was embedded in the tire's slit sidewall. He took off his jacket and, with her shining the flashlight for illumination, got the spare loose.

"You rob the rich to keep yourself in mink and ermine?" he asked as he rolled the tire toward the rear, where the flat was.

"Not exactly," she allowed.

"Mystery woman, huh?"

"You got a name, nosey?"

"What's yours?

"Rosealee."

"Jimmie, Jimmie Clayton. And what did you mean, 'not exactly'?" He was now getting the jack out of the trunk, unbothered by the unconscious man.

"I mean I'm not telling you anything else."

He was getting the scissor jack in place. "Maybe you're a Garveyite and financing our people's return to the motherland."

"Is that what you do in your off-hours?"

He looked over at her. "Not exactly."

She grinned.

As he worked, he took out a flask from his back pocket and tipped it toward her. "Like a taste? It's quality. Smooth."

"Okay." He handed it over, and she had a sip, then handed the flask back to him. "Not bad."

"We make a good product."

"'We'?"

He was loosening the nuts with the lug wrench. "Yeah, I work for one of the bootleggers who supplies the hooch in the area."

Newton absorbed this information. "You work the events as a butler to talk up your boss's booze, so the sophisticates look to have his gin at their functions."

"Yes ma'am." He got the flat tire off.

She regarded him for several moments. "But that's not all of it, is it?"

He shrugged. "Salvation for a race, nation or class must come from within. Freedom is never granted; it is won. Justice is never given; it is exacted."

"You sound like a friend of mine." Using a rag, she hefted the flat tire. "Enough philosophizing and more elbow grease." She rested the tire against the still chauffer in the trunk.

The passenger stirred, and both stopped dead. But he resumed snoring, and Clayton finished changing the tire.

Later that day, not much after sunrise, Rosealee Newton rode the subway, taking her to the East Eighteenth Street stop in New Zenith. It was as cold outside and in the car as it had been on Cape Egg. Across from her a man with a brush mustache, topcoat and large cloth cap slept, partially laying across the seats. He was between two women, one standing, absorbed in reading the morning paper, in a dark blue cloche hat and matching coat. The other sat staring straight ahead. She had round glasses, a light green cloth coat and a modest fascinator on her head. Dull pearls were around her neck and kidskin gloves on her hands. She looked to be returning home, preoccupied with what had transpired the night before—an unpleasantness, it seemed to Newton. Random pages of yesterday's bulldog edition of the *Graphic* were strewn about.

At her stop along the elevated portion of the tracks, Newton got out and went down the steps and walked the several blocks to her destination, a drugstore on the edges of Devil's Corner. The shades were already up in the shop, and she waved at the counterman in there who was readying to open for business. Around the side toward the rear, she let herself into a metal door with her key. In a compact space filled with twin lab worktables, beakers, test tubes, chemicals and electrical and mechanical parts sat an old man with a wild tangle of white hair and a drooping white mustache on a stool. He had on a crisp white smock with two fountain pens in the pocket and looked very much the part of the friendly neighborhood pharmacist. That was only one of several degrees Dr. Elias Baumhofer possessed.

Looking up from the device he was tinkering with, he said in Yiddish, "As you're not in the hoosegow, I take it the Satin Fox was again successful."

"Yes, but it was quite the evening," she responded, also in Yiddish. She took out the ruined electro-stethoscope from her purse and filled him in, speaking in English. While she did so, she dumped the swag, transferred to a grocery bag, onto one of the few open spaces on a tabletop.

"He was quoting Mr. Randolph," the old man said reflectively, when she'd finished. He referred to the socialist labor leader A. Philip Randolph, the head of the Brotherhood of Sleeping Car Porters, the largest black union in the nation. A man the late president Woodrow Wilson once called the "most dangerous Negro in America."

"I think this Clayton is a dangerous Negro," she observed.

The old man shook the end of his screwdriver at her. "I suspect you'll be seeing him again. Maybe going out of your way to, eh?"

"I've got my head on straight."

"As you say."

"Oh, Papa, it's not all work all the time, you know," said a woman who also entered the shop. She was dressed plainly and looked much different than she had out on Cape Egg with her martini and cigarette holder. Patricia Baumhofer kissed her father on the forehead and grinned at Newton.

"Nice touch with the fox hunt," Newton said to the inside woman. She knew the younger Baumhofer was attending that particular party to case the place.

The daughter produced a hand-drawn floor plan of the mansion on the hill. "We can go over this later."

"Yeah," the other woman said, a hand in front of her mouth as she yawned.

Pat Baumhofer said to her dad, "You've got to give Rosealee some kind of Buck Rogers ray gun. Something to zap a goon." She added, noting Newton's arched eyebrow, "To disable, not kill."

"That's not a bad idea," the inventor agreed. "But right now," he continued, rubbing his hands together, "the count, shall we?"

After they'd totaled the cash, some two thousand five hundred dollars, and calculated what they could make on the jewels from their fence, the three had coffee and fresh apple strudel from the delicatessen up the block while they talked.

"With this and the Talmont haul, we've got enough to make the down payment," the daughter said. "I'll call the lawyer."

"Good," the old man said, nodding his head.

"I'm going to hit the hay," Newton said.

"Gonna be dreaming about your dreamboat?" the other woman said.

Newton made a face but didn't answer.

After disembarking the subway at her stop back in O'Goshen, she went up the steps from underground and crossed the street as a streetcar clanged past. Soon in sight of her apartment building, she was still amazed at being one of its owners. Using some of the monies derived from their thievery, they'd bought the building from the landlord, who gouged the rents on the working people who populated the structure. The new phantom owners had reduced the rents and hired a super who actually repaired things. Same for a Baptist church, a gathering place for labor and Negro advancement groups, saved from foreclosure and a few other such efforts.

Their enterprise had started because the elder Baumhofer sought revenge on a fat-cat industrialist who lived in Cape Egg. This man had cheated the gadgeteer out of a lucrative patent. But soon the three realized they had the option to be greedy or altruistic . . . that they could accomplish something meaningful as modern-day Robin Hoods.

An hour or so after Newton got to sleep, a woman stopped outside her building, looking up at it. She was the hired maid the Satin Fox had encountered the previous night in the opium room out on the Peninsula. Curious about the green-eyed robber, the woman had asked a few other maids she knew if they had encountered her before, using the pretense that she needed to find her to return a lost item. Ironically an unsuspecting Ruby Teasdale had called her this morning with the information. Now as the woman smoked a cigarette, her coat buttoned to her throat, she wondered if them crackers out there on the Egg would really pay a colored girl to know the identity of the thief who'd been plaguing them the past year. Or could be she'd knock on the Fox's door to cut herself in for a piece of the action. If she objected, she'd bring along her pappy's straight razor and help herself to whatever cash Little Miss Green Eyes had laying around. That just might be the trick, she figured. She finished her smoke, ground out the butt with the toe of her sensible shoe and walked off, weighing her options.

*While **John Sandford** is best known for his two long-running series featuring Lucas Davenport and Virgil Flowers, he's also written four books about Kidd, a computer whiz, a good-guy criminal—and a professional artist. The author's own enthusiasm for art ("I have two thousand volumes on painting!") led him to find room in his schedule for "Girl with an Ax."*

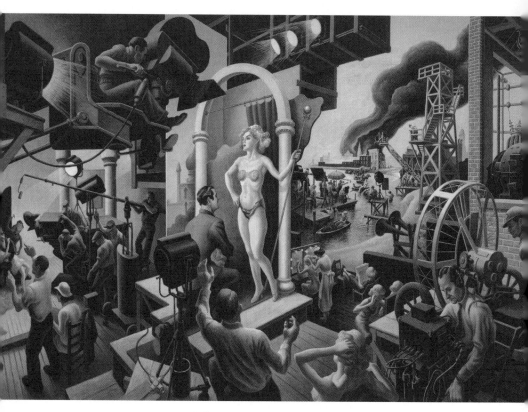

Hollywood by Thomas Hart Benton

GIRL WITH AN AX

BY JOHN SANDFORD

The girl with the ax got off the bus at the corner of Santa Monica Boulevard and Gower Street and started walking the super-heated eleven blocks down Gower to Waring Avenue, where she lived by herself in a four-hundred-square-foot bungalow with an air conditioner designed and manufactured by cretins.

The girl was slender, with wheat-colored hair cut close over high cheekbones and pale blue eyes, bony shoulders under an unfashionable blue shift from JCPenney. She had a nice, shy smile that could light her face when she let it out; she wore cross-training shoes chosen for their durability, and golf socks.

The ax was heavy in its hard case and banged against her leg as she carried it down the sidewalk. She'd spent all morning and half the afternoon at the Bridge recording studio in Glendale, and her amps were still there, along with two less-valuable guitars.

Her name was Andi Holt.

The name, the pale eyes, the shy smile and the wheat-colored hair were all relics of her Okie ancestors, who'd come to California out of the Dust Bowl. Andi knew that, but she didn't care about it one way or another. They were all dead and long gone, buried in cemeteries that bordered trailer parks, along with that whole *Grapes of Wrath* gang.

Gower Street ran down the side of the Paramount Studios lot, but like most native Angelenos, she didn't care about that, either. To care about Paramount would be like caring about Walmart.

Waring made a T-intersection with Gower, and she took the right, tired with the day's work and the bus ride, which had required three changes. She'd be riding the route in reverse the next morning, for the last session of this set. Her car's transmission had gone out, and she was temporarily afoot in Los Angeles. She could have called an Uber for the ride, but money was money and the bus was cheap.

Andi lived a few houses down Waring, a neighborhood of tiny bungalows worth, now, absurd amounts of money. She didn't own hers, but rented it, for what was becoming an absurd amount of rent. Somebody once had told her that Waring Avenue was named after the inventor of the Waring blender and she'd believed it—why would anyone lie about something like that?—but when she'd repeated the story, she'd been ridiculed: the street was actually named after a long-dead band leader named Fred Waring, who had nothing to do with blenders.

But the guy who told her *that* story had been massively stoned on some primo Strawberry Cough, so she'd never repeated the Fred Waring story.

Andi's house was gray.

The one just before it was a faded brick red and larger—six hundred and twenty-five square feet, or a perfect twenty-five by twenty-five. Andi's was twenty by twenty. She obsessed over the numbers. Hers was like living in a closet; the red house, small by any sane standards, felt expansive by comparison.

Just the way it was, in L.A.

As she passed the red house, she stopped to peer at it. The house was partly owned by Helen McCall and partly by a rapacious reverse-mortgage company called Gray Aid, which hovered over McCall like a turkey vulture, waiting for her to die.

Andi was friends with the old woman. They'd share a joint or a margarita or even two on a warm evening, and Helen would tell her about Hollywood days, or, as she pronounced it—you could hear it in the words—Hollywood Daze.

Helen had been an actress, once . . . or almost an actress. She had the stories to prove it.

And it occurred to Andi that she hadn't seen Helen for, what, three days? She thought three days. Helen was ninety-nine years old.

With the ax banging against her leg, Andi continued to her house, but the thought of Helen stuck like a tick on her scalp. Inside, where the ambient temperature was possibly 120 degrees, she turned on the air conditioner and took the ax out of the case—a 2007 Les Paul custom—and stuck it in a cabinet that maintained a temperature of 72 degrees and a relative humidity of 40 percent. Five other guitars resided in the cabinet, not counting the two of them still at the Bridge, with her Fender and Mesa amps.

The instruments were all sturdy enough, but even with the ocean, L.A. got dry enough in the summer that Andi liked to keep her guitars somewhat humidified. She'd like to keep herself somewhat humidified as well, but in the tiny house, with the piece-of-shit air conditioner that she suspected had fallen off a truck, probably in Chechnya, that was difficult.

She was a dry-looking girl; parched.

And she hadn't seen Helen.

She got a beer from the refrigerator, popped the top, and since the house was too hot to stay in anyway, she walked next door and knocked. No answer. Knocked harder. Still no answer. She trudged back to her place, a little apprehensive now, a little scared, and found the key that Helen had given her.

She opened her neighbor's door and smelled the death.

Not stinky or especially repulsive, but death all the same. To be sure, she walked back to Helen's bedroom, where the old lady lay on her bed, in a nightgown with embroidered flowers across the chest, her head turned to one side. She looked desiccated, like a years-old yellowed cigarette found under a couch when you move.

"Helen?" Andi knew she was dead but called her name anyway. Then she called the cops.

Of all the stories Helen had told Andi, the most interesting was about a famous artist who'd painted her back in the late thirties, and that the painting itself had become famous, and now hung in a Kansas City museum. Helen had never been the star of a movie, or even the third banana, but she'd been the star of Thomas Hart Benton's *Hollywood*, standing straight, tall and only skimpily clothed in the center of the work. She'd shown Andi a book about Benton's relationship to motion pictures, and to *Hollywood* in particular; and a black-and-white photograph of herself with Benton, who was holding a paintbrush and whose head came barely to her shoulder.

Andi knew some famous people—singers—but they were workaday people who'd happened to push all the right buttons and had gotten rich and famous, or one or the other. Just people. To be in a famous painting was something else: something that would carry you into the future, long after you were gone, and your music was gone, and your songs were gone. . . .

The cops came and were quick and professional. They looked at the undisturbed body, sat Andi down, interviewed her and took a few notes, especially emphasizing the time between her discovery of the body and her call to 911—Andi estimated it at thirty seconds. She was allowed to return to her house but was asked to stay around, until a medical examiner's investigator could speak to her.

That happened an hour and a half later. The investigator, a weary-looking woman in shoes like Andi's, named Donna, told her that the cops had been interested in the timing of her call to be sure she hadn't looted Helen's house after she discovered the body.

"She didn't have anything to loot, except maybe her wedding ring," Andi said. "She was living on Social Security and payments on a reverse mortgage."

Donna asked if Andi knew about survivors.

"Her son died two years ago, from being too fat. That's what Helen said. She has a granddaughter and some great-grandchildren who live in San Diego, I think. She has one of those old Rolo things with their names written in them. Their name is Cooper. The daughter's name is Sandra Cooper. I met her once, a couple of years ago."

"A Rolodex, I saw that. I'll notify the Coopers. . . ." Donna made a note and asked, "Do you think she might have taken her own life? There was no note, no pill bottle or anything."

"No, I don't think so. She was a lively old lady. Not in pain or depressed or anything, as far as I could tell. She was looking forward to turning a hundred next fall. She was ninety-nine."

They talked a while longer, and Andi cried a little, and Donna patted her on a knee, and when she was leaving, told her, "I kind of think that most people wouldn't want somebody to say this after they die, but . . . her death looks to me like it was totally routine. She got old and died."

Andi nodded. "That's what I think. But she lived so long. She knew so much. Now that's all gone. Gone."

"You gonna be okay?"

"Sure. I'm okay. Sad."

"And you're a musician?"

"Yes. Play guitar, I do session work. I work a couple nights a week over at the Guitar Center on Sunset," Andi said.

"I think you're probably good folks." Donna nodded. "You take it easy, girl."

The girl with the ax got off the bus at the corner of Santa Monica Boulevard and Gower Street and started walking the super-heated eleven blocks down Gower to Waring Avenue, where she still lived by herself in a four-hundred-square-foot bungalow with an air conditioner designed and manufactured by cretins.

She took the right on Waring, and the first thing she saw was a U-Haul truck and an SUV, parked outside Helen's house. The truck's back doors were open, and she could see Helen's two-cushion couch and television inside it. She walked past, looking through the open door, and could see a man pushing a desk across the wooden floor. He looked out and saw her, and she lifted a hand and went into her own house, unlocked it and put the ax in the humidifier cabinet and got herself a beer.

It had been two weeks since Helen died, and a piece of cop tape had been stuck on the door ever since, to keep people out. Andi had gotten her guitars and amps back from the Bridge and had been working at a place called Grassroots in Pasadena, laying down tracks for a Bakersfield country band that was, she had to admit, really pretty good. The front man had spent some time chatting her up, and she'd liked it; and she'd noticed that the band's own lead guitarist had some kind of ego conflict going with the front man.

She was thinking about the singer, whose name was Tony, and thinking that if he lost his lead guitar and she went on the road with the band, how she'd wind up sleeping with him. That prospect was pleasant enough—the sex part, not the road part—but then she'd lose her place in the L.A. session world, which kept her in a house, and the job at Guitar Center, which kept her in fish sticks and fries.

The fact was, she was $1,450.88 from being broke, and the transmission was broker. Summer was slow; even with no crises along the way, she needed every dollar she could find to keep her head above-water until the busy season started again, in October. She wasn't desperate, she'd been here before, financially, but from where she was, she could *see* desperate.

Halfway through the beer, the man she'd seen at Helen's house rang the doorbell. He was sort of piggish, she thought, as she walked toward the door. Probably her age, in his later twenties, middle-height, overweight, with a short, oily flattop over heavy pink cheeks. He was wearing a black T-shirt and tan cargo shorts. The T-shirt showed a slogan: "That's Too Much Bacon" and in smaller letters, beneath, ". . . said no one, ever." He apparently tried to live up to it.

"Can I help you?"

The man looked at a piece of paper in his hand. "Are you Andi Holt?"

"Yup."

"You found my great-grandma when she died?"

"Yes, I found Helen."

"Could you come over for a minute? My brother and sister and I are going through the place, checking out what she had."

"Sure."

On the way over, she asked, "What's your name?"

"Don Cooper. My brother's Bob, my sister's Cheryl. There's about a ton of paper shit in there; we're trying to figure out what to do with it."

The three Coopers were a matched set: dark hair, overweight, shorts and T-shirt with slogans. Cheryl's read, "Nope, Still Don't Care." Bob's read, "PETA" and beneath that, "People Eating Tasty Animals." All three shirts were sweat-soaked; Helen had had a window air conditioner, which was sitting in the middle of the living room.

Helen's house had only one bedroom, but it had another small room, which might have accommodated a twin bed, and which Helen had used as a home office: a couple of filing cabinets, rarely used, a mid-century office chair, a tiny desk, pictures on the wall. No computer. An elaborate old steamer trunk, probably dating back to the 1930s, substituted for a coffee table. It had been full of scrapbooks and other memorabilia, which now lay on the floor with the contents of the filing cabinet. The filing cabinets and trunk were gone, apparently loaded into the U-Haul. All the pictures that had been on the wall had been stripped of their frames, which were gone, the pictures scattered on the floor.

"Here's the deal," Bob said. "If we don't leave for home in an hour, it'll take us three hours to get down the Five. We need to get all this crap outta here so we can sell the place. We were thinking we could throw you a few bucks and you could bag it and stick it in Helen's trash can and your trash can over the next couple of weeks, and that way, we don't have to pay to haul it and you get a few bucks, which you look like you need anyway."

Andi ignored the implied insult. "What's a few bucks?"

"Fifty?"

Andi looked at the mess on the floor. "Fifty is a pizza for two and a couple of beers. For cleaning out this house?"

"Well . . . tell you what. You play the guitar, right? I saw all those guitars. Helen had a guitar in the closet. We'll give you the guitar."

"Let's see it."

Bob went out to the U-Haul and came back a minute later with the guitar. Solid body, weighed a ton. Two rusty strings still attached, four broken and curled around the neck, specks of rust on the bridge and the tuners.

"Electronics are probably shot," Andi said. She squinted down the fretboard. "But . . . neck looks straight, anyway." She grimaced and hefted the guitar. "Okay."

"Great," Don said. He waved at the paper, the photos, a round rag rug on the floor. "Just dump everything. The rug smells like a cat shit on it."

"Cat died a couple of years ago," Andi said. "It was seventeen."

"Good. Hate fuckin' cats," Bob said.

"I gotta ask," Cheryl said. "You didn't help yourself to anything when you found Helen, did you?"

"What? No! Jesus!"

Cheryl shrugged. "Had to ask. You'd think she would have built up a little more of an estate, you know. She was ninety-six or something. We got her rings, the diamond was like a half-carat, about the size of Don's dick."

"And she'd know," Bob said.

"Fuck you," Cheryl said.

"We got that camera," Bob said. An old camera sat on a windowsill, an Argus C3. "That's gotta be worth something."

"She was ninety-nine," Andi said, still pissed about being asked if she'd taken anything.

"Whatever," Cheryl said. She had a cigarette in her hand, lit it with a yellow plastic Bic lighter, blew smoke. "Got the house, anyway. We looked at houses around here on Zillow; that's a nice piece of change. One down the block like this sold for eight-fifty. Mom said the three of us could split half and she keeps the other half."

"Hello, cherry-red Camaro," Don said.

"Piece of shit," said Bob. "I'm going ZR1!"

"What's that?" Andi asked, waving smoke away from her face.

Bob did a spit take. "Corvette. Play your cards right, I'll give you a ride, sweetpuss."

"Yeah, well, before you spend the money, you better talk to Gray Aid," Andi said.

"What's that?" Don asked.

"Reverse-mortgage company. Helen had a reverse mortgage," Andi said. "I'm not sure, but I don't think there was much left. Maybe some."

"What the fuck? The old twat spent the house?"

"Most of it. Not all of it yet," Andi said. "She told me that she wouldn't get paid anymore after she turned 102, so she planned to die before then." She gestured at the papers on the floor. "The contract's probably in there. I'll go through it, see if I can turn it up."

Cheryl slapped her forehead. "Ah, Christ! She spent it? What about us?"

"Let's see if we can find the contract," Bob said, and kicked a pile of the papers.

"That won't do it," Andi said. "It's only going to be a few sheets of paper, probably."

They spent fifteen minutes looking, then Cheryl said, "Let's get the air conditioner in the U-Haul. We gotta get moving. If there's a mortgage, the hired hand can find it."

"We called and had the water company turn off the water," Bob said, "The toilets don't work. You think anybody would see me if I took a dump in the backyard?"

Andi: "Hey, I gotta live here. . . ."

"And I gotta go," Bob said. He walked down the hall to the bathroom, reappeared with a half roll of toilet paper and went out the back door.

"He's a real classy guy," Cheryl said. She lit another cigarette. "He'd take a dump on the White House lawn if he had to go. One time at a rock concert—"

"So fuckin' hot in here," Don interrupted. "Shoulda left the air conditioner to last."

"You really don't want all the pictures and photo albums and stuff? You don't think your mother would?" Andi asked. "It's Helen's whole life in here."

"Shit-can it," Bob said. "We don't care about that shit."

"You know, Helen once told me that she posed for a painting for a really famous painter," Andi said. "Back like . . . eighty years ago."

"You see a painting in here?" Don asked.

"No, but . . ."

"Then fuck it," he said.

Bob came back, threw the remnants of the roll of toilet paper on the floor, and he and Don staggered out of the house with the air conditioner. Cheryl was stacking plates and glasses into cardboard boxes and said to Andi, "Don't just stand there; you want the fifty," so Andi helped out. The dishes were old and never had been expensive: "I'll unload them on the wetbacks down at the flea market," Cheryl said. "That's a hundred bucks right there."

Bob and Don came back and carried boxes out to the U-Haul. Helen had had a couple of hundred books, many of them old *Reader's Digest* versions of fifties novels, along with a complete set of *Encyclopedia Britannica*, which Andi knew from her own flea market experience were virtually worthless. It amused her to see the two men sweat them out to the trailer.

And it went on for an hour like that: "Fuck her, fuck this place, fuck you."

When the house was empty, except for the thousands of sheets of paper and folders of old memorabilia, the Coopers headed out for San Diego. Bob gave a final kick to the stuff that had been in the steamer trunk, the photo albums, sending it exploding across the floor, faces of forgotten men and women, forgotten times, black-and-white images of men in army and navy uniforms. . . .

"Old bat," he said.

Andi: "How about my fifty dollars?"

The Coopers had gone.

Andi took a closer look at the guitar, decided to leave the broken strings on it, placed it in a clear corner of the living room and went to work on the paper. There was a lot of it: she went through it carefully, into the evening, and halfway through one of the stacks that had apparently been dumped from the file cabinet, she found the reverse-mortgage papers, and also the original mortgage on the house, which apparently had been paid off in the sixties.

Most of the paper on the floor really was trash and should have been thrown out years earlier: old bills, old warranties, old cancelled checks. Some of it was interesting, though: fliers for movies in which Helen had appeared, a stack of love letters bound together in their original envelopes, with a rubber band, from her husband, Gary, who'd fought in World War II, then Korea, and finally Vietnam, where he'd been killed in a car accident in Saigon. The letters all began with the same five words,

"Hey Babe,

"Miss you bad."

Bob Cooper had left his cell number with her, and when she called it and told him she'd found the papers from Gray Aid, he gave her an address and she said she'd mail them. "How long before you get the place cleaned?"

"I'll have the papers cleaned out tonight . . . and I'll sweep it tomorrow, as a freebee, 'cause I'm not working. All these pictures and stuff . . ."

"We told you to shit-can it."

"You mind if I take them? She was a friend of mine."

"We don't care, just get them the fuck out. We've got a Realtor coming around to look at the place on Monday, gotta be cleaned by then. Could you wash the windows?"

"Not for fifty bucks, no. The Realtor can take care of that."

She finished with the paper that night. One of the last things she looked at was a crumbling brown file-pocket, the kind with a fold-over flap. When she opened it, she found a carefully folded sheath of semitransparent paper. She unfolded the sheets, each about three feet by two, like the paper used by architects for their plans.

Drawings.

Men with old-fashioned movie cameras and microphone booms, some wearing old-timey workmen's hats. A man in what must've been an expensive suit, turned away, with a thirties haircut. One of Helen herself, holding what looked like a long dowel rod that extended over her head. Andi recognized it immediately: the star of the "Hollywood" painting, Helen as a nineteen- or twenty-year-old, wearing nothing but a bra and underpants. Another drawing was perhaps a different view of Helen, she thought, the blond woman shown from an overhead view; she might have been nude.

She stared at it for a bit, then carefully folded all the papers and put them back in the file pocket and set it aside. The house was still hot, but she crawled around the floor, picking up photographs, glancing at them, setting them aside, until she finally found the one that Helen had shown her, of herself with Thomas Hart Benton. She put the photo in the brown file-pocket with the drawings.

By midnight, it was done. Andi had five garbage bags of paper but had been unable to throw away the photos and the movie memorabilia.

Helen had told her about her movie life.

"You'd look at me on a screen, and you'd hardly see me," Helen had said one night, as they sat in her backyard, sharing a joint. "Some of the girls— Lauren Bacall—they'd light it up. You'd look at me, and you wouldn't even see me," she said.

"I'm sure that's not true," Andi said.

"It was true. You had to figure it out, and that took a while, but it was true. Still, I made a living. I even have a SAG card. Haven't seen it in years. I'd be a secretary who'd bring in some papers, and I'd say, 'Here are the papers, Mr. Shipley,' or whatever. I was in seventy movies like that, because they knew I was reliable. They'd call me in, I'd sit around for a couple of days, I'd get thirty seconds on screen and I'd go home. One time, this Japanese guy—Japanese American—got in an auto accident on the Pasadena Freeway on the way to the studio, and they were shooting a war film and they needed a Jap to fire a machine gun from a bunker, and I was small and they put a lot of makeup on me and a helmet and had me in the bunker firing this machine gun, and then in another shot they had me charging with a gun and bayonet and screaming, 'Banzai! Banzai!' That was sort of the peak of my dramatic career."

And she laughed, and she blew a little pungent smoke out into the evening air, passed the joint back and said, "You get the best shit, Andi. Musicians always have the best shit."

As Andi was locking up Helen's house, she noticed an unfamiliar and unhappy odor at the back door and stepped outside: Bob had indeed taken a dump in the backyard, in fact, in Helen's flower bed.

She locked the door and went home.

Andi mailed the reverse-mortgage papers to the Coopers. She had a spotty series of gigs over the next couple of weeks and picked up three extra shifts at Guitar Center when a salesman quit unexpectedly. A "For Sale" sign went up in Helen's yard, and one day she saw Bob and Cheryl Cooper talking to an agent. When the agent left, she walked over, and Bob said, with a grim shake of his head, "Bad as we thought—we're gonna get a hundred thousand if we're lucky, and my mom is backing out of the deal. She's gonna throw us ten grand each and keep seventy, greedy bitch."

"Don't talk about Mom like that," Cheryl said. She was smoking, dug a second cigarette out of her purse, used the first one to light it and flicked the used butt, still burning, into the street.

"You suck up to her 'cause you're trying to get more," Bob said.

"Fuck you. You're an asshole."

"You want a ride home?"

"Fuck you."

The house sold in August, but Andi never saw the Coopers again. The deal had probably been done electronically, and she never found out exactly how much they'd cleared. She had a very nice ten-day gig at Fox for a TV series that needed some blues guitar and got the transmission replaced on her Cube.

Then she waited, and waited, and waited.

On October 1, a warm Wednesday evening, the girl with the ax turned down Gower Street at the corner of Santa Monica Boulevard, down to Paramount Studios, and then right, to her four-hundred-square-foot bungalow with an air conditioner designed and manufactured by cretins.

She unloaded her Les Paul and an Asher version of a Strat, went inside, put them in the guitar cabinet, turned on the air conditioner, got Helen's old guitar out of a closet and went back outside to the Cube.

The trip to the Valley, to Van Nuys, took forty minutes because of a fender bender on the 101. Loren's Fine and Vintage Guitars was located in a neatly kept strip mall next to a hat store; Loren was an old pal. She carried Helen's guitar inside, and Dale Loren came out and looked at it, and said, "Holy shit. I think . . . a '58?"

"When I first saw it, I was hoping it was a '59," Andi said.

"It's not. The neck's too fat. Come on back, Andi, let's look it up."

They went into the back room, where a worktable was covered with a soft rubber sheet. Loren examined the neck from the end, and both sides, ran his finger down the ends of the frets. "Neck is good. Frets are original."

"I thought so. I put a ruler on it, and there's no waves or twist, as far as I can see."

"We'll have to do a little more than put a ruler on it. . . . Let's check the serial number."

The serial number was stamped on the back of the headstock. Loren had a paper printout of Gibson Les Paul serial numbers. He ran a finger down the list and said, "Here it is: 1958. So, 1958 cherry-red sunburst, even still shows a little bit of the red. They're usually pretty faded; they go yellow."

"Cherry red, like a cherry-red Camaro, almost."

"The same. . . . The bridge and tuners will clean right up, the rust, that's not a problem at all."

He turned it over. "Has some buckle-rash"—he rubbed the rough spots with a thumb—"but not bad. Where'd you get it?"

"An old lady left it to me. She said it belonged to her husband—he was killed in Vietnam. He was in World War II and Korea and then Vietnam, and it finally killed him."

"Have any more guitars?"

"Not as far as I know. . . ."

"Tell you what," Loren said. "I'll give you a receipt, and I'll have Terry clean it up. It'll take a while. . . . I'll call you in two weeks."

"What's your cut?" Andi asked.

Loren shrugged. "I've got to make a living, too, honey, and I have the techs who can restore it. I even got a guy who I think will buy it, like *right now*. I'll take thirty percent, and I'll tell you what, Andi, you won't do any better anywhere else. If this had been used by some famous rocker, then it'd be more, but . . . you say you don't know about that."

"Take it," Andi said. "And, Loren . . . let's keep this under our hats, okay?"

"Absolutely."

Ten days later, she got a text: "I got a buyer for $130,000. Your end will be $85,800. Yes or no?"

Yes.

Okay, so the late-model Porsche Cayenne was a basic version and used, but not very—thirty thousand miles. The Porsche dude said it would be good for two hundred thousand if she took care of it. He was mildly perplexed when she told him about the trade-in, but he walked out to take a look at the Cube. "Tranny's real good," Andi said.

And on a cool, bright day in December, she drove over to the Getty and parked the Cayenne in the underground ramp. A curator and her assistant carefully unfolded the drawings on a library table, and the assistant said, "Oh, my God. You got them at a flea market?"

"I did," Andi said.

"If these are real . . . we'll want to look at them for a while, but that looks like Benton's signature on this one and his initials on that," the curator said. "Thomas Hart Benton had a very distinctive way of . . . you know, this might be one of his finest . . . a flea market? Really?"

"Sure. And I want to do the right thing," Andi said. "You can look at them as long as you want. If you could give me a receipt?"

"Of course, and we'll take some photos," the curator said. "If you'd consider selling them, I'd hope that you'd let us bid."

"Yes. I'd like to keep them in Los Angeles," Andi said. "I read about the painting, so they must've been here for eighty years. Los Angeles is their real home. I'd hate to see them go to someplace like . . ."

"Back to Missouri?"

"I was thinking, *not even San Diego*," Andi said.

That night, out in the backyard, lying in a lounge chair, with the L.A. glow overhead, Andi sparked up a fatboy and looked to where the stars should be.

"Thank you, babe. Miss you bad."

And she cried a little, but not too much.

Lawrence Block *has embraced a late-life career as an anthologist* (In Sunlight or in Shadow, Alive in Shape and Color) *as a comfortable way station on the road to senescent decrepitude.*

Office Girls by Raphael Soyer

THE WAY WE SEE THE WORLD

BY LAWRENCE BLOCK

see they spelled his name right. Or at least they spelled it the way he spelled it: L-I-C-H-T-E-N-S-T-E-I-N, but you could argue that was a mistake on his part. Or that of his parents. Or some factotum at Ellis Island."

The painting in front of her was indeed by Roy Lichtenstein, part of a show the Whitney had chosen to call *The Way We See the World*, and the man who'd just spoken to her was standing a little behind her and a little to her left; if she'd been driving a car, he'd be in her blind spot.

Was he someone she knew? She didn't recognize the voice, and something kept her from turning to see if the face was familiar. He'd spoken with such casual assurance that one would think he knew her, or at least that he thought he knew her, but without looking she somehow decided that this was not the case, that he didn't know her at all.

That the intimation of familiarity, the casual assurance, might in fact be the point.

"One has to assume," he went on, "that the family name derives from the country, the Grand Duchy of Liechtenstein, but that's spelled with an *E*. Well, several *E*'s, actually, but the country begins L-I-E-C-H-T and the artist's name, as you can see, does not."

It struck her that the two of them might have been in a painting, a woman looking at something, a man behind her and to one side, invisible to her but not to the viewer, who could see them both and would know what he looked like. There was a particular painting that came to mind, and she could see it now in her mind's eye but couldn't summon up the name of the artist.

She remembered the man in the painting, his features ill-defined, his eyes peering out beneath a cloth cap. And she could imagine the man behind her, but what did he look like? She still did not turn toward him, but she was unable to keep from glancing at the painting's label and confirming the spelling of the name.

He wouldn't let it go at that, she knew. He'd say something else, and she'd have to turn then and find some remark, polite but uncompromising, to turn him away. She'd lived long enough to have developed the requisite coping mechanisms and could surely make it clear to him that they were not going to have a conversation, about this painting or the man who'd painted it or anything else.

She waited, sifting phrases in her mind, and he didn't say a word. He hadn't moved—she could sense his presence—but he'd answered her silence with silence of his own, and now she felt somehow off-balance.

There was a word for it, a term from the world of chess. Her ex-husband had had a half-serious interest in the game, and she'd learned the word from him. But had evidently not learned it terribly well, she thought, because she couldn't recall it now. It was German, or at least it sounded German, and what it meant was that it was your turn to move but that no move you could make would be advantageous.

Remarkable, really, that the Germans could get all of that into a single word.

So it was her turn to move, and she couldn't find a move she liked, and she felt something and recognized it as anxiety. Low-level anxiety, nothing that would send a person on a hunt for the Xanax bottle, but still—

"But you don't really need the label, do you? The Ben-Day dots, the comic-book imagery, it's unmistakably the work of this painter and no other. That may be why I like it."

She turned.

To see a man looking not at her but at the painting. He was a couple of inches taller than she, and perhaps as many years older. Clean-shaven, dark hair, strong features. Jeans, a blue button-down shirt, a tie, a blazer that might have started out as the jacket of a dark pinstripe suit.

Zugzwang. That was the German word. The compulsion to move.

She said, "You like the painting because of the dots?"

And now he turned to her, and his face seemed to light up at the sight of her. "Not the dots," he said, "although it would be hard to imagine the painting without them. But what predisposes me to like the painting is that it's so instantly recognizable as this artist's work. A single glance and one says to oneself, 'Ah, of course, Roy Lichtenstein.'"

His shoes were cordovan slip-ons. His tie bore red and blue diagonal stripes. He wore eyeglasses but would probably have looked as studious without them.

He was not wearing a wedding ring.

"I *think*," he said, "that part of my favorable response to the painting is a matter of ego. I congratulate myself for being immediately able to name the artist, even as I respectfully acknowledge him for the individuality of his work. Good on ya, Roy, with your Ben-Day dots."

"And good on you," she said, "with your eagle eye. Do you have other favorites?"

"Oh, yes," he said, and paused to consider the question. "Very different artists in the main, and it's something else that gets me."

"Not dots."

"And not the recognition factor either, if we may call it that. There are some paintings—some painters—that achieve their effect on a more primal level. Unless it's a work I've seen before, I can't look at something by Rembrandt or Picasso or Vermeer or Albert Bierstadt and know for certain whose work I'm seeing. All I necessarily know is that what's in front of me is magnificent, that it touches me."

She hadn't expected to get drawn into conversation, and caught up in it in the bargain.

"Once in London," he said, "I was in either the National Gallery or the National Portrait Gallery, and I found myself in front of one of Rembrandt's self-portraits, and I could only stand there and look at it."

They weren't in a painting, she thought. They were in a story, reciting the dialogue someone had written for them.

She recalled that Rembrandt was said to have painted almost six hundred oils. "Of which two hundred are in European galleries," she said, "and three hundred in the United States of America. I may have the numbers wrong."

"I'd say you're close enough."

Close enough, she thought, so that either of them could reach out and touch the other. But if someone had in fact written that line of dialogue for her, she'd let it remain unspoken. Internal monologue was where it belonged.

If it belonged anywhere.

"Now with Rothko," he said, "there's never any question. It's his work and nobody else's."

She'd been looking at a Rothko just minutes earlier. Had he been observing her? At her elbow, perhaps?

Or perhaps not. That was the way the gallery traffic was flowing. One looked at the Rothko, one moved on to the Lichtenstein.

"I suppose one could forge a Rothko," she said, "although it would be difficult."

"A sufficiently skilled forger could imitate anyone, although some would be easier than others. There was one fellow they caught a while ago who never copied existing works. He'd paint in the style of Gauguin or Corot or Manet. His defense was that he wasn't forging anything; he was making new paintings."

"Imitating rather than forging. Did the argument get him acquitted?"

"No, but it was an interesting contention. He'd misrepresented the work to buyers and was accordingly convicted of fraud, but were the paintings themselves forgeries?"

She recalled a remark of some renowned wit of the last century: *Imitation is the sincerest form of plagiarism.* She might have said it aloud if she had remembered who said it.

"Jackson Pollock would be interesting," he said. "As instantly identifiable as Lichtenstein or Rothko, but an actual line-for-line copy would be out of the question. You couldn't possibly do it. On the other hand—"

"You could do your own drip painting in the manner of Pollock."

"Exactly, though it would almost certainly be more difficult than it looks. Easy enough to splash the paint around, but hard to make it look right."

Like so many things, she thought.

"Mondrian," he said. "Anybody can imitate him, and everybody does. On highball glasses and T-shirts and shower curtains and God knows what else. Surgical masks?"

"I like his paintings," she said.

"Yes, so do I. And not just because I can recognize them."

"Wasn't he Dutch? Or was it Belgian?"

"Dutch."

"So what's he doing in the Whitney? Don't they limit themselves to American artists?"

"He came here during the war."

"To America?"

"To Manhattan. Lived here for four or five years until his death, spent his days painting and his nights at the jazz joints on Fifty-Second Street."

"*Broadway Boogie-Woogie*," she said. "Of course, New York and jazz on the same canvas. But that's at MOMA. I don't know if I've seen this one."

"His work evolved, but certain constants never changed. Primary colors and right angles. It was more than a style for him; it was an article of faith. There was a fellow countryman, Theo van Doesburg, and they were great good friends, and both painted the same rectilinear abstracts. And then van Doesburg started painting diagonal lines, and Mondrian wouldn't speak to him for years."

"Seriously?"

"Well, accounts differ. But it's a hell of an offense. I mean, sleeping with a man's wife is one thing, but painting diagonal lines . . . "

"Unforgivable."

"Evidently."

Not a painting. A short story, spare in prose and rich in dialogue. A story that held you in a loose grip. You can't stop reading because you need to know how it comes out, but you proceed with caution because you're afraid you won't like the ending.

They moved as one, from painting to painting. A few he studied in thoughtful silence, but more often than not he had something to say about a painting or an artist. He didn't lecture, it didn't feel as though he was mansplaining the show to her, but there were things he knew and views he held, and she found herself engaged.

And there were things she knew that he didn't. Hedda Sterne, for instance; they'd both responded strongly to the Abstract Expressionist painting, dark in color and mood, and he'd leaned in to read the label: "'Hedda Sterne, 1910 to 2011.' If those dates are right, she had a long run."

"They're right. She lived a hundred years and was still painting well into her eighties."

Born in Romania, she told him. Her first husband was named Stern, and she followed him to New York when war broke out. They changed Stern to Stafford, but when she showed her work, she became Stern again, but added an *E* to it.

"She kept the name but ditched the man and married Saul Steinberg." She found a few more facts to spout, then explained she'd read Sterne's obituary in the *Times* and found herself moved to surf the internet for more information.

"I may have been looking for the secret of her long life," she said. "If she had one, she kept it to herself."

He nodded and gave Sterne's painting another long look.

A story, as she'd heard, required a beginning and a middle and an ending. Theirs had been fitted out with a decent beginning, catching one's attention, drawing one in. But she sensed that the beginning was winding down.

Even as she had the thought, he glanced at his watch. "Two thirty," he reported. "Do you like the café downstairs? It's the middle of the week, and what lunch crowd they might draw will have thinned by now. Would you like tea or coffee? Or a glass of wine?"

Ah, the end of the beginning, easing its way into the beginning of the middle.

She breathed in; she breathed out. She said, "Why not?"

While the waiter served their scones and poured their tea, they fell silent. The museum café, as he'd predicted, was mostly empty. The waiter withdrew, the silence stretched. Zugzwang?

She asked him if he was an artist.

"No," he said, "though I sometimes envy those who are. What makes you ask?"

"Well, you look as though you could be."

"That must mean I need a haircut."

"I've no idea what it means, actually. But you know a good deal about art."

"And that must mean I've been talking too much."

"Hardly that. I've hung on every word."

"I wouldn't want to leave you hanging. But no, I've never painted. I sometimes imagine paintings. Lying in bed, on the verge of sleep, and I'll get this visual image. And then I'm asleep, and then I'm awake, and whatever it was is gone."

"A lost masterpiece."

"More the artistic equivalent of the brilliant insights that come just as one's dropping off. Those I do manage to remember, once in a while, they're always gibberish. Or tautology, some roundabout version of A equals A."

"Oh, I know what you mean," she said. "When I used to smoke, I'd get that more often than not. And it always seemed brilliant, and it was anything but."

"You don't mean tobacco."

"No, I never smoked tobacco. And I only smoked dope in college and for a year or two after. It started to make me paranoid."

"It always made me paranoid," he said.

"And I noticed that my doper friends were not as interesting as my straight friends, and they kept getting less interesting over time. I haven't smoked in years."

"Neither have I. I did smoke tobacco."

"Cigarettes?"

"And a pipe, because it made such a good prop, but that didn't last. Cigarettes were harder to quit, but I stopped for good a little over ten years ago. What about you? Did you ever paint?"

"I took a class."

"Oh?"

"Three, four years ago. I needed something. I thought that might be it."

"But it wasn't?"

"I was hopeless," she said. "And it was no fun at all. I just wanted the hour to be over. I went three times, and then I remembered the piano lessons my parents made me take."

"And you never went back."

"The piano lessons made me hate classical music," she said, "and it took me years to get over it. I wanted to make sure I quit painting before it killed my appreciation of art."

She sipped her tea. When they'd sat down she had almost ordered a glass of wine, and she sensed that if she had, he would have followed her lead. But she'd chosen tea instead, a Taiwanese oolong the menu was proud of, and he'd echoed her choice, and it seemed to her now that she'd made the right decision. Having a glass of wine with a new acquaintance was somehow different from sharing a pot of tea.

If this were a story, she thought, tea would be a good touch. It would make the narrative a little less typical, a bit less predictable.

They'd exchanged names earlier, first names, so she knew he was Philip and she was Kate. Now she said, "One reason I thought you might be an artist is that here you are in the middle of the day."

"In other words, what do I do for a living?"

"Oh, I didn't—"

"Sure you did, and why wouldn't you wonder? I sometimes wonder myself."

"Oh?"

"When I was at Colgate," he said, "I wanted to be a poet."

"Is that when you tried smoking the pipe? I'm sorry, I didn't mean that the way it sounds."

"It sounds okay to me, and it's right on the money. The pipe and the poetry seemed to go together, or to want to go together. And neither one was a pose. I wanted to be a poet, and I wanted to be a pipe smoker."

"And they didn't work?"

He shook his head. "They worked," he said, "until they didn't."

"What happened?"

"I'm not sure. All I can conclude is that I used up the poetry. Or stopped being the boy who wrote it. I know it wasn't any good, but it may have been promising. You know, the sort of work a person does on the way to finding himself as an artist. But one day it was over and the promise was broken." He was silent for a moment, then said, "I smoked the pipe a few more times. I wonder where it is. I don't think I would have thrown it out, but I haven't seen it in years."

"It could still be a good prop," she offered. "You wouldn't actually have to smoke it."

Dialogue, she thought, that managed to be light and effortless and yet had some depth to it. It occurred to her that he still hadn't told her what he did, and before she could raise the question, he answered it.

"I went to work on Wall Street," he said. "Isn't that what a young man does when the poetry gets away from him? I didn't do anything dramatic, shouting on the trading floor, trying to balance the Laphroaig and the cocaine. I was a nerd in a back room, analyzing stocks, playing with numbers. And no, it wasn't interesting."

"It wasn't?"

"Not once the novelty wore off. 'Look at me, I'm holding a responsible job.' I was married by then, which also seemed responsible of me, and the novelty of that wore off around the same time. For her as well, and she at least had the sense to find somebody else, and the next thing I knew I was divorced and in a job I hated."

"Not fun."

"But hardly torture. I had a nice apartment; I was making enough money to live comfortably. And then I had lunch with my freshman roommate."

"From Colgate."

"From Colgate, and we'd lost touch completely, but he looked for me and he found me. He'd designed this app. He'd always had that kind of a mind, and he'd quit his job at a tech firm because he got this idea and wanted to work on it. And now he had this thing, this app, and I'd explain what it does, but it would be even less interesting than what I did when I was crunching numbers in the back office. The point is that it filled a need, and it worked."

"And you teamed up with him, and your business chops were just what his geekiness needed, and the two of you made a fortune. I'm sorry, I'm butting in and telling your story, and I'm sure I'm getting it all wrong."

"No," he said, "as a matter of fact that's pretty much the way it played out. He'd figured out how to make it work and I figured out how to monetize it, and we did okay with it. I wouldn't call it a fortune, not in a world full of billionaires, but we got a fair amount of cash, and there's a continuing income stream, which will eventually reduce itself to a trickle."

"But meanwhile you can spend your afternoons at the Whitney."

"And my mornings at the gym. It's a little like being retired, except I'm not."

"You're between engagements."

"That's exactly right. Colby's on a beach in the Seychelles, thinking about the next app when he's not thinking of something else. And I'm waiting for him to come back with it all worked out."

"And if that doesn't happen—"

"Then something else will. Somebody'll come to me with something loaded with potential, and I'll figure out what to do with it."

"And you'll once again make what you wouldn't call a fortune."

"Or not," he said. "Colby and I did everything right, but we were also lucky. You can't count on that."

"No, I don't suppose you can."

And, he wondered, what did she do?

"Ah, what is it wise guys say? 'A little of this and a little of that.' Which is literally true. I teach a couple of yoga classes, I do some motivational therapy, I'm a freelance proofreader and copy editor, except I said that backward."

"So it should be copy reader and proof editor? Really?"

She laughed. "No, but a book gets copy edited before there are proofs to read. But I think you knew that."

"I probably did. What's motivational therapy?"

"Pretty much whatever you want it to be," she said. "I have four clients, one man and three women, and I meet with each of them once a week and tell them how to get on with their lives."

"Like Lucy in *Peanuts*? 'Advice—five cents'?"

"Kind of. I'm more nondirective than Lucy; I try to steer my clients to decisions they've already made or help them turn decisions into actions. I don't really have any answers, but more often than not they already know the answers. Although they may not know that they know them. You're smiling."

"I was thinking what my mother would say."

"Oh?"

"'From this she makes a living?'"

"I know, it's a little sketchy, isn't it? But it's interesting, and I get to tell myself I'm making a difference. Right now I've got a woman who wants to lose weight and another who wants to get out of her marriage. And a man who can't commit, and a woman who's fighting her way through in vitro fertilization."

"What can you do for the in vitro lady? Isn't her problem a medical one?"

"And she's seeing the right specialist for it. But it can be very stressful, the whole business, and what I can do is help her stay with it. Or, if she reaches the point where she really wants it to be over, I can help her pull the plug."

"So basically you see which way people are facing and give them a push."

"Pretty much."

"Jesus," he said. "Where were you when I needed you?"

Udine's lighting was softer than at the museum café. The music was jazz, but the sort that would be at home on an easy-listening station. Never frenzied or insistent, and unlikely to pull you away from your conversation.

When they'd poured the last of the tea, he'd suggested a glass of wine. "But not here," he said, and she'd waited for him to tell her about his apartment, not too many blocks away, where they'd find a very nice bottle of an interesting Napa Valley red. Instead, he'd brought her here, and there was no bottle on the table, just their two glasses of Valpolicella.

Udine, he told her, was in northeastern Italy, between the Adriatic and the Alps, and not far from Trieste. But the owners, he said, were not from Udine, or from Italy at all. They were Albanians, and like many of their countrymen who'd immigrated to New York, they'd been quick to open an Italian restaurant.

"Rather than an Albanian one," she said. "Because who'd come to an Albanian restaurant?"

There were a few in the Bronx, he said, and he'd read about one that he wanted to try sometime. But Italian food was certainly an easier sell in New York. Had she been to Italy?

She'd been to Florence and Rome and talked about that, and he said he'd always wanted to go to Florence but hadn't gotten there yet. He'd been to Venice, and it was beautiful but full of tourists off the cruise ships. He returned during the winter, when the weather was awful, and the city was still too crowded.

They talked about Italy, and they talked about food and wine, and she said, "The way we see the world."

"How's that?"

"Oh, the show we just saw. That was what they called it."

"Of course. It slipped my mind."

"Well, it was out of context. But I have to wonder. Do you suppose the artists' view of the world is as different as what winds up on the canvas?"

He cocked his head, thought about it. She liked that he would take a moment to consider a response, liked the way his face looked when he did so.

"I don't know," he said. "I like the question."

"Did Mondrian see a world of right angles and primary colors? Did Roy Lichtenstein see a world of dots?"

"We can know what they painted," he said, "but not what they saw."

"But do you suppose Lichtenstein saw a comic-strip universe? Or did he see the universe in a comic strip? And what about the people who'd been drawing comic strips all their lives, and here's this fancy-pants artist getting rich copying what they've been doing for years just to pay the rent."

She was holding an empty glass, and she looked at it and put it down. "I think that may have been the wine talking," she said.

If it was, he assured her, it had been well-spoken and raised an interesting question. And would she care for another glass? Not just yet, she said.

"As for how the comic-book people felt about Lichtenstein," he said, "I suppose some of them felt he was ripping them off. Others probably appreciated that he was finding beauty in what the world tended to dismiss as hackwork. Comic art is taken far more seriously than it used to be, and I don't know if that's a result of Lichtenstein's work."

"But it could be," she said.

She picked up her empty glass, frowned at it, put it down. Was she really feeling the wine? Or was that simply the attitude the story called for her to take?

"I should probably eat something," she said.

They shared an order of calamari, followed it with pasta and a salad. They each drank a second glass of wine with dinner.

Over coffee she said, "When you first spoke to me? I was standing in front of the Lichtenstein, and you were a few feet behind me and off to the side."

"And?"

"It reminded me of a painting, but I couldn't think which one. It still does, and I still can't."

"A man looking at a woman?"

"And she's oblivious. Except I wasn't."

"There must be any number of paintings that would fit. A man looking at a woman, himself unobserved in return."

"Except for the all-seeing eye of the artist. Oh, I remember the painting. She's pretty and nicely dressed and on her way to work, I think. And he's kind of shabby and lower-class, you know, wearing a flat cap. And there's something furtive about the way he's looking at her."

"Menacing?"

"It could be menacing, but not necessarily. It might be wistful, like he knows he can never have her. It's funny, I can see it clearly, and I can't remember who painted it."

"It sounds Depression era."

"Yes! And I saw it at the Whitney, but not today, not in this show. Oh, a year or two ago. It was by one of the Soyer brothers. Moses or Raphael or What's-his-name, and don't ask me which one."

"I'll bet it was What's-his-name," he said.

"Isaac," she said, "That's what his name was. Except I think it was Raphael whose picture I remember."

"And that was us? You on your way to the office, me in my flat cap?"

"That's how it felt," she said. "Like a painting."

And now it felt like a story, and they were well into the middle of the story. Approaching the end of the middle, actually.

And where was this story going?

Oh, she knew where it was going.

But how would it resolve itself? That depended, she thought, on what sort of story it was. Thus far it had no end of options as far as genre was concerned. It could certainly be light romance, having begun with a meet-cute that could have worked for Tracy and Hepburn, or Nick and Nora, or Harry and Sally. But it could be something darker. Suppose Megan Abbott was writing it. Or Stephen King . . .

"I don't want the evening to end," he said.

What could she say to that? Nothing, she decided, and left the zugzwang ball in his court.

So he waited, and she waited, and he said, "We could go hear some music. But I'm not sure I'm up to it tonight."

"Tables jammed together. People talking through the numbers."

"Exactly. Sometimes I don't mind, but—"

"Not tonight."

"No," he said, and let his fingers graze the back of her hand. "Would you like to see my apartment?"

One needn't render the scene in detail, she thought. Not in this story. One could draw a veil. Or could toss in a trio of dots or an asterisk.

Or, simpler still, skip two lines and get on with it.

She lay there and began to notice that of which she'd been unaware. The whirr of the air conditioner. The not-unpleasant chill of perspiration cooling on her skin.

The sounds of the city outside. A siren, police or ambulance, a few blocks away, receding in the distance.

Well, that was that, wasn't it? And she had nothing to complain about. He'd hit on her, and she'd been uncharacteristically receptive, and one thing had led to another. And, in return for whatever it was she'd brought to the party, she'd had a couple of hours of good conversation, warmed by the satisfaction of knowing that an attractive and personable man found her attractive and personable.

And half a pot of tea, and a couple of glasses of wine, and a good meal. And that part over which she'd drawn a veil: they'd done the deed, to her satisfaction and apparently to his as well. And now it was time to put on her clothes and go home.

"So that's the story."

"How's that?"

Quite without realizing it, she'd spoken the words aloud. "Oh," she said. "Oh?"

He'd be sitting up, she thought, and it seemed to her that she could feel his gaze upon her, more on her face than her body. Her own eyes were closed, and she kept them that way.

She said, "It's nothing, really. I was thinking out loud."

"I gathered as much. Thinking what?"

"Oh," she said, and opened her eyes and sat up. "I'd been running this tape in my head, that you and I were characters in a story."

"I thought we were images in a painting. By one of the Soyer boys."

"Raphael. But that was only until I turned around and saw you."

"It was just a virtual painting," he said, "hanging on a virtual wall."

"And it turned into a short story," she said, "and somehow we both knew what lines of dialogue to speak, and I wanted to see how it came out."

"And?"

"And it might have turned out to be a crime story or a horror story. The ending could be straightforward, or it could have an O. Henry twist."

"Or it could be straight out of *The New Yorker*, with no ending in sight."

"Oh, I wouldn't have cared for that."

"It's unsatisfying enough in print," he said. "You turn the page, and instead of more story, there's a profile of some community organizer in, I don't know, Belize? Moldova?"

"Liechtenstein."

"There you go," he said. "I liked the story a lot better the way we wrote it."

"So did I. And now, well, it's as I said."

"'That's the story,' were your words, as I recall."

She nodded, suddenly unable to speak. She felt wonderful—exalted, really—and at the same time she found herself on the brink of tears.

"I think," he said, "that you may have made a mistake. First in thinking it was a painting, and then on the first page of your story. You didn't notice the title."

"*The Way We See the World*," she said. "No? What then?"

His hand on hers. "On my copy," he said, "what it says is *Chapter One*."

PERMISSIONS

We gratefully acknowledge all those who gave permission for material to appear in this book. We have made every effort to trace and contact copyright holders. If an error or omission is brought to our notice we will be pleased to remedy the situation in future editions of this book. For further information, please contact the publisher.

Patti Abbott, "The Prairie is My Garden"
Harvey Dunn (1884–1952), *The Prairie is My Garden*, 1950 (p. 2)
Oil on canvas, Height: 104.14 cm (41 in.), Width: 180.34 cm (71 in.). Digital image and reproduction permission courtesy of the South Dakota Art Museum, Brookings, SD.

Charles Ardai, "Mother of Pearl"
Piet Mondrian (1872–1944), *Broadway Boogie Woogie*, 1942–43 (p. 20)
Oil on canvas, 50 in. × 50 in. (127 cm × 127 cm). Digital image © The Museum of Modern Art / Licensed by SCALA / Art Resource, NY.

Jan Burke, "Superficial Injuries"
Andy Warhol (1928–1987), Detail from *Thirteen Most Wanted Men*, 1964 (p. 32)
Andy Warhol, Most Wanted Men Exhibition Poster, 1988. Poster (Gagosian), 29.5 in. × 37.5 in. Digital image and reproduction permission © 2019 The Andy Warhol Foundation for the Visual Arts, Inc. / Licensed by Artists Rights Society (ARS), NY.

Jerome Charyn, "The Man from Hard Rock Mountain"
Rockwell Kent (1882–1971), *Twilight of Man*, 1926 (p. 50)
Wood engraving, 8½ × 16⅛. Digital image courtesy of Ralf Nemec. Reproduction permission courtesy of Plattsburgh State Art Museum, State University of New York, USA, Rockwell Kent Collection, Bequest of Sally Kent Gorton. All rights reserved.

Brendan DuBois, "Adrift Off the Diamond Shoals"
Winslow Homer (1836–1910), *Reefing Sails Around Diamond Shoals, Cape Hatteras*, 1905 (p. 60)
Watercolor on paper, 35.2 cm × 55.2 cm (13.9 in. × 21.7 in.). WikiArt, public domain.

Gary Phillips, "A Matter of Options"
Reginald Marsh (1898–1954), *Why Not Use the "L"?*, 1930 (p. 202)
Oil and tempera on canvas mounted on composition board, 36⅛ in. × 48⅛ in. (91.8 cm × 122.2 cm). Digital image courtesy of the Whitney Museum of American Art, New York; purchase 31.293. Reproduction permission © 2019 Estate of Reginald Marsh / Art Students League, New York / Artists Rights Society (ARS), NY.

John Sandford, "Girl With an Ax"
Thomas Hart Benton (1889–1975), *Hollywood*, 1937–1938 (p. 220)
Tempera with oil on canvas, mounted on panel, 56 in. × 84 in. (142.2 cm × 213.7 cm). Digital image courtesy of the Nelson-Atkins Museum of Art, Kansas City, Missouri/ Jamison Miller. Bequest of the arrist, F75-21/12. Reproduction permission © 2019 T. H. and R. P. Benton Testamentary Trusts / UMB Bank Trustee / Licensed by VAGA at Artists Rights Society (ARS), NY.

Lawrence Block, "The Way We See the World"
Raphael Soyer (1899–1987), *Office Girls*, 1936 (p. 238)
Oil on canvas, 26⅛ in. × 24⅛ in. (66.4 cm × 61.3 cm). Digital image and reproduction permission courtesy of the Whitney Museum of American Art, New York; purchase 36.149. Reproduced with permission from the Estate of Raphael Soyer.